HIS ARMS

P. B. Parris is an Amer_____ __our. Her
publications include nu_____ ...stories, one of which
received a PEN Fiction _____ ....first novel, *Waltzing in the Attic*,
was published in this country in 1991. Her fascination with Charlotte
Mew took some fifteen years to become *His Arms are Full of Broken
Things*. She is currently at work on another novel set, in part, in
England.

His Arms are Full of Broken Things

P. B. PARRIS

PENGUIN BOOKS

PENGUIN BOOKS

Published by the Penguin Group
Penguin Books Ltd, 27 Wrights Lane, London W8 5TZ, England
Penguin Putnam Inc., 375 Hudson Street, New York, New York 10014, USA
Penguin Books Australia Ltd, Ringwood, Victoria, Australia
Penguin Books Canada Ltd, 10 Alcorn Avenue, Toronto, Ontario, Canada M4V 3B2
Penguin Books (NZ) Ltd, 182–190 Wairau Road, Auckland 10, New Zealand

Penguin Books Ltd, Registered Offices: Harmondsworth, Middlesex, England

First published by Viking 1997
Published in Penguin Books 1998
1 3 5 7 9 10 8 6 4 2

Printed in England by Clays Ltd, St Ives plc

Names, characters, places and incidents are either the product of the writer's imagination or are used fictitiously.

ACKNOWLEDGEMENTS

Chapter epigraphs are from the poems of Charlotte Mew.

The publishers wish to acknowledge Papermac for permission to reproduce copyright material from the following poems by Thomas Hardy: stanzas one, two, eight, nine and ten from 'Dead Man Walking'; 'Nobody Comes'.

All poems by Charlotte Mew are reprinted by kind permission of Carcanet Press Ltd, © The Estate of Charlotte Mew.

Research and writing of the novel was supported in part by the Mills Endowment and the University of North Carolina at Asheville, for which I am most grateful. I wish to acknowledge the invaluable scholarship of Mary Celine Davidow, in her unpublished 1960 dissertation, 'Charlotte Mew: Biography and Criticism', and Penelope Fitzgerald, in *Charlotte Mew and Her Friends*; and the diligence of Val Warner in collecting into one volume Mew's *oeuvre*. Also, I want to thank Andrew H. Leah, Curator of Max Gate; Paul Woodhuysen of the Fitzwilliam Museum, Cambridge; Professors Martin Ray and Lee Zacharias; the tarot lady at St James, Piccadilly; Christopher Parris, Cathy Mitchell, Pamela Nickless, Dershie McDevitt, Geraldine Powell, Virginia Sampson, Elizabeth Daniel Squire, Flo Wallen, Margaret-Love Denman, Jenny Newman, and all the others who comforted and encouraged me throughout my lengthy search for Charlotte Mew.

P.B.P.

For
Elizabeth Bartlett, poet

Let us not take for granted that life exists more fully in what is commonly thought big than in what is commonly thought small.

Virginia Woolf

. . . one who surely stands with Emily Brontë, Christina Rossetti . . . many will be on the rubbish heap when Charlotte's star is at the zenith where it will remain.

Siegfried Sassoon

Miss Mew is far and away the best living woman poet – who will be read when others are forgotten.

Thomas Hardy

Charlotte Mew 1869-1928 (approx)

1877

You can hear the whole world whispering;
    The shy green grasses making love,
    The feathers grow on the dear, grey dove,
    The tiny heart of the redstart beat,
    The patter of the squirrel's feet,
The pebbles pushing in the silver streams,
The rushes talking in their dreams,
    The swish-swish of the bat's black wings,
    The wild-wood bluebell's sweet ting-tings,
        Humming and hammering at your ear,
        Everything there is to hear
In the heart of hidden things,
    But not in the midst of the nursery riot,
    That's why I wanted quiet,
        Couldn't do my sums, or sing,
        Or settle down to anything.
And when for that, I was sent upstairs
I *did* kneel down to say my prayers;
But the King who sits on your high church steeple
Has nothing to do with us fairy people!

                        from 'The Changeling'

He promised. Father promised. I was a very naughty girl, Nanny
Elizabeth said so. Anne cried for my sake, and Mama sent the
maid up to ask for quiet in the nursery.

The door-knocker banged. Footsteps in the front hall.

It took two of Father's draughtsmen to carry it up the narrow
steps, up three flights to the top of the tall house. Rain fell on the
frosted glass of the oval skylight overhead. The dusky stairwell
echoed with my shouts. 'Hurry! Up here! Hurry!'

The canvas cover was dripping on the bare floor. Nanny

made that *tsk-tsk* sound with her tongue and called down over the banister for the maid to bring a cloth, to wipe up.

We girls danced round the hidden box-shape under the wet canvas, nearly as tall as me. I was whooping and laughing, and Anne was imitating whatever I did. Nanny spoke sharply: 'Lottie, stop at once. Or I shall tell the men to come and collect it and carry it away.'

I was eight years old, and my real name was Charlotte. Charlotte Mary Mew. I took Anne by the hand and pulled my little sister to my side, holding tight to her fingers. 'Father promised,' I said, solemnly defiant.

'He promised a surprise for two young ladies, not a pair of Red Indians.' Nanny pinned me with *that look* and grasped Anne's free hand and pulled her across the room to the round table in front of the dormer windows, towing me along behind. 'We shall unwrap your father's gift after you've had your tea.' Her voice was surprisingly deep and well suited to statements not to be questioned.

Nanny lifted Anne on to her chair. Caroline Frances Anne was her full name, and she was four-going-on-five and small for her age. Both of us were. Mama said Anne was her most beautiful child, fair-skinned, with eyes the colour of spring violets.

As soon as Nanny's back was towards me, I studied the promising shape under the wet canvas. So hard to wait. I dragged my chair away from the table and over to the window and climbed up on it. I folded my legs in itchy black stockings under me and pressed my forehead against the smooth, cool window-pane. Deep in my pinafore pocket, I fingered the piece of coloured chalk – bright crimson – I'd hidden there when Nanny made me clear the table of the drawings Anne and I were making. I squeezed the chalk hard and felt red run up my arm and into my heart, up my neck and into my cheeks. I thought of all the reds I knew: roses and sunset skies, the coats of Father Christmas and the guards at Buckingham Palace, redcurrant jelly and blood when I pricked my finger with a sewing needle.

I rocked back on my heels and stole a look at Father's present. Behind me, Nanny was poking at the coals in the grate and making the sounds of brewing tea and setting the table. So hard to be good. I watched the raindrops light on the window-pane, draw towards each other and join to run down in teary streams. Beyond the glass, the plane trees of Mecklenburgh Square across the street shone black and wet. No outing today. No going through the locked iron gate – Nanny had a key – to play croquet on the thick green lawn. No smelling the flowers, the red, red roses. Mustn't pluck them. Mustn't run. Mustn't get flushed and perspire. Mustn't take off one's hat. Mustn't dirty one's hands or wrinkle one's frock. Mustn't, mustn't . . .

Out of the nursery, free of the house where we were supposed to tiptoe and whisper so as not to disturb Mama, I choked with energy and excitement that drove me half mad. I had to run, I had to shout, I had to disobey. I couldn't help myself. One day, a gentleman in a bowler hat was walking his dog inside the Square. The biggest, loveliest dog I'd ever seen, an Alsatian as tall as me. Its tongue lolled pink velvet. I wanted to touch the dog, stroke its black and tan fur. Suddenly, a pair of angry crows swooped down from the trees and flew at the dog, cawing and flapping their great black wings. Neither the dog nor the man paid them the least bit of attention, and they kept on walking. Again and again the crows attacked the Alsatian, clawing the air over its head. I was fascinated, a wonderful show. I started running across the grass towards the appealing danger of the man and the dog and the birds. Nanny called to me, angry as the crows.

I stopped. 'The eye that mocks his father and despises to obey his mother, the ravens of the valley shall pick out.' One of Nanny's proverbs from the Bible. Nanny, who was a kind of mother, must be obeyed. Or the crows – they were the same as ravens, weren't they? – they'd come and peck out my eyes.

So I walked sedately back to the wooden bench where Nanny sat with Anne beside her. Nanny reminded me, again, I must act like a young lady. And if I would not – or could not – why then, maybe I wasn't my mother's daughter after all, and right across the way, beyond the Square, was the Foundlings' Home, which might suit me better.

So I climbed up on the bench and folded my reluctant hands in my lap. My feet stuck out in front of me. I studied the scuffed toes and the round black buttons. Miserable in my fettered waiting – for what? – I listened to the raucous crows on the far side of the Square. A hansom cab went *klip-klop* along the street, its brasswork jingling. I had to resist the impulse to twist round and spy out where the dark, blinkered horse might stop in the neighbourhood. Instead, I watched as a lady does who doesn't want to be caught watching, out of the corner of my eye without moving my head. The cab passed behind the bordering hedge and disappeared.

I loved pretending. I hated pretence. I was soon bored with the pretence of little-lady behaviour. A minute later, the muffin-man came *ting-ting-tinging* along our grey, dull street, the chime of his bell like brass confetti, and I was off running again.

My brothers could run as much as they liked. Henry was the oldest and could run fastest. He was at school, and I scarcely ever saw him. Richard was only five to my almost-seven last summer. He beat me in every race. Then, he took ill, and they called it scarlet fever. Scarlet was another name for red. Nanny said, 'You must give him a kiss goodbye.' His cheek was white as the satin cushion under his head, and cold. Where had the fever heat and the scarlet red gone?

Christopher's coffin was smaller, a white box for a doll baby. He was the first dead brother I remember. He was born on 15 November 1875, my sixth birthday. Mama was in her bedroom, and grown-ups kept coming and going, up and down the stairs. I watched from the landing above, where they couldn't see me.

Nanny was in there with Mama. Nanny had been Mama's nanny when she was a girl. I fell asleep, my head resting against a stair rail. Nanny woke me. She wasn't angry. She was smiling. 'You have a new brother,' she said. 'His name is Daniel.'

But it wasn't. He was tiny and red and squealed so much I thought of the baby pigs at Uncle Richard's farm on the Isle of Wight. Night and day, my new brother cried. Mama cried, too. She told Nanny to take him away, to find a wet nurse. Then, Mama changed her mind and called for her to bring her darling back. Next day, Mama changed her mind again. And again. Finally, Mama decided the baby had been given the wrong name. That was what was upsetting him. He was to be called Christopher from then on.

It didn't help. The crying went on for weeks. On and on. Until it stopped. Nanny took me into the parlour, where the curtains were drawn and I couldn't breathe properly in the candle-heated air. I clutched Nanny's hand and stared at the waxen baby face. I stood mute, scared I'd wake him and start the crying again. What bothered me was the lid of the white box and what would happen when it was closed. Everything blurred together then, like the stripes on a spinning-top.

Two black wreaths hung on the street door. For months, everyone was dressed in black, even me and even little Anne. Mama wouldn't leave the house. She didn't want her children to go out either. Henry found ways to, I know he did.

Angels, Nanny called them, the dead brothers. I tried to think of them flying round on their little white wings, circling in the air like the crows in the Square. I wanted so very much to believe in the goodness of God and the existence of angels. Believing gave Nanny so much comfort. With some effort, I imagined angels were God's attendant fairies. God I couldn't picture at all. When I thought about Richard and Daniel—Christopher and about baby Frederick, who'd died before I was born, I saw smiling little boys, playing in the deep green hollows among the fern and foxglove, sitting on rainy days under giant toadstools, sleeping under coverlets of fallen leaves in a vast wood, just like in my nursery-rhyme book. Fairies had stolen the brothers away. And some day I'd follow them into the woods, and there we'd laugh and run as much and as far as we liked. No one would say 'Mustn't'. And no one would cry ever again.

'Let me look at you.' Nanny's no-nonsense voice, right behind me. I blinked and crept off the chair. The window's tears were running down my cheeks. Nanny gripped my chin with a firm hand, lifted the corner of her starched white apron and wiped them away.

In her plain black frock, Nanny Elizabeth was stick-stiff and tall, taller than Mama, who barely reached Father's shoulder. Nanny didn't much like him. She didn't make any secret of that, faulting him for making Mama unhappy. Just the same, she made a great pretence of being properly respectful when she was in his presence. My father, Frederick Mew, married my mother, Anna Maria Kendall, in 1862. His abiding sin was bringing them – Mama and Nanny – here to this house at 30 Doughty Street, to a block of similar terraced houses, where nothing was as refined, as pleasant, as elegant as what Mama had as a girl at the Kendall house in Brunswick Square. And Father and Nanny and Cook and the maids and we children had to work very hard to make up for Mama's disappointments.

Nanny's hair was grey round her face. She kept the rest of it hidden under a gathered cap, white and starchy like her apron. Her eyes were pale blue and chilly, with a sorrow that never left them, even when she smiled. Her life had been a hard one. She told us stories about her stony upbringing in a Yorkshire village, her struggle to rid herself of rough ways and country accent so she might live in a fine household in London and teach Christian morals and proper manners to her young charges. She never tired of reminding us it matters not whether one wants to do a thing, one does it because it's one's duty. For myself, I was tired of hearing about duty. I wanted more of her stories about cows that kicked over milk pails and rain barrels that froze and burst with a loud bang in the middle of the night.

Nanny read her Bible and quoted from it daily. She led us in saying the Lord's Prayer each night. I hated the part about 'Forgive us our trespasses' because she required us to confess in detail every one of the day's sins. Those I couldn't remember, I simply made up. I didn't see how it made any difference to God, who, according to Nanny, was up there somewhere, watching all the time anyway.

I tossed my head now, freeing my chin from Nanny's grip. If I'd had long curls like Anne's, it might have been a charming sight, I suppose. Instead, my curly brown hair was boy-short since I'd taken the scissors to it, and the head-tossing was simply a gesture of wilfulness. 'I want my tea.'

'Sit down, then, miss, and mind your pleases and thank-yous.'

I considered the canvas-covered shape in the middle of the room. Nanny must be obeyed, or appear to be, for she had the power to withhold all good things: gifts, food, affection. I smoothed my pinafore. 'Please, Nanny, may I have my tea?'

After grace was mumbled and my boiled egg cracked and its soft yolk spooned out, I dipped my toast in the sticky yellow and winked at Anne. My little sister giggled. Nanny gave us both *that look*, and the room fell silent. Bright coals shifted in the grate. I squirmed on my chair and glanced again at the tantalizing gift waiting to be uncovered.

Nanny stacked the cups and plates on a tray and wiped her hands ritually on her spotless apron. 'Yes, you may,' she said, in answer to the unasked question.

I hopped down from my chair and lifted the damp canvas and tugged it off on to the floor. There, in front of us, stood a doll's house, a cunning replica of our own Number 30 Doughty Street. For a heartbeat, Anne and I stared. 'Oooh,' she said in amazement. We exchanged grins and began bouncing up and down, shrill and joyous.

'Lottie! Anne!' Nanny pulled us apart. 'Back it goes if you can't behave properly.'

I put my hands over my mouth. I examined the tall wooden box painted to look like the yellow-grey brick house where I'd lived since I was born. The street door, with its half-round fanlight, was enamelled shiny black. The window sashes were white. Anne pointed. 'Glass,' she said, 'real glass.' The roof was made to imitate slate, with a large brick chimney at one side. Two dormer windows were set into the roof. I touched the glass in the window of the attic nursery, the very room where I was standing now. I shivered. There was a kind of magic to it. It was large and small, inside and outside at the same time.

Anne stepped round to the rear of the doll's house and squatted to peer inside. 'Oh, Lottie, come see. Mama's room and the parlour.' I joined my sister. The toy house had only one room on each level, not like our house that had many. The doll's house did have an entry hall and stairs climbing up the side, and the little rooms opened off the stairwell: Father's ground-floor study, the first-floor parlour and Mama's bedroom on the second. Fireplaces waited in the wallpapered rooms. The nursery was at the top under the sloping roof. A tiny, tiny doll's house stood in the middle of the room. This room. It was this doll's house. I shivered again.

'Where's the kitchen?' Anne piped, already the practical one.

Nanny bent over her and explained that the basement was the province of Cook and the laundress and the various maids who came and went without reason, and should be of no interest to young ladies.

I listened and wasn't listening. Something was wrong. Something was missing. 'Where are the people?'

Nanny straightened up. 'Bring me my workbox.'

I didn't move. I'd do anything for Nanny, if asked. When I was ordered, the way I'd just been, a steel rod slid up my spine.

Nanny spoke again. 'Bring me my workbox.' She stared hard at me. I stared hard up at her in return.

Anne ran across the room for the battered mahogany box with brass hinges. 'Here it is, Nanny,' she said, with conciliating sweetness.

Nanny turned away from me, holding my gaze to the last, and set the box on the table. She opened it and took out several wooden clothes pegs covered in bits of cloth. Anne snatched one from Nanny and held it up. 'Mama,' she said, dancing the doll in black ruffles and ribbons and lace about in the air. Nanny handed her another and another and another.

'Father . . . Henry . . . me!' Anne hugged a bouquet of dolls to her flat little chest.

Nanny held out the last one to me. I hesitated. She cleared her throat impatiently. I took the clothes peg. It wore my own grey smock and white pinafore. I slid the wooden doll into the pocket of my pinny, keeping my self for myself.

Anne was kissing the father doll. 'Thank you, thank you, thank you, Father.'

Nanny pulled a long face. 'Well, now. Your father didn't make those dolls.'

'Who did?'

'Miss Bolt it was.' Miss Bolt, Bolty, was the Cockney needle-woman who came twice weekly to turn collars and darn socks and mend linens and repair and let out our clothes. 'When I told her what your father was planning, she offered to make a family to live in the doll's house.'

I was very fond of Bolty. She reminded me of a plump brown sparrow. No matter how long she might be with us, she never removed her hat, a rusty black crushed affair tied under her chins with mismatched ribbons, and she had a funny way of biting off the thread instead of using the scissors. 'Saves the price of grinding, dear.' I quite liked sitting on the nursery floor by her chair and threading needles for her, as her sight was beginning to fail. I gobbled up Bolty's stories about her adored, feckless relatives in Lambeth. The brother who'd failed to make a living at bookbinding and carpet-beating, gone of late into the theatre where he shifted scenery and suffered through various wonderful misadventures. The nephew subject to fits, who used up too much paint doing watercolours and wrote comic songs for the music-hall stage. The niece who was expected at any moment to go into a decline. I've no idea what a decline was, though it sounded deliciously ominous.

Some of Bolty's stories were so outrageous I suspected her of tale-telling. I loved tale-telling. I engaged in the sport myself whenever I could get away with it. Nanny was a stickler for the truth. 'The Lord hates a proud look and a lying tongue' was one of her favourites from Proverbs. A story had to be carefully thought out and well told not to be spotted by Nanny as a lie. I took it as a challenge to my ingenuity.

'Next time Bolty comes, I'll say thank you, thank you, thank you to her,' Anne sing-songed and made her doll-self prance across the doll's house nursery floor.

I agreed with a nod.

'And the Almighty?' Nanny asked.

Anne folded her hands together with her clothes-peg doll between them. 'Oh, I shall say thank you, thank you, thank you in my prayers tonight.'

Nanny shut the lid of the workbox with a thunder clap. 'And you, miss,' she said to me, squinting, 'you must go down on your knees at your bedside and thank the Almighty for the blessing He sent you today.'

I tossed my head. 'I shan't.' I reached into the pocket of my pinny and gripped the doll that was me. A terrible whipping was coming, the certain consequence of defying Nanny. I didn't care. I was too excited by our doll's house, mine and Anne's. 'Father made it,' I said, with anxious honesty. 'God didn't have a thing to do with it.'

1885

Red is the strangest pain to bear;
In Spring the leaves on the budding trees;
In Summer the roses are worse than these,
   More terrible than they are sweet:
   A rose can stab you across the street
     Deeper than any knife:
   And the crimson haunts you everywhere –
Thin shafts of sunlight, like the ghosts of reddened swords have
   struck our stair
As if, coming down, you had split your life.

   I think that my soul is red
Like the soul of a sword or a scarlet flower:
   But when these are dead
   They have had their hour.

I shall have had mine, too,
   For from head to feet,
I am burned and stabbed half through,
   And the pain is deadly sweet.

The things that kill us seem
   Blind to the death they give:
It is only in our dream
   The things that kill us live.

From 'The Quiet House'

The downy paleness of Miss Harrison's neck drew me on, step
after step. The sight of bare white skin above a black collar
held me, kept me walking along block after block of brick and
stone buildings between Gower Street and the house in Hampstead. The six of us walked to school on weekday mornings

and back in the evenings, the hours of light shortening and getting longer with the seasons.

Behind me, Ethel Oliver and Edith Scull walked in Quaker silence. Next to me walked Amice Macdonnell. Ahead, leading the procession, walked Miss Harrison and Miss Greener. Teachers and pupils, the pairs held hands as we crossed the rackety streets, checking right then left, dodging drays and carriages and hansom cabs, their bells jingling to warn unwary pedestrians.

The other girls and I were boarders with Miss Harrison, even though my father's house in Mecklenburgh Square was only a short distance from Gower Street. I'd pleaded with him last year, 'Please, Father, please. You *must* let me go to live with Miss Harrison. She can tutor me in English literature.' My argument was a spontaneous mixture of temper and logic. 'I'm not a child, Father. Surely, I ought to be allowed to leave that rotten old night nursery.' And Nanny Elizabeth, although I didn't say it. She and I were more than ever at daggers drawn. I was growing up too quickly, she said, and was still much too headstrong. 'Yes, of course, I'll miss the family. But Mama has Freda' – her new favourite, born in 1879, named after Father – 'and Henry's so busy with his own friends and working in your office he'll hardly notice I'm not here. I see Anne every day at school. And I shall come home to tea every Sunday faithfully, I promise. I *must* go! Father, please.' Mama said I was giving her a migraine with all my begging and badgering. In the end, Father had agreed to my going.

This pastel spring evening we passed shop windows and painted signs and window-boxes sprouting flowers. Iron-rimmed wheels clattered on the stone street, and a flight of sparrows fluttered up from the pavement in front of us. Miss Harrison turned to Miss Greener, who said something that made them both laugh – what were they laughing at? – and quicken their pace. I gripped my partner's hand and lengthened my stride, towing her along. At sixteen, I was small, not much taller than ten-year-old Amice. I was fine-boned but sprightly and determined and more than able to keep up.

To my private satisfaction, I matched the rhythm of my steps exactly to Miss Harrison's, my black boots shadowing hers. But inside mine I'd a secret – red stockings. I always wore red stockings. No one could see them, but I knew they were there. For myself, I liked having secrets no one around me would ever guess.

Ahead of me, Miss Harrison's thick blond-almost-white hair was waved and cut unfashionably short. I was allowed to keep my hair short, too. Miss Harrison wore black and white: black skirt and jacket, white shirtwaist. My school-day frock was a black-and-white check. I wore a pert black hat, straw with the brim rolled jauntily up in the front, very much like the one Miss Harrison had on.

My hands were damp and uncomfortable inside black kid gloves. No lady went out without gloves. I detested gloves in warm weather when all they did was imprison my fingers and deny them the pleasure of touch.

I focused my sight and my mind on Miss Harrison and did my best to ignore my discomfort and everything else: the coarse shouts and haggling whines of the street vendors selling combs and lavender and roasted potatoes, and the crossing-sweeper boys in Euston Road and Camden High Street. I followed Miss Harrison as closely as I dared and tried to imagine what it would be like to be in Miss Greener's place, holding Miss Harrison's gloved hand in mine and making her laugh with my own witty chatter. And yet if, right at that instant, I'd been magically transported into Miss Greener's favoured position, I couldn't think what I might say. My walking daydream never got beyond the moment when I took Miss Harrison's hand and started off towards Hampstead.

Marvellous Miss Lucy Harrison, forty-ish, headmistress of Gower Street School, lover of books and music. In the school-room, the faces of all us girls turned up to her like flowers to the sun as she read aloud to us from Shakespeare and from the Brontës – especially the melancholy poetry of Emily Brontë – Blake and Wordsworth and the Brownings. And when she gazed upwards, her hands clasped behind her, and recited from the English Romantics – Byron, Shelley, Keats – I, too, fell half in love with easeful death. Oh, the morbid joy, to die for one's love. I'd gladly have died for the sake of Miss Harrison. Somehow, in my fantasy, I was splendidly, tragically deceased, laid out like Sleeping Beauty, and at the same time standing at the side of a weeping Miss Harrison, my arm round her, comforting her.

Sometimes, when I was supposed to be doing my lessons, French or geography or the dreaded mathematics, I wrote my own poetry. I wrote it and tore it up, and when no one else was there, I tossed it into the fireplace, watching the flames take my poor efforts and char them to ash. In spite of the fact I knew almost nothing about how to do it, I was determined to create the perfect poem, one Miss Harrison might some day read with the same breathy mixture of awe and excitement she brought to her recitation of Christina Rossetti.

Among ourselves, we Gower Street girls whispered confessions of adoration for our headmistress, flushed with unembarrassed enthusiasm. I joined in, nodding my agreement, but kept mum. Secretly, I hated their schoolgirl crushes, so fleeting and foolish. I was sure what I felt was more profound and everlasting. Not silly like the others, with their blushing and giggling, but fine and ennobling. On our daily walks from school, I trailed Miss Harrison with a longing I'd no name for, sick with a happy misery in her presence.

Stepping along now as we neared Haverstock Hill, I watched the regular swing of Miss Harrison's arms, the taut black serge of her jacket stretched constant and smooth over her shoulderblades. The beckoning white of her neck. The unchanging firmness of her jawline. The poignant lost profile. The tiny pillow of her ear lobe, naked of jewellery. Mama wore earrings, jet or black onyx or marcasite, mourning jewellery. Miss Harrison needed no adornment. Her beauty was of a transcendent kind, perfect in itself.

As we turned in at the front gate, Miss Greener broke from the group and rushed to the flower-bed next to Miss Harrison's house. She was a tall, slender woman, maybe ten years younger than Miss Harrison, with broad, boyish shoulders and what I considered unbecomingly large feet. I was a bit vain about my own small feet, buttoned into custom-made boots of black kid.

'Oh, Lucy, look,' Miss Greener cried, as she hurried back, 'the first rose, just opening.' Breathless, she held out the bright red bud, making a gift of it to Miss Harrison.

I was furious. The idea! Picking Miss Harrison's flowers. Without even asking. She should be punished, sent away, right this second. But Miss Harrison accepted the rose and put it up to her face. Not simply to smell. She touched it to her lips. 'Thank you, Amy dear,' she said. Her tone was calm and gracious and something more. And the smile she gave Miss Greener: I'd have given anything for such a smile. I felt a pain in my chest, as if a thorn were caught there.

Inside the house, I lifted my skirt and led the way as the girls and I clambered up the stairs to our rooms. I chattered excitedly about nothing, bewildered, distracting myself. As I went by, I plucked a stalk from an arrangement of dried pussy willow and sea grass in a basket on the first landing. In the upper hallway, I dropped my book bag, tossed my head, and pirouetted round to face the other three. I held out the brittle branch daintily between thumb and forefinger. I bowed deeply and presented it to a surprised Amice, who took it with a stifled giggle. I clasped my hands together under my chin and twisted my face wickedly and mimicked Miss Greener's high-pitched voice. 'Oh, Lucy.' I rolled my eyes. 'The first rose.' I gestured widely, nearly knocking a fern off its stand. 'Just opening.'

'Oh, Lottie!' Ethel said, grinning. Amice giggled again. Edith laughed and called me a scamp, and the girls all clapped their hands and danced from foot to foot, and the thorn began to withdraw from inside my breast.

The upright piano in Miss Harrison's front parlour stood against the wall opposite the fireplace. A sofa and several chairs with needlework cushions of wild flowers were arranged round the hearth. An open book lay on a side-table, where *she*'d been reading, a stack of others near by. Dun and grey-green watercolour landscapes decorated the walls. With the curtains drawn and the oil-lamp on the piano lighted, the room was my retreat. In the evening before dinner, I came here to practise my music. As I fingered an ascending scale, I imagined myself climbing the rocky slope of a snow-capped Alp with Miss Harrison, who'd studied in Germany and France as a girl. I wanted especially some day to visit France and practised talking to myself in French as I played . . . *n'importe quand . . . n'importe qui . . . n'importe où je suis . . .*

I was finishing my warming-up exercises when Amice slipped in, closing the parlour door. I ignored her and launched into a new Chopin Étude I was learning. Miss Harrison had said it reminded her of a misty evening with the streetlights along the Seine, fading off into the distance, as if they were melting. I pictured that and saw myself and Miss Harrison walking hand in hand under those dreamy lights, going . . . where? Amice said something. I lifted my fingers from the keys. 'What did you say?' I swivelled round on the piano stool.

Amice half-skipped across the faded Persian carpet and stopped in front of me. She raised her chin. 'I said I know a secret you don't.'

I folded my hands in my lap. I liked Amice. I'd play along with her childish game. Besides, my curiosity, once roused, was beyond my control. 'And what's that?'

'I was in the dining-room. I was putting fresh napkins in the rings.'

'Yes? So?' The boarders took turns helping with the table.

'I overheard Miss Harrison talking to Mrs Newcombe in the kitchen.' Mrs Newcombe was the housekeeper.

'And what did you hear, Miss Eavesdropper?' I teased.

She put her hands over her mouth, and tiny doll's titters escaped between her fingers.

'Don't be tiresome, Amice. Do tell me what you heard.'

'Miss Harrison is going to leave.'

I was stung. 'You must be mistaken, Amice. You've got to be.'

'No, Lottie, I heard her tell Mrs Newcombe she's going to be leaving at the end of term.'

'No! Never!' I was overwhelmed by wild grief. I wanted to stamp on the floor so hard and shout so loud I'd bring the whole house down about me in splintered timbers and plaster dust. Instead, I spun round and pounded the piano keys with my fists in broken, wrathful discord. I left off, and the sound rolled on like distant thunder.

Poor little Amice, her eyes were saucer-wide and her mouth gaping. Perversely, I wanted to shake her like a rag and make her take back everything she'd said.

I jumped to my feet and dashed at the wall beside the piano, banging my forehead against it, over and over again. The pain was dizzying. And necessary. Behind me, Amice was shrieking for me to stop. I stepped back. A bright red shape, like the silhouette of a rose, bloomed on the striped wallpaper.

The pain wasn't in my head but in my heart. The thorn pierced deeper than ever. I lay curled in bed, my eyes squeezed so tight tiny suns and stars wheeled and burst against the inside of my lids. 'Find rest in Him,' Nanny Elizabeth used to say. When I thought of God, I imagined Him as Someone like Father – but larger, much larger, and more pompous, puffed up, solemn and judgemental, His waistcoat buttons sewn on too tight.

I put my palms together under the sheet, dubious and desperate. 'Dear God, Heavenly Father,' I prayed, 'let Amice be mistaken. She must be. Please, please make it Miss Greener who's going away.' My prayer was interrupted by footsteps in the hallway outside and the sound of the bedroom door opening.

'Charlotte?'

Miss Harrison. I kept my eyelids shut. There was a pounding in my chest, all heart pain gone.

'Charlotte.' The way she spoke was gentle, and insistent. 'I must talk to you.'

Her spiritual presence filled my narrow room with its low, slanted ceiling, up under the roof.

'Look at me, Charlotte.'

I blinked my lids open. She sat on the edge of the bed. She was holding a candlestick to one side in such a way that the light seemed to be shining from her ethereal blue eyes. Her pale gold hair, combed from a high parting, fell in waves, touching her temples like angels' wings. I remembered a painting I'd seen at the National Gallery: a Flemish Virgin with a small, square chin and high, broad cheekbones. All that was missing with this miraculous vision was a halo.

'Yes, Miss Harrison?' I said in a reverent whisper.

'I hope you're feeling better now. And more composed.' She set the candlestick on the floor beside the bed, and the light shifted, casting a distorted shadow against the slanting wall behind her. As if some dark giantess were lurking there. 'You're a lovable and infuriating child, my dear. You've a highly emotional nature. There's no denying it and no escaping it either. What we're born, we will be. I grant you, strong emotions are the source of creative energy, but they're also the instrument of our own torture. Isn't that correct?'

'Yes, Miss Harrison.' She was so wise. As if my thoughts were written on my face for her alone to read.

'Now, you must listen calmly to what I have to say to you.'

'Yes, Miss Harrison,' I said, with limited certainty.

'Amice has told me what prompted your behaviour in the parlour.'

'But you can't leave!' I raised myself up on one elbow.

She put a hushing forefinger to her lips. I lay back, pressing my head, hard, into the pillow. I turned my face away in frustration. The candlelight shadow wavered on the white plaster beside my bed.

'Promise me you'll listen and not let yourself become overwrought again.' After a silent moment, I nodded my head, and she went on. 'At the end of term, I shall be leaving London, as Amice told you.'

I turned towards her, searching the Virgin face for some bit of hope. 'And after your holiday, when will you return?'

'I shan't.' A pause. 'I'm moving to Yorkshire.'

I wanted to say, 'You mustn't! You mustn't go! Because I love you!' I couldn't. It would be like giving her a cane to whip me with. I hurt too much already.

After a long silence, I said, 'But why?' More a demand than a question, spoken much too loud for the small room.

'I'm afraid there's no explaining, beyond telling you I'm building a house near Wensleydale, where I'll have my gardening and, of course, my books and my writing. I may even complete my history of England, finally.' The chuckle in her last word hung in the air, alien and unaccepted.

I waited, hoping hopelessly for a consoling hand to touch me. With gentle desperation, I said, 'You can't go off and be all alone.'

'Miss Greener will be joining me.'

I was speechless with outrage. I wrapped my arms round myself tightly, pressing together the bosoms that weren't yet breasts, squeezing until my chest hurt, inside and out.

'Don't be cross, please. Perhaps one day a little intellectual window will open and make clear what is obscure now.'

I gritted my teeth.

'You and I shall always be friends, you know. We shall write letters, and one day you must come and visit us in the north.'

No, I would not. Never. My body went rigid. The swelling on my forehead began to throb. I closed my eyes again. The light glowed through my lids, then darkened as she stood and moved off from the bed, taking the light with her.

'You will always be dear to me, Charlotte.'

A flicker of mitigating joy.

'You and all the other girls,' Miss Harrison added. She wished me a good night and left the room.

I lay there for several minutes, listening to her retreating footsteps. The house was unnaturally quiet. When at last I opened my eyes, the sight of a skewed patch of moonlight stretching across the floor was so sad and white it made me sob out loud.

1888

Do roses grow
Beneath those twenty windows in a row –
And if some night
When you have not seen any light
They cannot move you from your chair
What happens there?
I do not know.

From 'Ken'

It was nothing to do with me. Mama was the reason Father purchased the lease on the house at 9 Gordon Street just off Gordon Square, a more fashionable Bloomsbury neighbourhood than Doughty Street. Number 9 was in a terrace of similar four-storeyed houses with brass door-knockers, balconies with iron railings across the three tall windows of the first-floor parlours, and basement stairs behind black palings. Together, the houses formed a single façade, varying in details of facings and stone cornices and mouldings. The new house was of mud-brown brick trimmed in light grey Portland stone. The interior order was much like the house in Doughty Street, with a side hall and stairway. The new rooms were larger, but the stairs darker, lacking a skylight. The house seemed to press down on me every time I entered it. The light and lightness of my early years remained in the house in Mecklenburgh Square. Night-time dreams of home took me again and again to where I was born. And waking, I felt my childhood had left me, mysteriously and without farewell.

Gordon Street ought to have pleased Mama; it was a good address and had the added advantage of being nearer the Gower Street School, for Freda, who was nine, and the Royal Female

College of Art in Queen Square, where Anne, now sixteen, was a student. When Father announced we were moving house, Mama had been delighted. But after the removal men arrived and departed and the furniture and fittings were settled, she wept and pouted and found fault with every new arrangement. She was most unhappy about Father's offices on the ground floor. 'Like living over the shop,' she wailed.

True, the walls of the front hall and the stairwell were lined with framed architectural drawings and finely calligraphed building plans. I thought they were all works of art as worthy as the one Mama had hung in the first-floor parlour: Grandfather Kendall's watercolour drawing of basilicas and bridges and spires, which had been displayed at the Crystal Palace in 1851. Later, it was exhibited in Paris, where Baudelaire himself saw it and was inspired to write his poem, 'Rêve Parisien'. Or so the story ran in Mama's family. I liked to think it was true; I still cherished secret literary aspirations.

But Mama considered the plans and drawings in the hall nothing more than crass advertising. To her mind, art was the oil painting over the fireplace in the parlour. Her portrait, made some five years before her marriage, hung above the sepia family photographs and cards of invitation set on the mantelpiece. In its gilt frame, the painting shone, a radiance on the wall. The artist had created a young lady like a flower in a spring garden, her eyes the colour of delphinium. She held her dainty head high, ringlets covering her ears. The painted smile was strangely shy, half haughty and half sweet.

Thirty years later, Mama had become a shrunken imitation of the portrait. Her small, thin nose had become sharp and disapproving. Her hair was greying in a cluster on the crown of her head and curly fringe in front, her forehead pinched and creased by discontent.

'I haven't had such a fine frock since I married,' Mama lamented again this afternoon, gesturing up at the painting. 'Is it any wonder my old friends no longer come to call?'

That wasn't true, of course. Mama had had callers yesterday.

'And see how my hands have withered.' She splayed her ringed fingers across her lap of aubergine silk taffeta. 'I might as well have been scrubbing floors.'

Nanny murmured soothingly as she poured Mama's tea from the china pot decorated with cherubs and garlands and silken swags. She spooned up two mounds of sugar and stirred the cup while quoting from Psalms: 'Let the beauty of the Lord God be upon us and establish the work of our hands.'

I put aside my embroidery, came over from the sofa and knelt beside Mama's chair, on the Axminster cartouches and cabbage roses. I took her soft hands in mine and told her what she wanted to hear, expected to hear: that she was still as beautiful as the painted girl. 'More beautiful because more loved,' I said, a practised litany, 'by me and Nanny and Father and Anne and Freda and Henry.'

'Henry,' Mama echoed. 'Where *is* Henry?' She pulled her hands away. 'I haven't seen him in days. He lives in this house, doesn't he? Why do I never see my son?' She touched a lace-edged handkerchief to her nose. 'There is such a thing as filial duty. Why does he neglect me?'

I was ready to say that wasn't so, she'd seen him this morning at breakfast. 'Henry is . . . ,' I began. Nanny gave me *that look*. I got to my feet and began again. 'Father has taken him to inspect a building site in Highgate,' I lied.

At that moment, Wek, the ancient parrot, began squawking loudly from his perch by the middle window. Behind him, the afternoon outside was a hazy grey. Like Nanny, the large blue and yellow bird was Mama's from before her marriage. His eyes were like shoe buttons, his beak an ivory scimitar. He became excited when Nanny uncovered a plate of iced cakes on the tea table. Sounding like a hoarse old man, the bird demanded, 'Biscuit! Biscuit!' Mama crossed the room and fed him bits from her plate, making kissing noises, calling him her dear, sweet one.

I was feeling particularly oppressed today by this gilded, fringed and tufted room, where all comfort had been lost to ornament and ostentation. The parlour was a botanical garden of needlework footstools, pillows and chair cushions – birds, fruit, foliage, flowers – worked in coloured wools. 'I'm going for a walk,' I said. No response. I left the airless, over-stuffed room and shut the door behind me.

I pinned on my black hat, snatched up my gloves and handbag, and fled to the misty little park that was Gordon Square.

I envied the trees. They were so much nearer the stars. They lifted their arms above the city's shout and rumble, above the sooty brick façades, the grimy pediments and slates, the smoking chimney-pots. As I walked through the misty grey-green of Gordon Square, I envied the trees their strength and stalwartness, dependably there, in wind and weather, bright day and dark night.

I glanced back towards Gordon Street. Where was Henry? I went on. This gloomy late afternoon, the gravel path crunching under the soles of my boots, I envied the trees' rootedness. No one would expect one of them to leave behind the place of their lives for eighteen years. No tree had to endure the fuss and discomfort, the packing and unpacking, the troubling dislocation, and the constant stream of demands and complaints from Mama. Dismayed, I was more than half inclined to agree with her, to blame our current unhappinesses on the move to the new house.

In the fading light, I found a seat on a damp bench under a plane tree, its grey bark peeling away like old wallpaper. I took a deep breath, inhaling the sour-green smell of wet leaves, and continued my meditation on trees. They didn't have mothers. They didn't have brothers. They didn't have any family obligations at all.

My dear older brother Henry had always been so clever and promising and quick at drawing. At twenty-three, he was

Father's assistant in the architectural firm and expected soon to be a junior partner. After Grandfather Kendall died three years ago, in 1885, Father had been left with running the business of Kendall and Mew. And yet, as he relied more and more on him, Henry grew more and more unreliable. I'd become aware of his changing personality about that same time, when I returned from boarding with Miss Harrison, my schooling for ever ended. At first, Henry seemed to be working himself too hard – often irritable, distracted and distant. Father expected great things from his only surviving son; as a result, Henry had a good deal on his mind.

Always before, Henry had been openly affectionate with us, his three sisters, indulging us as much as he was able. He was especially fond of Freda, laughing and swinging her off her feet and calling her his little rosebud, his coat tails flying. Over the years, I'd taken him as my measure of what a young gentleman ought to be, so the changes in his temperament confused me. All the same, he was my older brother, my *beau idéal*. And my co-conspirator. He taught me to roll and smoke cigarettes, and each week he bought the makings for himself and me at the tobacconist's in Malet Street. He introduced me to the few swear-words in my vocabulary, exhilarating sounds I delighted in saying to myself under my breath. If I'd let one burst out unawares, Mama would have been appalled; Nanny would surely have made me wash my mouth out with soap.

Also, Henry gave me a greater freedom than any of my friends had. Mama said it was improper for me to go out alone, so he escorted me to night-time concerts and lectures. What she didn't know was that most often he only went as far as the door of the performance hall and left me on my own, reappearing to collect me for the walk home as the crowd dispersed.

Then one afternoon some weeks ago, shortly after the move to the new house, Henry and I had arranged to meet in Trafalgar Square. He had an appointment near by, delivering some blueprints to a client; he promised that after his errand he'd join me for a walk through an exhibition of Italian Masters at the National Gallery. I arrived promptly at the agreed-upon time, three o'clock according to the blue clock in the steeple of St Martin-in-the-Fields.

I wore my weekday costume: black jacket, white blouse with soft tie, and black-and-white tartan skirt. And red stockings, of course. My skirt was plain, no drape or gathering-up behind, no crinolette or flounce or any other modish furbelows. I detested tight-lacing and refused to wear a corset with metal stays or a wire bustle frame. I was unwilling to suffer the limitations of such underpinnings, intended for women who did nothing but look decorative.

Mama often bemoaned, 'You have no sense of style, Charlotte, in your manner or your dress.' For myself, I thought I'd developed a style very much of my own. I continued to have my curly hair cropped short, and I refused to shape myself into the mincing doll that was the current fashion in females. I wanted the freedom to stride along with the boyish gait I'd known since I was a child. I strode now with brisk purpose to a spot between the paws of one of the lions below Nelson's Column, and there I waited.

According to Mama, the acceptable feminine manner was reticent and demure, but I was simply incapable of dimpling and simpering. I sometimes spoke my mind with a candour she called a glaring liability. 'No man will marry a girl who isn't modest and obedient, or at least agreeable in all things.'

Ah, the sweet irony of my mother, whose manner was consistently disagreeable. I said, 'I wouldn't marry any man who couldn't bear a little frankness and honesty now and again.' In truth, in spite of Mama's expectations, marriage held no immediate appeal for me. Several of my schoolfriends were already married. I was nearly nineteen and supposed that some day – but here my imagination balked. For the present, I meant to enjoy the leisure and latitude that were mine as a single young woman of a certain class, not obliged to earn a living.

This sunshiny day, Trafalgar Square was thick with throaty cooing and the airy rush of pigeons' wings. Sleek and fat, born middle-aged, the birds waddled on pink feet across the stone pavement. They moved in shaggy ranks like badly drilled soldiers in coats of grey and white and black. In the slant of afternoon light, gleams of pink and purple and green came and went on their feathers. I was reminded of Wordsworth's rainbow.

I lost track of time, watching the way passers-by were surrounded by pigeons and trailed and finally given up by the silly, scurrying birds. When shadows crept to where I stood, chilling the air, I frowned up at the clock in the steeple and realized Henry was over an hour late. Apparently he wasn't coming after all. I passed my small black handbag from one set of restless gloved fingers to the other and sighed.

I truly loved Henry. But I was losing patience with him. We'd all put his increasing forgetfulness down to pressures of business. It had become something of a family joke, but I no longer found anything amusing about it.

When I got back to the new house, teatime was long past; no one was in the darkened parlour, just Wek dozing on his stand by the twilight window. I climbed the dusky stairs to Henry's room and rapped on the door. No answer. I rapped again, louder.

The door opened a few inches. Henry, slender, with high forehead and dark arched brows, peeked out. His eyes darted wildly, searching beyond me, as if someone were lurking there in the empty hallway.

'I waited for you, Henry,' I said, charged with righteous anger. I cocked my head at a defiant angle. 'Why didn't you meet me as you promised?' I shoved at the door.

He stopped it from opening any wider, continuing to scan behind me. 'The Queen made me wait here,' he said in a conspiratorial whisper.

'The Queen? Do you mean Mama told you not to meet me?'

He waited, as if listening to a voice from far away. 'I cannot disobey a royal command. Lions stalk their prey in Trafalgar Square.'

'Henry, are you joking?' But his steady gaze, turned now on me, was chillingly serious. I took a shocked, frightened step backwards.

Then, as if *I'd* said something funny, he let out a high-pitched laugh and slammed the door.

Now, as the misty evening gathered round, I left the bench and strolled back along the path towards the Gordon Street entrance to the Square. I couldn't make up my mind whether it was better to return to the house and wait for Father and Henry or to watch for them from here and speak to them before they went in. All day, I'd worn a face as bland as milk to hide my concern for my brother. I'd tried again and again to pray for him.

But God surely must have known my prayers were merely expedient. Not that I didn't want them answered, just that I hadn't any certainty they would be. Although Mama and Anne and I regularly attended Christ Church in Woburn Square, I felt a perfect fraud. The appeal of the services came from the music; I gloried in it. When the organ swelled triumphant, every nerve of my body sang with it, in awe and excitation.

I was attracted to Christ Church, too, by the knowledge that the piously columned and candlelit sanctuary was where Christina Rossetti often worshipped. Each Sunday, I watched over the top of my prayer-book, secretly hoping to catch sight of the famous poet with her great, sorrowful eyes.

And sometimes during services, I thought about Miss Harrison – dear Miss Harrison. The name, the remembered face, she was altogether forgiven for having abandoned me. What a passionate, possessive child I'd been! Lucy Harrison was enshrined in memory, like a patron saint. I recalled some lines from Rossetti she'd read in class years ago:

> Though I till now have put forth thorns, yet now
>   Strengthen me Thou
> That better fruit be borne.

I longed for the comfort of firm belief. At the same time, the wrestling with my dark angel of disbelief went on. I wore a silver cross on a silver chain on weekdays, gold on the Sabbath, as if the outward and visible sign could draw down like lightning to a lightning rod the inward faith I yearned for. Religion is like music, I decided. One must have an ear for it. I didn't seem to, although God knows I kept trying in my own way.

The lowering sky touched the treetops. Ahead of me, another bench squatted, heavy and empty, near the break in the hedge along Gordon Street. From this vantage point, I could see the front of Number 9. The curtains were drawn shut in the parlour on the first floor. The gaselier in the entry hall was lighted, yellow glowing through the transom window above the street door. By this time, Freda and Anne, coming from their schools, must already have gone in through that black door and up to their rooms at the top of the house. They must have knocked at my bedroom and, when no answer came, gone on down to the parlour.

If I'd been at the house, they'd have come into my room, bringing kisses on cheeks, brightening the dreary afternoon. I'd have asked, 'Did you have a good day?' Anne would have chattered on about her fellow students at art school, a jolly lot. And Anne and I would have smiled at Freda's tales of her own adventures at school. What an imagination possessed our little sister: St George slew dragons in the hallway, scaly corpses thick on the ground, and King Arthur jousted with his knights in Gower Street.

And no one would have mentioned Henry. Or the events of this morning.

On reflection, our brother's behaviour had been deteriorating steadily over recent months. He often went on long walks to clear his mind, he said, and came in, complaining of headaches caused by the heavy traffic and the noise of all the foreigners in the streets. He took to his bed with cold compresses on his forehead; Nanny had to change them precisely every ten minutes until he fell into a deep sleep. Since the move to Gordon Street, it was no longer possible to think of Henry's illness as a temporary nervous condition that would soon pass. Still, we were forbidden by Father to speak about it; Mama refused to acknowledge it in any way. She preferred to go through her days as if she didn't have a son who behaved oddly, who some days wouldn't leave his room because he swore – loudly through the closed door – that someone had stolen all his clothes.

This morning, the rest of the family had been sitting at the breakfast table when Henry came in, humming to himself. Father was at the head, Mama at the foot, Anne and Freda on one side, I on the other. The silver gleamed, the crystal and glassware glittered, the centre epergne overflowed with fresh grapes. Mama prided herself on setting an elegant table.

Henry was newly shaved, several clotted cuts on his chin and cheeks, and was wearing his business suit and stiff collar. He pulled out the chair at his customary place on Mama's left, next to me. 'Good morning,' I said, smiling, pleased he'd recovered enough to join the family for a meal. The guard I'd become used to raising with Henry lowered. I reached for his cup and filled it with coffee from the silver pot.

He seated himself without saying a thing. His manner was intense, his shoulders held stiff, his movements small and awkward, almost mechanical. He took his table-napkin from its ring, refolded it diagonally, arranged it round his collar and knotted it like a cravat. He examined his reflection in the blade of a butter knife.

When Mama asked what he was doing, his hand began to shiver, and he dropped the knife. It fell with a sharp clatter on his plate. Not used to being ignored, Mama looked stricken and offended.

Henry spun round in my direction and said, 'One can't be presented at Court with an untidy cravat. They're sending round the carriage at three, so I must be ready on time. I mustn't keep Her Majesty waiting.'

My smile shrank to nothing. He was off and ranting again.

'Henry, dear,' Mama said, blinking in bewilderment, 'what *are* you talking about?'

He leant towards Anne and Freda across the table. They were staring at him, their forks suspended over their plates. 'And you two must henceforth address me as M'Lud.' He hurried on, speaking to no one in particular. 'When the invitation arrived in the post, I was quite certain it was a forgery.' He interrupted himself with a silly giggle. 'I have enemies everywhere,' he said, 'waiting for me to make a bloody fool of myself.'

Mama put down her toast. 'Language, Henry!'

Disregarding Mama for a second time, he rattled on. 'They disguise themselves. All the same, I recognize them by their eyes. Like cat's eyes, they glow red in the light.' Perspiration stood out in fine droplets on Henry's forehead, and he spoke more and more rapidly, like an automaton with its spring wound too tight. 'When I tell them to look into the light and they refuse, I know them for what they are' – he waved his arms stiffly over his head as if fighting off a swarm of insects – 'the minions of the King of France.'

Slowly, shaking, I pushed back my chair and said in a near whisper, 'Maybe you'd like to have a little lie-down, Henry.'

At that instant, he noticed me beside him and drew away as if I'd threatened him. 'Don't come any nearer. You're one of them. Your eyes are as red as hot coals.'

Father dropped his napkin by his plate and came round the table towards Henry.

'Damn it! Keep them away from me!' Henry shouted, half rising, causing his chair to tumble over backwards. Unbalanced, he grabbed the tablecloth and pulled it towards himself, upsetting his cup of coffee. The brown stain spread silently across the white damask as everyone spoke at once: I was pleading, Henry cursing, Father ordering, Mama objecting, Anne placating and little Freda weeping and begging to be protected from her brother's evil enemies.

Henry dashed round the table and out of the rackety room. My last, brief glimpse of my brother was of his feet, bluish, bare and vulnerable. And from below came the sound of the street door slamming shut.

In the vaporous twilight, Gordon Square had faded to monochrome, black tree-trunks, dark grey grass, rose bushes delicate silhouettes, their blooms a paler grey. I chewed the tip of my gloved finger and diverted myself by trying to remember their lost colours. From far along the block in the direction of Tavistock Place came the jingle and *klip-klop* of a hansom cab. At last! I hurried towards the house.

Father had been out all day, searching for Henry. He stepped down from the cab and paid the driver. He was alone. I called to him as he started to go up to the door. In the sallow glow from the window, he waited for me. His face above his dark moustache was hidden under the shadow of the brim of his top hat. I reached out but didn't touch his arm. 'What is it, Father? Where's Henry? Did you find him?'

'Yes, daughter. I found him.' His tone was heavy and flat as granite.

I looked up at him, head and shoulders taller than I, and tried to read in his expression what had happened and not have to ask. Stoic. Indecipherable. I glanced down. One of the pearl buttons was missing from his waistcoat. Had Henry done that?

'Best discuss this before we go in to your mother and sisters,'

Father said, thick with authority. 'You're the strong one, Charlotte. You can bear what the others can't.'

I waited for what was clearly bad news, not wanting to have to hear it.

'I won't tell you where I found him. In a pitiful state. I've consulted two doctors. They're unanimous in their diagnosis. Dementia praecox.'

I wasn't sure what that meant. 'What can they do to make him well again?'

'Not a thing.' Father passed a hand over his face. 'He's mad. Incurable.'

'Oh, no! That's not possible!' I was frantic. 'Where is he? What are they doing to him?'

'Control yourself, Charlotte. Listen to me. Henry is in Peckham Hospital. He'll be well looked after. That I promise you. We must accept that what remains of his life will be spent in care.' Father sounded so grave, so hopeless. 'Otherwise, he'd do himself or others injury. Became violent, you know. Had to be restrained.'

'Oh, poor Henry.' And I added, 'Poor Father.' Despair hung round us like the fog in the streets.

'Your mother must be spared this agony, do you hear?'

I nodded.

Father went on to explain with weary patience, 'I'll tell her he's ill and in hospital, attended by a private nurse. All true. We must bear this burden for her. Comfort your mother. Don't let her lose hope, false as it may be.'

'Yes, Father.' My words were obedient but spoken from the lips only. I was unaccepting. I twisted my handbag between my fingers. Good God, how could he be so soon resigned to this? There must be something more that could be done, surely. I tossed my head. 'I want to see Henry.'

'No. Absolutely not. You mustn't go there. Must never go there,' he said sternly. 'Charlotte, do you understand me?'

I ran down the steps to the pavement.

'Daughter! Come back . . .'

I barely heard the last of my father's words. I was already walking quickly towards Euston Road and the omnibus.

I was alone in the dark, hours from Bloomsbury and miles from Gordon Square, south of the river in a part of London I hadn't even known existed: a crumbling neighbourhood of open stairway doors and shuttered shops and unlighted street lamps. The night without stars smelled of coal smoke and stale milk and rotting fish. I stood in the sordid gloom across from the entrance to the soot-blackened hospital and counted the rows of dimly lighted windows of clouded glass on each floor and imagined Henry locked behind every one of them, and my courage failed me and I could not go in.

1889

No year has been like this that has just gone by;
    It may be that what Father says is true,
If things are so it does not matter why:
    But everything has burned, and not quite through.
    The colours of the world have turned
    To flame, the blue, the gold has burned
In what used to be such a leaden sky.
When you are burned quite through you die.

from 'The Quiet House'

Freda wouldn't leave her room. On the morning of Henry's final outburst, she'd been so terrified by his ranting about his enemies that she'd run howling and stumbling upstairs, pulled the bedclothes up over her head and wouldn't come out. That day and the next, Nanny Elizabeth carried Freda's meals up on a tray but couldn't coax her to take even one bite.

Mama refused to get the doctor in, insisting all this be kept within the family. Ten-year-old Freda had been her angel-child since birth, the darling of her mother's extravagant heart. 'Bright as a flame,' she'd tell callers. In recent years, she'd often summon Freda to the parlour to recite for them. This Freda did with coy drama (and suitable gestures), her blue eyes liquid, her cheeks charmingly rosy –

Satan is glad (grotesque leer)
When I am bad (deep frown, pursed lips)
And hopes that I (index finger to chest)
With him shall lie (finger pointing to floor)
In fire and chains (eyes wide with horror)
And dreadful pains (hands clutched under chin)

– ending with a dimpled smile and a low curtsy, the skirt of her frock spread wide. She'd then spin round, her long auburn hair a triumph of Nanny's curling iron, and with a merry skip return to Mama's side, where a sliver of teacake was popped into her mouth. That was our Freda as she'd once been.

Mama stepped now from Freda's bedroom. She'd taken to wearing black, as if Henry had died. Her lips were like a drawn white thread. I'd been told to wait outside in the hallway. After she closed the door behind her, I folded her hands in mine. 'How is she?'

'It's no use. She won't speak to me. She won't eat. My poor, poor baby. Oh, Charlotte, you must do something, for your sister's sake.'

'We need to be patient,' I said, as much to myself as to her. 'Freda's had a terrible shock. It will pass, you'll see.'

But Freda stayed in her room. By autumn, the situation had been accepted within the family as normal and permanent. Anne came in from her art classes; she and Mama and Nanny and I took our tea with Freda every afternoon. Freda blamed Father for failing to rescue Henry, and she strictly commanded him: 'You may not enter my room.' So he stood in the open doorway, conversing awkwardly with us – 'Unseasonably cool today, an early frost likely' – while we women of the household sat crowded round the bed on straight-backed chairs, sipping our tea and eating ginger biscuits. Soon, the empty pleasantries were exhausted. Mama's black taffeta rustled in the terrible silence. I sat there mute. I was afraid for my little sister, but I wasn't allowed to say so.

Freda crouched on her bed. The front of her nightdress was stained with tea and broth and fruit juices, the only nourishment she'd take. Solid food, she protested, was Cook's plot to make her choke and die. Her uncombed hair hung in knots and tangles. She wouldn't let anyone touch her, not even Nanny, who'd always bathed and dressed her. And she shrank from the kisses and caresses she and I had always shared in the past.

It hurt me to have my little sister scramble to the far side of the bed when I came near. She'd become all eyes, shrinking inside herself in mourning for her missing brother, her lost cavalier, now the prisoner, she said, of the evil King of France.

I escaped to my bedroom to write. From my second-floor window, I could see the thick foliage of the sycamore in our back garden, now yellow-leafed and hung with winged seeds. I glimpsed between the leaves a sky as hard as blue stone. Below my window, geraniums, lobelia, lavender and other flowers had blossomed through the spring and summer, sprawling round the paving and against the enclosing brick wall. Today, the aged plants were grey in the dying season, in our garden and the neighbours' as well, all narrow, proper, private and empty.

An autumn wind on the other side of the glass fluttered the leaves of the tree like ten thousand silent wings; I fancied myself lifted up, briefly leaving the quiet, sorrowing house. The illusion passed. I stepped away from the window and pulled out my desk chair. Earlier, I'd gone out into the garden and cut the last full bloom from a rusting chrysanthemum, white, with a sharp scent like black pepper. It stood on my work table in a vase beside the brass tray of pens and pen nibs, and a cork-stoppered pot of black ink.

I sat down and took the makings from the shallow drawer of my work table and rolled myself a cigarette, licking along the seam with a flick of the tongue, sealing the fragile white paper to the rough brown shreds of tobacco. Every time I performed this minor ritual, I thought about Henry and considered it a sort of benediction, like lighting a penny candle in a Catholic church, hoping for its power to bless and doubting it at the same time.

I twisted a discarded page of manuscript into a spill and went over and lighted my cigarette from the coal fire in the grate. After shifting my chair nearer the table, I gathered the rest of the pages together, unstopped the ink pot, and took up writing where I'd left off yesterday.

Just then, without knocking, Nanny came into the room and shut the door with an elbow's shove. She seemed to enjoy interrupting me. Over the years, her shoulders had grown stooped, her hair, pulled in a tight bun, chalk white, but her censorious stare, *that look*, was still as piercing as a darning needle. She said nothing but started to dust the candlesticks, the pin boxes and the Staffordshire lion and lamb on the mantelpiece – a cherished birthday gift from Anne. Nanny returned each exactly to its proper place. She was the tidiest person I'd ever known. She'd have brought order to the night sky if she'd been given the chance; she'd have rearranged the stars in straight rows according to size and brilliance.

Nanny came next to stand over my table. She still treated me as if I were a little girl in the nursery, rather than a young woman of nearly twenty. While I smoked my cigarette and scratched away at my work, Nanny swept stray ashes and scraps of paper into her dustpan. She emptied the cracked saucer I used as an ashtray. The crease between her brows deepened as she lectured me: 'This smoking and that constant writing, why, you know, Lottie, both are bad for the brain.' I'd heard this all before, more times than I cared to remember. When she got no response, Nanny quoted Proverbs with a knowing inflection: 'When pride comes, then comes shame.' I went on jerking my pen impatiently across the page until I heard the bedroom door shut again.

Never mind the smoking. For myself, I wasn't prepared to give up writing, the thing that made me most happy. Nanny said writing was harmful. Mama said, 'It's the very sort of pastime that puts men off.' But to me it was like a gift bestowed on me at my christening by a fairy godmother no one but I remembered. My writing was different from my needlework or playing the piano or reading aloud to Mama. More than merely a way for a respectable young lady – how I hated those words – to fill vast, arid stretches of time. In the parlour, I was often overcome by a numbing ennui; on those days when I was kept from my work table by social obligations, I was abstracted, irritable and mildly unhappy. I'd stare up at the corner of whatever room I happened to be in, up where the wall-paper seams met or a stray cobweb lingered, and try out words and phrases in my head.

I attempted to write every day, even on Sundays, when I'd regularly fabricate a mid-afternoon headache so I might go up to my room. I didn't mind the solitude of writing. I welcomed it, relished it. Writing for myself alone had all the clandestine excitement, the subterranean allure, of a solitary vice. I climbed the stairs each day with a curious eagerness to work on the manuscripts locked in the travel trunk at the foot of my bed. The key on a red silk ribbon round my neck, next to my skin, was a hidden shadow of the silver cross on a chain, gold on Sunday, that everyone else could see.

With a mixture of impulse and trepidation, I'd committed myself to a writing apprenticeship, with the authors of my own reading as my mentors. Otherwise, I was cutting my path as I went. My ability as a writer was a mystery: I might well have no talent, or at best a very modest one. I hadn't tested it pub-licly. Maybe I never would. I was well aware doubt and shyness lay behind my bold public manner. What I wrote was intended for that other Charlotte – the one who saw without eyes and knew without reason – who remained hidden from Nanny and Mama and all the others. Except for Anne. We had no secrets between us. She understood and waited, without asking, for the day when I was ready for her to read what I'd put on paper.

For several weeks, I'd been drafting the story of a young woman's visit to a dark, alien place, much like the one where my search for Henry had ended. The experience of that night had been profound. I'd been absolutely alone, not able to cross the street to the grimy brick hospital, forced to wander through a urinous maze of foggy streets to find transport back to Bloomsbury and Gordon Square. I wanted to write about that, about the appalling neighbourhood and my failed courage. Something between a catharsis and an act of contrition. I hoped it might rid me of that memory.

At first, I'd tried to make a poem about my feelings for Henry, but the result was sentimental twaddle. Sentiment was a second-rate emotion, an avoidance, a fearful turning away from Medusa's gaze. I didn't want to be one who turns away. But such pain must be approached slantwise, with something like Perseus's mirror-shield. I had to find a way to do that. Finally, after many scribbled and crumpled false starts, a short story re-creating that night and transformed into someone else's, a fictional character's, experience seemed to be the solution.

I reread the last sentence I'd written. I shook my head and crossed it out with a furious stroke, and reached for a fresh sheet of writing paper.

I laid my pen down. I thought I'd heard someone knocking. I waited. When it came again, a tentative *rap, rap*, I pushed back my chair and opened the door.

Calm and glassy-eyed, Freda looked up at me and said, 'We have swords.'

What was this?

My little sister stood in the hallway, in a stained, wrinkled nightdress burdened with flounces and ruffles at neck and sleeves and hem. The pink ribbon threaded through the eyelet trim trailed, dingy and unravelling, along the floor behind her. She waited there in Henry's high-button shoes, black and gaping round her bare feet. Her small bony hand was raised in a gesture of pathetic bravado, holding an imaginary blade. Seconds ticked by, and she smiled a gay little shadowy smile. 'A devil-angel is coming for me.' Her face contorted into the grotesque leer of her parlour recitation. 'It was Satan snatched Henry away and now he's coming for me.'

*

At dinner, Father told us he was taking Freda on holiday to the Isle of Wight. He'd been born there; his people still lived in and about Newport. When I was a girl, Nanny used to take us children to spend our holiday there. Mama preferred the more fashionable Brighton, where Grandfather Kendall had a summer house, and Father was bound by business to London. I cherished sunshine memories of the freedom I'd found on the island: charging down the steamer's gangplank and clambering up into the open carriage at the landing with seagulls bickering overhead, hide-and-seeking in haycocks on Uncle Richard's Newfairlee farm, shouting and shooing the flock of maddened chickens, climbing trees – impossible, unthinkable in London – windfalls in the apple orchard, pigeons and dog-roses, cider and gingerbread, noisy piglets and a silent dead rat in the lane.

'The sea air will do wonders for Freda,' Father assured us. Yes, I hoped, holding to my memories, yes. The doctor came to the house in the evening. Mama held a lace handkerchief to her lips and said nothing. The doctor left. The next morning, Father and Freda were gone.

Early in the afternoon, Anne and I were in the parlour, reading together. Mama was out paying calls. I heard no bell at the door, but there were heavy footfalls in the hall; Father stepped into the room – where was Freda? – and set his suitcase down. He removed his hat and put it, upright and hollow, on a side-table. Wek, who disliked all men, began squawking rudely. Over the din, Father told us to join him in his office. Dutifully, we followed him down the stairs. He closed the door after us and went to stand behind his broad mahogany desk.

With Anne at my side, I waited a nervous eternity, staring at my father.

He wasn't a large man nor a tall one whose top hat might be distinguished above a crowd, although the women of the family, all of us small in stature, had literally to look up to him. He leant on his spread fingertips. The cuffs of his frock-coat were beginning to fray along the edges. The pearl button had been re-sewn on his waistcoat, Nanny's doing. Grey bristles sprouted among the brown in his moustache. His hair had begun to thin and recede above a broad forehead creased with gravity. 'Freda is in hospital,' he said.

Anne moved closer to me. 'Where, Father?'

'Is she with Henry?' I asked, suddenly angry. 'She's not, is she?'

'No.' He shook his head. 'She's on the Isle of Wight, at Carisbrooke, committed to Whitelands Hospital, with a private nurse to tend to her.' His expression was grim, weary. 'For the rest of her life.'

'But, Father,' I cried, 'she's just a little girl. She's only ten years old.'

Anne covered her face with her hands.

Father sank into the leather-covered chair, slumped forward, his hands clasped before him on the desktop cluttered with envelopes and papers and sketched-out plans. 'The doctors . . .' His voice faded away, a pebble dropped into a shallow pool.

I'd never before seen Father so empty and discouraged, so close to despair. I could feel Anne trembling beside me.

'I've fathered seven children,' he said. 'All but the two of you taken. One by one. A failure. I'm a failure.'

'No!' I burst out.

He raised a hand to stop me. 'I failed to protect them. Had I been a better provider . . .'

'Rubbish!'

He shook his head. 'If only . . .' He faltered, and then pushed himself to his feet. 'I promise you' – in a breathing space, he raised his chin – 'I promise you shall never know want . . . go unprotected . . . be unprovided for.' He straightened himself and made a firm new beginning. 'I bear this guilt. My burden. Don't make your mother's any greater. Be concerned for her.

She's not strong, you know. Never has been. This double disaster could be a killing blow. We must protect her, accept what God has sent and not question why.'

I clenched my hands into useless fists. 'Oh, Father –'

He cut me off. 'We shan't speak of this again.' And he left the room.

Anne turned her face down into my shoulder and began weeping. Tenderly, wordlessly, I comforted her as best I could, my eyes streaming. The house settled round us and the still, dark civility of our lives.

The coals in the grate burned low, tiny yellow-gold and blue flames like distant stars in the black of night.

The door to my bedroom opened and closed, and Anne slipped under the covers, as she hadn't done since she was a small child. She nestled close to me, smelling faintly of violet sachet. Her feet and hands were icy. I pulled her closer, willing my warmth to pass to her.

She whispered, 'One of us may be next.'

'You mustn't say that.' I'd been troubled by the same idea since Henry's breakdown, and Freda's had sharpened my dread. 'Don't even think it.'

'Oh, Lottie, why does Father keep saying it's all his fault?'

'That's Mama's unreasonable reasoning. The Kendalls blame the Mew blood for Henry's condition. It's so unfair. They ought to look at themselves. Do you remember Uncle Edward, Mama's brother? Maybe you were too young. He sometimes behaved oddly. In the end, his affairs had to be managed for him. Naturally, it was never talked about openly, merely hinted at. And never, ever mentioned in front of outsiders.'

'Yes,' Anne said, sighing it out.

'Once when I was a child, I laughed at something he did, no, more his wild way of speaking, I suppose. I couldn't help myself – he sounded so funny – and, of course, I was punished. Mama said, "It's rude to show that you find another's behaviour in any way out of the ordinary. You must remember he is your uncle.""'

'Poor Mama,' Anne said. 'Keeping up appearances means so much to her.'

'Poor Mama, indeed. They're *all* hypocrites. It may be unkind to say so, but it's true. Have you noticed when Aunt Mary and the Kendall cousins ask about Henry's health, somehow the conversation becomes a criticism of Father?' Anger made my words harsher. 'Accepting what's happened to Henry and Freda as God's will, well, it wasn't Father's fault, surely, so God can have all the credit this time.'

Anne raised herself, a faint white face hovering over mine. 'But it's as they say, a family curse, isn't it, the dementia?'

'They do say it runs in the blood.' A flutter of fear at the notion of madness already pulsing through my veins. No. I mustn't let myself think about it.

'So one would be wrong to pass tragedy on to another generation?'

I could see where my sister's questions were taking us. 'Yes,' I said, 'to marry would be wrong. Even to encourage a suitor would be cruel.'

'Oh, Lottie, and you so fond of Sam.' Sam was the older brother of our schoolfriends, Elsie, Edith and Margaret Chick.

'Only for the girls' sake,' I reassured her. 'The whole family has been so kind to us. He's a pleasant enough fellow, but I never loved him or any other man in that way.' And I added, 'I never shall.'

I was startled at myself, saying aloud what I'd already decided somewhere inside, deep and unheard. Raised in blackest ignorance, I'd had so much hidden from me. I knew almost nothing about the relations between men and women, so how could I measure what I was forsaking? But for some time I'd been worried about the whole idea of courtship and marriage. Henry might have explained it all to me if he'd been there and still been Henry. The one time I'd tried to learn something about intimacy between the sexes from Mama, she pretended not to hear my question. I went next to Nanny. 'Put it out of your mind, immediately!' she'd insisted. 'You'll learn all you need about *that* from your husband after you're married.'

I decided nothing pleasant could inspire such conspiracy.

Anne lay back, her head on the pillow next to mine. 'You may say you'll never love any man, but some day you might change your mind.'

'No, I think not.' I turned towards her. 'But you, Anne, you're the pretty one, so bright and witty.' I reached over and smoothed back her hair, as if to see her eyes in the unseeable dark. 'And you're barely seventeen. You should soon have flocks of beaux.'

Anne shook her head under my hand. 'I've thought quite hard about it. I can't let myself be tempted into passing on this sickness.' Anne, the sensible, the practical one, her words absolutely serious. 'It's a sacrifice we both must make. It's our duty, don't you see?'

I lay down again, flat on my back, searching the ceiling lost in the high darkness. My usual response to the word *duty* was incipient rebellion. But now, I agreed with what my sister was saying. 'Yes, dear, I see. We have a kind of moral obligation not to carry this any further.'

'And as a guard against natural temptations, we need to make a pact,' she said. 'And we must do it together, a vow of chastity such as nuns make.'

Ritual had a certain appeal, I admitted.

Anne cleared her throat and began solemnly, 'I swear to Almighty God . . . Say it with me, Lottie.'

'I swear to Almighty God . . . ,' I echoed.

'I shall remain chaste . . .'

'I shall remain chaste . . .'

'Never marry . . .'

'Never marry . . .' No sacrifice for me to give up what I'd never really wanted. Why was I all at once so sad?

'And never bear children . . .'
'And never bear children . . .'

Infants in prams, toddlers with their nannies, younger brothers and sisters in the houses of my friends, my own little sister – *oh, Freda!* – I loved children. I'd never given any thought to their care or conception, about which I was almost wholly in the dark. What attracted me was their energy and candour, their short memories for sorrow, their amnesia for disappointment. They responded to me with eagerness and laughter, recognizing a fellow spirit who'd grown older, if not much taller. I squeezed my stinging eyelids shut, forbidding any more tears.

'Amen,' Anne whispered.

I repeated the seal on our vow, and we clung to each other like frightened children until the fireplace embers burned out and we fell asleep in each other's arms.

1892

– before I die I want to see
The world that lies behind the strangeness of your eyes,
There is nothing gay or green there for my gathering, it may be,
Yet on brown fields there lies
A haunting purple bloom: is there not something in grey skies
And in grey sea?

from 'On the Road to the Sea'

Beyond the high iron fence, the British Museum's classical pediment teemed with allegory. I crossed the courtyard warmed by the early spring sun, climbed the broad steps and passed through the shaded colonnade. Inside, the darker lobby echoed with mingled voices and shuffling feet. I held my handbag up in front of me with both gloved hands and started to make my way through the crush of mid-afternoon visitors towards the doors of the Reading Room, directly opposite the entrance. Because of my small stature, I was forced to weave and shove and excuse myself across the stone floor with ingenuity and strained patience. 'Sorry,' I said, stepping round two stout men who'd stopped to consult a guidebook. 'Sorry.' A woman in trousers – how odd! – gawking up at a winged Assyrian lion on a pedestal. 'Sorry.' A man and woman paused, changed course, headed off in the direction of a side corridor, nearly colliding with me. I stepped back, losing ground, bumping into someone behind me – 'Sorry' – and went on inching across the dim, congested lobby, pressed on all sides by bustles and elbows.

Even though my formal schooling had ended years ago, I continued to educate myself in what interested me, especially literature and history. As often as I could, I came to the Reading Room of the British Museum, where I sat at one of the radiating desks in the huge sky-blue rotunda and drifted off on the hushed lap of page turnings to whatever exotic shore my reading carried me. I enjoyed the notion of being surrounded by books containing 'all the best that has been thought and written', to quote Matthew Arnold. And a good deal of useless drivel, as well. I was becoming widely read enough to question received wisdom, even when it came between pasteboard covers. Still, books could tell me everything I needed to know, although I didn't always know what that might be.

Occasionally, I attended a free lecture at University College, near the house in Gordon Street, and sometimes went out to night lectures and concerts without an escort, now that Henry was . . . gone. And that greatly distressed Mama and Nanny Elizabeth. I was twenty-two years old and perfectly capable of walking alone in our quiet, gas-lit neighbourhood. Still, my physical safety wasn't what concerned them. 'Keep thyself unspotted from the world,' Nanny said biblically, and Mama wrung her tiny hands and fretted about what others might think of her daughter. 'It's not right, and what's more, it is unbecoming in a lady.' She repeated apocryphal stories of other young women's misbehaviour and ultimate disgrace. In them, she always appeared as a child – 'when I was a girl' – pure and blameless, just as she assumed she was in the present.

These days Mama's greatest pleasure was fearing the worst, scanning the morning newspaper for accounts of disasters, studying the obituaries. She found a kind of reassurance in the pervasiveness of human tragedy, consoled somewhat that she hadn't been singled out for suffering. Father no longer did much to comfort her or counter her fears. Henry and Freda were never mentioned, and Father withdrew into his office and his work, saying hardly anything at meals and saying it in a clouded way. He was still the paterfamilias, but he governed from a distance, like a sorrowing Zeus on Olympus, stern and unapproachable.

In spite of Mama's dire predictions, I continued my outings, rather proud of myself for not letting pointless convention make me a prisoner. Ahead lay years of hours of willed idleness, of needlepointing superfluous fire-screens and cushion covers, of reading aloud from dully uplifting books, of keeping Mama from dwelling on the great unhappinesses of her life. In the meantime, I intended to have what intellectual and aesthetic pleasures I could.

Today, I was going to the Reading Room to find material for an essay I'd thought of doing about Emily Brontë. My forward progress was halted just then by a clot of elderly bonneted matrons, maps of the museum's galleries in hand, discussing which to do first. I was trapped in the echoing hall until the ladies reached a decision, and I wished mightily for a pair of stilts to lift myself over the congestion in front of me. Suffocating with impatience, I raised my chin, surveyed the pillared walls, the high coffered ceiling and the stairway off to my left. Several steps up the flight, a man in a grey suit and dove-grey felt hat was looking out disinterestedly over the museum visitors' heads. Although not a tall man, he stood erect, his face calm under dark brows and trim dark beard.

I'd never learnt to cast my eyes down coyly in front of a man as was expected of young women. I met his gaze directly and, in that instant, recognized him as the writer Thomas Hardy. I'd seen his picture a number of times in the *Illustrated London News*. Last year, reading his new novel, *Tess of the d'Urbervilles*, I'd been unsettled by its earthy candour and considered it vulgar and wonderfully daring. I'd been drawn on by the exceptional writing and couldn't help being touched by the plight of poor, wronged Tess.

Hardy returned my stare with a quick, faint smile. In the murky light, he descended the steps. I swear the crowd parted as he walked through to stand in front of me. He touched the brim of his hat and spoke over the low rumble: 'I'm afraid you have the advantage of me, miss. I'm sorry to say I seem to have forgotten your name.'

I was pushed towards him by the passing of the chattering matrons. 'Oh, we haven't met, Mr Hardy.' We were uncomfortably close; I tried to retreat but was hemmed in by the sluggish flow of frock-coats and fringed shawls.

'No? But you returned my glance in such a manner . . .' He blinked down at me several times, unexpectedly shy. An opening in the milling crowd allowed him to shift a few inches backwards. 'Please excuse me for presuming.'

Flustered, I said, 'No, no, it's I who was presumptuous, staring like that, and I'm the one who should apologize for my rudeness.'

'Don't you suppose we've apologized, both of us, enough and to spare? Surely, we've placated all the gods of *politesse*?' he said, with sly amusement. I couldn't resist smiling. In fact, I was grinning like the Cheshire Cat. Thomas Hardy. Imagine. He continued: 'Let's manoeuvre out of this teeming mass of culture-mad humanity and find a quiet place where we may introduce ourselves properly.'

My boldness fled. I was all at once too much in awe to speak. His touch on my elbow was firm and vaguely benevolent as he guided me beyond the stairway and through a series of over-peopled corridors and galleries until we came to a large, quiet room lit by frosted-glass skylights. He led me to a bench in the middle of the gallery, where we sat in opposite directions, facing each other as if seated on a *tête-à-tête* in someone's parlour. Even seated, he was a head taller than I. My attention fully on Hardy, I'd no clear sense of where we were, my peripheral vision a blur.

'I'm invited more places than I care to go,' he said, 'and I meet so many people that I often fail to remember. And your name is . . . ?'

'Mew. Charlotte Mew.' I hated that my cheeks were colouring. 'And I assure you, Mr Hardy, we've never met, except through your writing.' I bit my lip to keep from gushing.

'Your father, would he be Frederick Mew, the architect?' I

nodded, glad he'd found a connection that might support some minutes more of conversation. 'I remember him as a junior partner in Kendall's office when I came up to London as a young man to learn the architecture game under Arthur Blomfield.' Hardy was in his early fifties, only slightly younger than my father. His beard was flecked with the odd white hair, like Father's moustache. His ash-grey eyes were at once sad and teasing.

Hardy added, 'That would've been 1862 or 1863, if memory serves. Truly, I was a feckless lad.'

What I heard as Hardy spoke was a schooled accent with now and again a West Country inflection, a regional pronunciation. It suited him and reminded me of his fictional county of Wessex.

He chuckled. 'Can you keep a secret?' Again I nodded, happy to be taken into his confidence. 'Church restoration is what I was supposed to be training in. I spent every spare minute, however, scribbling bad poetry on stray bits of paper.'

I wanted to say something profound, something he'd remember. My mind was a perfect muddle.

His dark brows tilted; at their outside corners, his eyes narrowed and the folds of the lids went up, slightly mandarin. 'What brings you here today?' he asked politely, keeping up the conversation.

'I was going to the Reading Room.'

'Why then, you mustn't let me keep you.' He started to rise.

'Oh, no, it's not important. Some research.'

He settled again on the bench. 'You're a writer?'

I couldn't think how to answer. I wrote, yes.

'You mustn't be modest. We writers recognize one another, if only by the ink stains.'

'I want to be a very good writer, Mr Hardy, even though I haven't published anything. I haven't even tried to.'

'That will come.' He sounded so certain. I wanted to believe him. 'I came for research, too. But I made the mistake of going to the Egyptian galleries first.' He sighed. 'Girls and young men laughing and flirting round the mummies, thinking today is for ever.'

'But surely you're not old enough to worry about how much time is left before you die.'

He regarded me seriously. 'You almost make me feel that's true,' he said softly.

I turned away, embarrassed by the implications. Instinct told me I was being made love to and told me to escape. Reason told me not to offend such a kind and distinguished gentleman.

I checked for the first time round the gallery where we sat and realized where he'd brought me. Ranged along the walls in imitation of the original frieze on the Parthenon were the Elgin Marbles: ancient gods and goddesses with Homerically blind eyes, horses and flying drapery, pediment and metope, all chiselled from creamy stone, shattered by time and wars and rough handling, reassembled like a gigantic jigsaw puzzle, with many precious pieces missing.

I got to my feet and walked over to examine the nearest relief, a headless female torso, pleats of stone garment curving round a breast. A bare breast. My own breasts tingled, and my cheeks blazed. I hurried further along. When I stopped at the badly mutilated head of a warrior, Hardy came and stood beside me, his hands clasped behind his back.

'I find a kind of grandeur, a serene dignity in this work,' he said. 'I can return to it again and again without ever tiring.' He conducted me through the rest of the gallery – Zeus and Athene, Dionysus and Iris, Apollo and Venus – discussing the sculpture with the spatial sense of an architect and the myths they depicted with the ease of the born storyteller.

The light in the gallery was going grey as the day outside faded. The two of us were alone in the vast room. We came next to a girlish figure, clad in a diaphanous garment open along the side, pale thigh and calf, ankle and foot exposed. She was running towards the left, staring behind her in frozen horror. Hardy said, 'This is Hebe, the cupbearer to the gods, who was dismissed after she tripped and fell and indecently exposed herself while pouring nectar at a grand gathering.'

I was as horrified as Hebe looked by the picture his words conjured up. I didn't know where to focus my gaze. I couldn't speak. The air was too thin to breathe.

'She resembles you, Miss Mew,' he added mildly.

Shocked silence. I found my voice. 'I beg your pardon.'

'I mean she's small like yourself. So small she could easily be carried under a man's arm. And like you, she's distressed because she revealed what she meant to keep hidden.'

I frowned up at him. 'What are you saying? What have I revealed?'

'You've allowed yourself to make the acquaintance of a stranger, and now you're unsure that was wise. You've allowed your emotions to surface, and I've read them.'

I tossed my head. 'How can you know what I may be thinking?'

'You've shown me. Oh, not in words spoken but in expressions passing over your face.'

In the failing light, I could just make out the inscrutable greyness under the brim of his hat. Could he actually read my thoughts so easily? I was alarmed at being so transparent. I looked round the room. Shadows and silence. I said, 'We'll be locked in.'

'One moment, please, Miss Mew – may I call you Charlotte? – one more moment, Charlotte, and then we'll go.' He took both my gloved hands in his. 'When I was a young man, I once ran wildly towards the edge of a cliff overlooking the ocean on the Cornish coast, and stopped at the last second on the very brink. The immense power of the waves dashing themselves to death against the rocks, the breathless exhilaration mingled with the terror of falling from that great height, it was my only direct encounter with the Sublime. Until today. I experienced something very like it earlier when I looked down and saw you.'

Suddenly, it was as if I myself were falling from a great height.

He began quoting Tennyson:

> Break, break, break,
> At the foot of thy crags, O Sea!
> But the tender grace of a day that is dead
> Will never come back to me.

'You shall come back to me,' he said and bent and kissed me lightly on the cheek before he released my hands and turned to leave.

It is the only truth: it is the dream in us neither life nor death nor
  any other thing can take away:
      But if she had not touched Him in the doorway of the dream
  could she have cared so much?
      She was a sinner, we are what we are: the spirit afterwards,
  but first, the touch.

from 'Madeleine in Church'

After several weeks of doubting and hoping, I persuaded myself
I'd only caught sight of the famous man on the stairway in the
British Museum and everything after that was an especially
vivid daydream, concocted from admiration for Hardy the
writer and a desire for some bit of his genius to be passed on
to me by means of one kiss – a modest, paternal kiss on the
cheek, as if I were an agreeable, precocious child.

Then, Hardy came up to London for a meeting with his
publishers later in the spring, and a brief note arrived in the
post one afternoon, inviting me to accompany him to a performance of *Hedda Gabler*. It was signed with his spiky, slanting
scrawl, *Believe me to be, your sincere T.H.* I refolded the paper,
replaced it in the envelope and went upstairs to my room.

I sat at my work table for some time, uncertain, smoking
one cigarette after another. If I accepted Hardy's invitation, I'd
be stepping outside the strict bounds of convention. I'd done
it often enough, but this was different, a difference of degree
rather than kind, and a vast difference at that. I ticked off the
reasons to decline: although he was well-known as a celebrity,
Hardy was a virtual stranger to me; we hadn't been what Mama
would call properly introduced; and he was married. I'd seen
Mrs Hardy's picture in the newspaper. Not an attractive

woman, fat and frog-like. Still, married men with middle-aged wives seemed to be immune from public criticism if they went about socially with younger women. The Prince of Wales had set the fashion in that.

But if Mama or Nanny found out I'd gone to the theatre with Hardy, they'd be frantic about the loss of my reputation. Well then, I decided, I shan't tell them. Besides, what's a young woman's good reputation for but to make her an acceptable commodity on the marriage market, and I wasn't on offer.

With unsteady fingers, I took up my pen and wrote a reply. I'd never seen an Ibsen play. I'd be honoured to attend. I'd take a cab and meet him at the theatre. I thanked him and closed formally: *Truly yours, Charlotte M. Mew.*

I wore my Sunday frock, gravy-brown finely striped with black. Without shame and with very little envy, I took note of the bright satins and silks, the laces and long white kid gloves of the other women in the audience as we settled into our orchestra seats. Hardy, in stiff shirt and black evening clothes, didn't seem to care what I or anyone else was wearing. He was convivial and charming, and talked about some difficulties he'd been having with the garden at Max Gate, his home near Dorchester. I listened, anxious and excited by the company and the occasion, as we waited for the play to begin. The great red velvet curtain rose. The murmuring of the audience died away.

His elbow pressed against my forearm along the armrest between our seats. Feeling lumpish and clumsy, I debated whether it was more impolite to move my arm or let it stay. Soon, I forgot myself, caught up with the actors on the bright stage. Once, I slid my eyes sideways to steal a glimpse of Hardy. His hairline was receding, his thinning hair smoothed back like Father's. He watched the play with a half-shuttered gaze, his fingers steepled in front of him – brooding and wise.

Afterwards, as we came out of the theatre into the clear May night, he set his top hat rakishly on the back of his head and asked, 'What do you say we walk a while, away from the crowd? Further along it should be easier to hail a cab.'

The awe I'd felt before was altogether gone; I liked being spoken to as if we were old friends, and I agreed. As we were strolling past lighted restaurants and darkened shop fronts, Hardy rolled up his programme and stuck it into my handbag – a gesture so intimate and yet innocuous that it surprised and confused me.

'Tell me, Charlotte, what did you think of the play?'

I was no coquette. Honesty was all I knew, so I plunged right in. 'I can't accept Hedda's suicide as a solution to her problems.'

'Can't you imagine a time when one's life has become so unbearable that ending it is the only relief?'

I shook my head. 'Unthinkable,' I said. For myself, I didn't *want* to think about it, so I went on with my critique of the play. 'Also, I didn't care for the way the aunt kept prodding the new husband about his "expectations", his plans for a family.'

Hardy reacted with great energy: 'Don't you see how it paints his character? He's so much the intellectual, his mind supremely resident in his body, that he doesn't even understand what she's getting at. Tesman has no passion beyond that for books and ideas. He lacks the necessary sensitivities for a lover. No wonder Hedda is so bored and cross.'

'Oh, Mr Hardy, really.' I gave him *that look*, borrowed from Nanny Elizabeth. 'You're as shocking as Mr Ibsen.'

His brows high-arched in mock astonishment and scepticism. 'Are you truly shocked?' He indicated my short hair and my simple brown frock. 'You who appear to delight in defying convention?' His manner was playful, almost flirtatious. 'Are you, after all, a prude?'

'Of course not.' I tossed my head, in spite of a deep, doubtful stir. 'What does it matter if Tesman is no lover?' I went on defiantly. 'Hedda says herself she has no desire for children.'

Hardy chortled. 'I'm sorry, Charlotte. I'd forgotten how awfully young you are.'

My cheeks flamed. I wasn't willing to confess my ignorance about relations between husbands and wives. That mystery – and it was still a mystery, even though I was acquainted from my reading with the improbable mechanics of it – was both intriguing and fearsome. While we passed in and out of the glow of a street lamp, I fumbled to cover my embarrassment. 'And surely Hedda Gabler, a married woman, giving in to her feelings for a man who's not her husband, that can't be proper behaviour.'

Hardy stopped and looked down at me, laying a hand on my arm. His tone was half rueful. 'Do you imagine being married necessarily puts paid to one's love for any other?'

His hand burned through the sleeve on my arm. I pulled away. 'I don't know about being married.' My answer was abrupt, sour, disagreeable. I didn't want to hear any more about it. I didn't much like being reminded that Hardy had a wife down in Dorset. It brought me, in spite of all my bravado, too perilously close to sin and scandal. In any case, I calmed myself, ours was in no sense a similar situation to the play's. I was never going to marry; I was no Hedda Gabler, no trifler with men's emotions, no wretched suicide.

Oh! there was nothing, nothing that did not sweep to the
high seat
        Of laughing gods, and then blow down and beat
  My soul into the highway dust, as hoofs do the dropped roses of
  the street.

from 'Madeleine in Church'

Late September, a Sunday afternoon, we walked. Rain clouds
waited on the horizon, what horizon can be seen in city streets,
and the air was still and tepid. And as we walked through a
part of north London unfamiliar to me, we talked – or rather
Hardy talked and I listened, outwardly sympathetic and sub-
dued. Inwardly, I was choked with unseemly joy, joyous to be
the single audience for his angry reflections. His father had
died in the summer, and Hardy was preoccupied with his own
mortality. He raged against it: 'Why should a man's mind be
thrown into such close, sad, sensational, inexplicable relations
with such a precarious object as his own body!'

In an unfocused way, I was aware of other pedestrians, those
approaching, those whose backs were ahead of us. I kept my
eyes forward. If I met Hardy's, some troubling discussion about
bodies was sure to ensue. I didn't want any of that. As we waited
at the kerb for a coach to pass, the horses' hoofs clattering over
the granite setts of the street, I asked about his work.

'I've been making notes on the story of a young man who
couldn't go to Oxford,' Hardy said, 'his struggles and ultimate
failure.' Still early days, he couldn't say more. Instead, as we
crossed the street, he shifted the conversation to my writing,
urging me to concentrate on poetry: 'You're a born poet, I'm
certain of it.'

Always that unblinking certainty about my work, which I didn't share. Exciting, though, to listen to him discuss it as if it were genuine and of the same kind as his own. Next, he began coaxing me to show him something I'd composed.

'No, no,' I said. 'I've got nothing but fragments and false starts.' I was reluctant to show anyone, especially Hardy, what little I'd produced that I hadn't slashed through with cancelling strokes. Truth to tell, I wasn't willing to risk humiliation. 'Some day,' I promised. My plan, recently and roughly formed, was to wait until I'd got a piece published in one of the literary journals and then present it to him as a *fait accompli*. And as an offering, a gift, a reward for his faith and encouragement. He couldn't fail to be gratified at that. Once in print, it – and I – would be immune from any hurtful criticism.

As we passed shuttered shops and terraces of houses with net curtains drawn, I tried to divert him with questions about poetic form and metre, and his methods of working, how he managed to be so steadily prolific. He answered in patient detail. 'I never let a day go by without using my pen. Just holding it sets me off. It's important not to wait for the right mood. If you do, it will come less and less.'

We strolled along Beaumont Street and came to what looked to be a dead end, our way blocked by a two-storeyed, ochre-brick house with ginger-red cornices over the windows. But as we got to the iron railings in front of it, I noticed the street bent sharply to the left and connected with the Marylebone High Street. And ahead of us at the corner was a hot-potato man's cart on the edge of the pavement. Hardy brightened. 'I'll get us some, shall I? And we can have an impromptu picnic in Regent's Park.'

We found an unoccupied bench off the Broad Walk, by a clump of box near Queen Mary's Garden. The powdery scent of late roses hung in the air. From far away in the direction of the boating lake came the faint, wavering sounds of a brass band playing the final measures of a Strauss waltz. A pause and then the strains of 'God Save the Queen', the end of the outdoor concert. We sat and unwrapped the pieces of newspaper from round our roasted potatoes. I nibbled at mine. Something too sensual, too intimate about eating for me to do it so openly, in full view of passing strangers: courting couples, families with children in tow, nannies pushing prams.

Hardy, though, ate his potato with obvious gusto and said, brushing his palms together, 'Capital fare, better than the fancy cuisine served at the dinner parties I'm forced to attend in London. One can't always avoid such obligations. I'd actually grown to despise this city.' He added, meaningfully, 'Until early last spring.'

'Last spring?'

'Why, yes, one day in the British Museum I smiled at a bright-eyed, vivacious girl. She soon revealed herself to be thoughtful, intelligent, sensitive, touchy even' – he gave me a sly glance – 'light and slight, seeming to see wonders in the air.'

Being spoken of in the third person as something unique, held up for both of us to admire, flattered and delighted me.

Hardy was obviously savouring it, too, as he continued his appraisal of the person he'd met four months ago: 'She's all nervous motion, with the nature of a woman clipped and pruned by severe discipline. Yet she has a wildly tossed spirit and an underbrightness shining through from the depths, which discipline hasn't been able to reach. I've come to know her as a complex being, at the same time rash and prudent. She's a pert little thing, boyish as Ganymede, modest as Hebe . . .' He paused with the wicked arch of a brow.

The indecently exposed and shamed Hebe flashed in my mind. His teasing had crossed some unspoken, unspeakable boundary. I stared at my black-gloved fingers laced in my lap, feeling guarded and disconcerted.

'. . . with tight-strained nerves. She's something of a riddle to me, her conduct one lovely conundrum . . .'

I looked up. 'Mr Hardy –'

His expression was plaintive. 'Please, call me Tom.'

I hesitated. 'Thomas.'

'All right. Thomas, then.' He bent towards me. 'What's the matter, Charlotte?'

I shook my head in a quick, violent way. He leant back against the bench and resettled his felt hat on his head.

'Thomas . . .' I cleared my throat. I needed to explain myself to the both of us. 'When I was a girl, I imagined Sunday was the day of eyes, with God and all His saints and angels watching everything I did. In my memory of childhood sabbaths, I'm for ever confined to the nursery under God's – and Nanny's – scrutiny. I'm memorizing scripture passages and restlessly playing with the one acceptable toy.' It had been poor Henry's when he was a boy, but I couldn't tell Hardy that. 'I'm miming the story of the Deluge, using a painted wooden Noah's ark with pairs of lions, rooks and elephants. And God is watching my every move. I thought I'd outgrown that notion, but today, I feel as if those eyes are watching me again.'

'You, an orthodoxy believer?' he burst out, close to laughing. 'I wouldn't have thought it.'

I frowned to show him I was serious. 'I don't make any claims to orthodoxy. I honestly don't know what I am. A seeker and moral struggler, maybe. I want so to believe in Something that believes in me, do you see? Some Ultimate Cause.'

'I've long since concluded, Charlotte, that the Ultimate Cause is indifferent, neither moral nor immoral but with no moral concern, if one can attribute such a quality as concern to It at all.'

Such talk was both stimulating and uncomfortable. I sat listening, half expecting some cosmic response. I'd never before heard anyone state the agnostic case so boldly, but here it was, spoken aloud without bringing down a single clap of answering thunder. His boldness made me bold, too. I had an idea of my own: 'Maybe the gods of the ancients, the ones in the Elgin Marbles, were better suited to our human nature. They lacked perfection, so they didn't expect any mortal to be perfect either.'

'And your Sunday God of the eyes expects perfection?'

'He demands it.' A rain bird called and called in a tree somewhere across the way. The clouds couldn't be held off for ever. I turned fully towards him, letting myself get openly excited: 'There's a certain freedom, Thomas, an exhilaration, when one accepts entirely the responsibility for judging one's own behaviour. I've felt it at times.' In the next breath, I sat back, murmuring, 'Still . . .'

'Still,' he went on, picking up the dropped thread, 'one is left without anything beyond one's self on which to rely.'

'Yes, I suppose that's it. And I'm not quite prepared to abandon what I think of as my soul and accept being merely a creature of bones and nerves.'

We sat now in cool shade, the sun setting beyond the shrubbery behind us and the sky overhead blue-purple. I looked off in the direction of the thick trees along the eastern edge of the park. Their topmost leaves and branches were gilded against the plum-coloured evening clouds.

Hardy shifted on the bench beside me. 'I understand what it is to go seeking after a mystical Someone,' he said, 'whose transcendent love redeems and compensates for the solitary anguish of life. In the end, one finds only disappointment and despair.' He sighed. 'I shouldn't be so pessimistic and despairing if I hadn't, when I was young like you, had higher expectations.' He gave an ironic chuckle. 'Did you know that as a boy I wanted to be a clergyman?'

I studied his bearded profile and tried to picture the idealistic young Hardy. A tender sympathy was building in me. What terrible forces had worked to turn him inside out?

He stared into the distance, his jaw set under the short, dark whiskers. 'Travelling in France years ago, I came upon the carved wooden figure of Christ on a wayside Calvary. It appeared to writhe and cry in the twilight. I've never been able to rid myself of that image. It comes to me whenever I try to remember a poem I once heard. I don't recall its source, but it was about an old peasant who knelt one evening before just such a crucifix on the side of the road, and as he prayed, he slipped into an easeful death. In the morning, all that remained was a heap of dry brown leaves, which the wind stirred and blew away. That's how I'd like to die.'

In the ebbing daylight after a lengthy, weighted silence, Hardy said, 'Death is an absolution.'

'Will one be forgiven all one's sins? Won't God punish us? What about the loss of heaven and the pains of hell?' I asked, remembering Nanny's fearsome catechism.

'They are beyond that – the dead. They are divinely indifferent.'

Hardy had been pondering for years matters I'd only begun to consider. He'd reached conclusions while I had nothing but equivocations. All his thinking echoed one persistent theme, the best I could tell. 'Life, then, is simply a deathwatch?'

He faced me. 'Except for those moments when two – I was about to use the word *souls*, but I can't say with any certain knowledge they exist. This I can say: life *is* a deathwatch, except for those rare, brief moments when two imaginations meet and twine.' His grey eyes were earnest; he was near whispering. 'Such as we've had.'

A flicker of panic touched me, and passed. 'You're making love to me, Thomas, and it's wrong.'

'I can't explain or justify my actions, but in time the inevitable justifies itself.'

I felt watery inside. I gripped my handbag and got to my feet. 'It's late. I must be going,' I said and strode off across the grass. In seconds, Hardy was at my side, slowing me to a walk. As we neared the York Gate, he stopped and, without a word, took my hand and raised it to his lips, kissing the inside of my bare wrist at the throat of my glove. I pulled my hand away and hid it behind me, ashamed and bewildered, and oddly pleased.

1893

Lend me, a little while, the key
　　That locks your heavy heart, and I'll give you back –
Rarer than books and ribbons and beads bright to see,
　　This little Key of Dreams out of my pack.

　　　　　　　.　　.　　.

Give me the key that locks your tired eyes,
　　And I will lend you this one from my pack,
Brighter than coloured beads and painted books that make
　　men wise:
　　　　Take it. No, give it back!

from 'The Pedlar'

Up in my room, I put on Hardy like a pair of spectacles and reread the poems and stories I'd written, and burned them all, every one. Their flaws were glaring – spotty, false, self-conscious, and without life – in spite of any satisfaction I might have felt when I was creating them.

Sometimes when I wrote, I was given moments when I got completely outside myself, moments of such keen joy as I'd only had before, say, at a concert when I was wrapped round and lifted up by a Mozart concerto, or in a gallery when I was taken completely into a Constable landscape. In those scattered, joyous instants in writing, exactly the right word or phrase or metaphor flowed off the nib of the pen, and it seemed as if I'd tapped the vein of creativity leading directly to the heart of all things. Those moments were rare and exhilarating. They were what I hoped for every time I sat down at my table to write; this same hope kept me coming back and made me determined to start all over again.

Nanny came daily to interrupt my work. Since the days of

Miss Bolt, we no longer employed a regular seamstress, so our clothes were kept in good repair by Nanny Elizabeth. That was her excuse for coming into my room as I'd nearly finished burning my manuscripts in the fireplace grate. I must have looked furtive, poking at the feathery black ashes among the coals.

'My, it's got warm in here,' she said, accusingly. The distance between us was more strained than ever, with suspicion on her side and defensiveness on mine. Today, I'd no intention of explaining perfectly innocent behaviour. She opened the door to my wardrobe and rummaged round in the bottom among my shoes, setting them to rights in tidy pairs, and then rearranged the hats on the top shelf, well acquainted with the proper place for everything.

'What are you after?' I asked, replacing the iron poker in its stand.

'I intend putting white linen collar and cuffs on this.' Nanny held up my black-and-white-checked school frock, examined it fore and aft, and draped it over her forearm. 'Still lots of wear in it,' she said, as if I were about to argue with her. She left, closing the door emphatically behind her.

I hadn't grown at all in the last half dozen years – still under five feet tall – and wore the same white shirtwaists, the same tartan skirt and two others in fawn and grey. I had, as well, two black fitted jackets of summer and winter weight, and my brown Sunday frock. And in the far corner, one of black broadcloth for funerals and mourning. All perfectly adequate for a someone of my taste and activities.

I rarely even thought about what hung in the wardrobe, so I was surprised at myself when I was overtaken by an unexpected burst of vanity in late November. After trying on a number of shawls in front of a large looking-glass at Liberty's, I bought one with the money Father had given me for my twenty-third birthday: a Turkey-red paisley cashmere wool, shamelessly sensuous, soft as thistledown. After that, when I sat at my work table, I wrapped the shawl round myself like a magic mantle, and wrote.

Christmas came and went; the year 1893 commenced darkly, muffled in a sooty fog, with no word from Hardy. At one time, he'd confessed to me a fondness for home-made valentines, so I boldly went to making one, although not so boldly as to let anyone else know what I was doing. It was all white paper lace and water-coloured ribbons and rosebuds Anne had taught me to paint. Not used to having so many secrets from my sister, I worked on the valentine in my room while she was at the studio she'd taken with two other young women from her art school class. Over and again, I considered telling her – what? That I'd met a well-known author? That he was married; nevertheless we'd become – what? – something I'd no name for? What about our vows to one another, Anne and I, to avoid any entanglements? What would she think of me, other than I'd taken leave of my senses?

I loved her too dearly to suffer her bad opinion. Maybe some day, when we'd both got too old for such things to matter any longer, I'd tell her, entertain her some rainy evening with tales of my silly infatuation with a famous man. And we'd laugh together at my innocent folly and have another sherry – our one bit of decadence once safely into old age. For the present, though, I wasn't certain I could make her understand what I hadn't got clear myself. About Hardy, I was confused by feelings of awe and admiration and something murky. A mixture of fear and what? Attraction? Outside my heart, I was circumspect and silent.

I posted the valentine to Hardy at Max Gate – unsigned, a last-minute qualm – and decided to set myself to rights, to make amends for neglecting my sweet sister. In the afternoon, when she wasn't occupied with her painting of birds and flowers, Anne and I read aloud to each other by turns from the magazine serialization of Hardy's novel, *The Pursuit of the Well-Beloved* – ironically, Anne's selection – until teatime. On clear, chilly days, we went for walks in Russell Square or paid calls on old friends from school. Most of them had got themselves comfortably and complaisantly married, presiding over their own parlours and teapots, antimacassars and footstools. And some had been delivered of pink and gold babies, brought in for our admiration by starched nannies and whisked away again to distant nurseries before they could be handed round. No touching, no yearning allowed, I reminded myself.

I waited for each day's post to drop through the brass flap in the street door, ready to snatch up any envelope with my name on it before Nanny could spy the postmark and begin asking pointed questions. At last, his letter arrived:

Feb'ry 20, 1893

Dear, dear one,

My domestic circumstances make it impossible to extend hospitalities at this time, or I should invite you to visit.

Are you writing? You must. And you must write, in prose or poetry, those stories – however extraordinary or unorthodox – that one would never relate to one's family at the dinner table. We tale-tellers are all Ancient Mariners, and none of us is warranted in stopping Wedding Guests (in other words, the hurrying public) unless he has something more unusual to relate than the ordinary experience of every average man and woman. The whole secret of fiction and poetry lies in the adjustment of things unusual to things eternal and universal.

On a recent wet, black Sunday I caught sight of two lovers under one umbrella and thought of you. You reside vividly in my memory – pretty, liquid-eyed, light-footed, with your quick, high voice. You once said you knew nothing about marriage. To this dynamic involvement with life I have always been myself but a wistful spectator. As with so much of this world's business, I cannot untangle the paradox of the thing. Love lives on propinquity, but dies of contact.

I have watched women with some care and profound fascination since I was a small boy and have found those who run against the grain the most attractive. Therein lies, I suspect, my fondness for you, my fey, my little unsentimental maker of valentines. Yes, I saw at once whose tiny hand fashioned that sweet token of love. Which is returned, multiplied many times, by

Your admirer from afar,
Tom

In my room, I read the letter over twice, the second time aloud in the faintest whisper, and imagined Hardy saying the words to me. I went all over gooseflesh. Just then, I heard the slow footfalls coming along the hallway outside my door. Nanny! I slid the letter and its envelope into my work-table drawer and picked up my pen and got busy scrawling empty nonsense – *mustn't, mustn't, mustn't* – across a piece of paper by the time she let herself in.

After Nanny had been in to do her daily dusting and discouraging me from work on my writing, I read the letter one more time, put it into its envelope and tucked it under the lining at the bottom of my travel trunk, locking it with the key on the red ribbon round my neck. With a spill, I lighted a cigarette at the fireplace and leant against the mantelpiece, watching the flames finger the coals and wondering how to reply to the letter. Or if I dared to reply at all. Down what primrose path had I stumbled?

The next morning was cold and still. A light snow had covered the soot of the city during the night. Frost-lace edged the window-panes, and the back garden was transformed into a foreign country where pristine white was the only colour. The sun reflecting off the snow made spots caper in front of me when I stepped away from the window. I took out a fresh sheet of paper. In for a penny, in for a pound.

My dearest King of Wessex,

You have found me out. I confess; I am the unsigned valentine-maker. And you have read its unwritten message clearly.

I, too, often think of you. Sometimes, when the breeze blows from the south-west, I walk alone in Gordon Square among the leafless plane trees and think it has been in Dorset between one and two hours before, floating along the streets and lanes, pulling round the weathercocks, touching your garden, being breathed by you, and now being breathed by me, the very same.

I understand your 'domestic circumstances'. I shall never visit Max Gate, and I do not care; I care solely for its troubled chief resident, and you do sound troubled, which troubles me.

I work at my writing. I cannot say more than that, but you have inspired me to keep at it, no matter what. For that, and so much else, I thank you and remain

> Yours gratefully and devotedly,
> C.M.M.

Without hat or coat or gloves, the paisley shawl tied round my shoulders, I rushed out to the corner, to the red pillar box embossed with the intertwining VR. I dropped the letter in the slot. The instant it disappeared from sight, I regretted having written with such candour and realized how foolish I'd been to send it off without a second thought. Fretting and distracted, I went back into the house, where I was met in the front hall by a stern-faced Nanny Elizabeth. I shivered, not from the cold day but from her arctic blue stare. Her expression was so grave my first thought was for Mama.

'What is it, Nanny? What's happened?'

'I'm asking you.' She skewered me with *that look*, and my knees threatened to fold under me. 'You're a clever one,' she said, a remark with a sting in its tail. 'You always were a fractious, provoking child, wilful and impulsive. Now, you've added sly and deceptive.'

I gritted my teeth to keep from saying something vindictive or, worse, self-incriminating, and tried to step round her.

But she countered by moving sideways. 'Don't suppose I haven't seen your comings and goings. And now, running out into the street like that, without even a hat to cover your head decent. What will the neighbours say? Think how their gossip would wound your mother. What is it you're up to, Lottie?' Her mouth was creased and sour, drooping at the corners. 'No good, I'll warrant,' she said in a tone with an edge like broken glass. 'It's a young man, isn't it? You've ruined yourself with some scoundrel too evil or too cowardly to show himself like a proper suitor. Oh, you wicked, wicked girl.'

Sick and excited and ashamed, I stood my ground, twisting my fingers together behind my back. I kept my face as blank as I could, in spite of its reddening heat.

'When you go out night and day, where do you go?' She fisted her hands on her hips. 'Tell me. You meet someone. Who is he? What do you do?'

'I will not be catechized!' I burst out, shouting to be heard over my heart's thumping, and dashed round her and up the stairs.

At Christmas time we went half mad
For joy of all the toys we had,
And then we used to sing about the sheep
The shepherds watched by night;
We used to pray to Christ to keep
Our small souls safe till morning light –;
I am scared, I am staying with you to-night –
Put me to sleep.

from 'In Nunhead Cemetery'

I killed Nanny Elizabeth. My guilt was undeniable; no amount of prayer and bedside watches could lift it from me.

She'd collapsed, struggling up the stairs after me, calling my name; she lay on the first-floor landing for some time before Molly, the maid, found her and let out a scream that echoed up through the stairwell to my bedroom. I ran down the steps, nearly tripping, to find her standing over the crumpled figure. Mama came from the parlour and began a loud wailing. I knelt down beside Nanny and touched her bony wrist. Her pulse was weak, but she was breathing, still alive. I sent Molly for the doctor.

He could do nothing for her. 'A matter of time, Miss Mew. I'm so sorry.' So I sat, watching and waiting, where Nanny lay on her narrow bed, hardly making an impression on the sheets. She was a papier mâché shell of what she'd been. Some fierce substance had gone out of her in the hours since our angry meeting in the front hall. Or had it been evaporating over the years and I hadn't seen, hardly aware of what was happening in front of me every day?

Winter evenings arrive early. Outside, the city was inky-dark and distant. I'd never before been in this room at the top of the house. It had a camphory smell and was small and spartan, which suited Nanny: walls distempered the colour of egg shells, a white-painted cast-iron bedstead, a low cottage chest of drawers beside it, and a single wooden chair. Sepia photographs of us as children – Henry, Freda, Anne, and me – lined the shallow mantelpiece. Mama had banished all images of my lost brother and sister; they were too much for her. From my seat beside the bed, I stared at their pictures, re-memorizing the long-ago faces.

Jolly nursery times came tumbling back. Nanny smiling, petting and praising. Not all of it had been criticism and caning.

The sound of the door opening startled me out of the past.

'What a climb,' Mama said, fingers fanned across her bosom. I got to my feet and pulled out the chair for her. She put her candlestick on the chest of drawers. 'It's cold in here.'

The room had got chilly as night came on; I'd barely noticed, sitting in near-darkness. 'I'll stoke the fire,' I said and turned over the photographs on the mantel with one hand as I worked the poker with the other. Mama sat in the chair, and I came to stand at the foot of the bed, my back to the reviving heat of the fire. I buried my fingers in the folds of my shawl to warm them.

'How is she, the poor dear?' Mama asked. 'Has she wakened at all?'

I shook my head.

'How at peace she seems.' Mama sighed. 'I'd forgotten how she looks without a wrinkled frown.' Her hands fluttered to her face as if feeling for her own wrinkles. 'She was *my* nanny first, you know.' Mama raised her widened eyes and stared at me. With a kind of awe, she said, 'I think she's gone, Charlotte.'

I hurried round the end of the bed and touched Nanny's wrist for a pulse, my own beating in my ears. I stepped away, my arms dropping helplessly at my sides.

Mama rose with a rustle of taffeta as she fluffed and shook herself like a tiny black bird. 'It's God's will,' she said, resolved. 'She's gone before us, gone with the angels, waiting on the other side. We shall meet her again, by and by.'

I'd freely have given my own life right then to share such certainty.

Mama moved to leave, pausing in the open doorway with the candlestick in her hand. 'Your father will make arrangements for the undertaker in the morning. Someone must be with her tonight.' She faltered, tugged a lace square from her sleeve, and dabbed at her wet cheeks. 'I don't trust the maid. She'd likely fall asleep. You're the strong one, Charlotte. You must keep the vigil.'

'Yes, Mama,' I said.

She went, taking the candle's light with her, leaving me and the little room in shadow. The coals in the grate shifted; an eruption of sparks brightened the hearth, and then settled into blackness. I dropped on to the chair and pulled my shawl round me.

In the snow-light from the window, Nanny's face – her smooth brow, her domed eyelids, her benign and silent lips – all were the colour of the winter moon. Her hair was loosened, white and fine on the pillowcase. Her marble stillness held me for several minutes in a kind of mortal fear. This was the first death I'd ever attended, the first dead person – body – I'd been alone with. And it came to me, with a sad certainty, it surely wouldn't be the last. I leant over and lifted her empty hands, so cold and heavy. I crossed them on the front of her white flannel nightgown. White on white on white. Gone to the country of all-white things.

I *did* love her, even though she had a mind too angular, always poking and prodding. Her last days – oh, she couldn't know they were her last – were spent in petty tasks and worries. No denying it, I'd been her greatest worry for as long as I could remember. And I'd killed her. My shouted words, my hateful manner, my tart defiance had struck her down as surely as if I'd hit her with my fist. I *was* truly wicked, as she'd said, writing to a married man. My shoulders drooped. The weight of my sins was almost more than I could bear.

I bowed my head and worked at praying. Phrases of self-condemnation drifted up to the low ceiling and hung there with no further place to go, no One to go to. 'Forgive me,' I whispered to Nanny and was, all at once, so exhausted and scared I nearly fell forward on to the bed. Tears I'd bitten back all day until my underlip was sore started to flow. I wiped them away with the hem of the coverlet. And still they came, beyond my control. How I longed for her to wake up and carry me to my room, the way she did when I was ill as a child, and tuck the bed covers up under my chin and tell me all would be well in the morning.

On a piece of foolscap dated some years before and signed 'With Love and Duty', Nanny Elizabeth had set forth her will and portioned out among us her few possessions, to each one of us some carefully chosen thing: her mother's eight-day clock that stood in the corner by the kitchen door and her tea-caddy with the inlaid roses to Mama; her own much-dented mahogany workbox to Anne; and, for me, the china teapot commemorating the Queen's Silver Jubilee.

But a few hours after the blinds were drawn in the quiet room at the top of the house, these and all her other things were collected, packed and removed in a four-wheel cab, and the funeral loudly discussed in every bitter detail by a band of newly arrived relatives, among them a heavily scented niece and a brazen sister-in-law. With a great display of black-bordered pocket handkerchiefs, they overran the house, ransacking boxes, turning out drawers, and eating endless meals in the kitchen. They disagreed to the end, with all the noises of a Punch and Judy show. We were hampered by our own grief and Mama's insistence that we respect theirs, such as it was, so we were helpless before the barbarians' onslaught. I hoped wherever she was, Nanny couldn't see or hear them.

I went up to my room, as far from the squabbling as I could get, and tried to compose an obituary:

Elizabeth Goodman, born in Yorkshire (where exactly? when? 1806? 1807?), spent her adult life between the attic nursery and the basement kitchen, in cooking, washing, sewing; in planning for us, her charges, her children, small treats and great futures; patching clothes and sibling quarrels. She slaved, adored, fought for and occasionally whipped us with a calm crescendo of 'Will you? Will you? WILL YOU?' between spanks. She was the most rigorous with me, a strong-willed child, because I insisted upon growing into an independent young woman.

The obituary had got away from me and evolved into something resembling a eulogy. At the same time, writing about Nanny, even in such a roughly done first draft, was a way of explaining her to myself so I might get her fixed more clearly in my mind before I let go of her altogether.

Throughout the year her reading was limited to the Bible, but in December she flung into the festooned disorder of the nursery a pile of Christmas numbers, and we lived, for a week or two, in the world of pure romance. Lights gleamed from manor-house windows; we glided down broad oak staircases and through the halls of holly-decked mansions, where, above, ghosts stalked the corridors and, below, there was always dancing; or we lost ourselves on the great white road outside where the snow was falling, in a whirl of highwaymen and elopements.

My imagination and love of story had been fed on such holiday fare. Had Nanny known what she was educating me to be, would she have done anything differently? She'd been, for all of us, our first teacher, and she'd never left off teaching.

She trained a long succession of raw girls from the country. Under her tutelage, the housemaids, the Emmas and Marys and Mollys, learnt to go about their work with noiseless feet and downcast eyes;

answering the door, tending fires, feather-dusting parlour bric-à-brac; laying the table, serving meals, clearing; weeding and trimming in the garden; fetching hot water from the kitchen for baths; and running up and down stairs on a thousand other errands.

Nanny understood work without understanding any that wasn't active or obviously productive. No wonder she'd been so critical of my writing; to her it hadn't any practical utility at all. Even at her great age, she'd still scurried round like a clockwork mouse; no one dared to speak to her about rest. How were we ever going to manage without her?

It was the sun. The sunshine weaves
A pattern on dull stones: the sunshine leaves
    The portraiture of dreams upon the eyes
        Before it dies:
    All Summer through
The dust hung white upon the drowsy planes
Till suddenly they woke with Autumn rains.

from 'The Fête'

I couldn't let go of her, or she of me. I couldn't escape *that
look*. She persisted. My incessant moral guide. In the weeks
following Nanny's death, voices echoed in my head; I was
arguing with her over everything I did, no matter how trivial.
Letters arrived from Hardy whenever he was coming up to
London; I refused, politely, formally, his invitations.

Her whispering admonitions continued. But, damn it, she
asked too much, insisted on more than I could give. Finally, a
very touching note arrived from Max Gate late in the dry,
empty summer:

Charlotte, dear friend,

The Creator, Whose name we're told is Love, gave us the capacity
to feel deeply and set us in a world where mostly what we feel is
suffering. What have I done to deserve from you such ill-treatment?

What indeed. I was already a self-condemned liar and murderer.
'What is being a harlot to that?' I shouted at my Nanny-
conscience. Unrepentant, I wrote, agreeing to meet Hardy on
Wednesday next at St George's Gardens. To add further piqu-
ancy to my misdeed, I changed out of my mourning clothes –
Mama had decreed a year of black in remembrance of Nanny

79

– into the black and white frock she'd revived with new collar and cuffs. I put on my straw boater and crocheted gloves. Carrying a white cotton parasol against the sun, I hurried down the stairs, past the closed door of the parlour where Mama had callers, down to the ground floor and Father's office, silent and empty, and out into the bright afternoon to meet Hardy.

He was waiting for me at the gate in Handel Street. I nearly passed him by; since our last meeting, he'd shaved his beard, leaving a drooping moustache like Father's, flecked with silver-white. I felt the pinch of shyness. He was half a stranger after so long, with his chin so palely naked. We exchanged greetings. He regarded me from under the brim of his panama with an affection that made perspiration prickle on my upper lip. Was I mistaken to have come?

St George's Gardens, a skewed rectangle tucked behind terrace houses and a church fronting on Regent Square, had been at one time a cemetery; salvaged fragments of tombstones leant against the rust-red brick of the garden walls. Dusty trees, wooden benches and beds of flowers dotted the clipped lawn. Above it all, the sky was molten and caramel-coloured.

No one was in the gardens except ourselves. Nervous, aware of a strain between us, I shifted my parasol to my left hand. Hardy took my right one and folded his arm into mine. We began a leisurely stroll round the gardens, deciphering the inscriptions on the lichened, cracked and broken slabs of stone. They reminded me of the tablets on which Moses brought down the Ten Commandments from Mt Sinai. 'Thou shalt not commit adultery.'

Rubbish. Adultery was something vastly other than walking in a public park. We were old friends, Hardy and I, fellow writers who met on occasion to renew our acquaintance, nothing more.

I joined in Hardy's bantering speculation about the long-ago deceased. 'Look at this one,' I said, pointing with the toe of my shoe at a tilted piece of marble. Hardy brushed aside the long fingers of ivy to expose the full inscription. 'Linton Long-worth Harper, 1667–1713, Husband of Maria,' I read aloud. 'Father of Longworth, Arabella, Samuel, Cecilia, Agatha, Benjamin, Susannah and Bess.'

Hardy laughed. 'It's a good thing old Linton died when he did, or there'd have been no room on the stone for listing all his progeny.'

I smiled at him. 'I'm glad to see you so light-hearted,' I said. 'Our last meeting was mostly angry brooding and gloomy railing against death.'

'It's you, Charlotte. I'm so delighted you're here.'

'I've missed you, too, Thomas. Over these many months, I've wanted so to –' I stopped short. There was more emotion in those few words than I'd intended.

'I thought I'd never see you again,' he said. As quick as a cloud passing over the sun, his expression went dark, his eyes storm-grey and sad. 'We had people down at the weekend just past. We sat on the edge of a sandpit and talked of suicide, pessimism, whether life was worth living, and kindred dismal subjects, till we were all quite miserable. If your note hadn't come in the day's last post, I'm not certain what I might've done.'

'Oh, Thomas. Please don't make me responsible for your life and your happiness. I've enough difficulty with my own.'

The corners of his mouth lifted under his moustache. 'No more talk of death and dying, then. Let's go among the roses and leave the gravestones to the ivy.' We walked on. The day was quite warm, and the heat made me pleasantly drowsy and somnambulant. I listened as Hardy talked in a low, dreamy way about his boyhood and his family. 'Country folk, all of them, Dorset farmers and artisans. My father was a mason and builder, like his father before him, and his before him, back to Adam. And they were musical. I was, too, as a youth.' As he spoke about that earlier time, the squint left his eyes. His moustache no longer drooped; under it, his lips parted in a smile. His high cheeks went apple-y, round and ruddy, and the boy in the man shone through. It was like an image appearing on a photographic plate; I wanted to fix it for ever in my memory.

We halted under the shade of a great, thick plane tree. A slight breeze riffled the leaves, with a sound like whispering gossips. I checked round. We were still alone.

'Do you play?' he asked.

I was at a loss for a moment. What was he talking about? 'Oh. Yes. The piano. Well, I'm told, although not well enough to inflict myself on anyone outside my family.'

'Such modesty,' he said, clucking in comic disbelief.

'When you speak of your childhood, Thomas, your face alters, and you seem so happy.'

'Yes, that's true, but I don't delude myself. Childhood was no Wordsworthian idyll. The rainbow didn't come and go; it came once and departed, apparently for ever. At the age of six, I fell in love with a beautiful woman, gentry she was, and I never recovered. First love marks us, always.'

My mind went to dear, dear Lucy Harrison, somewhere in Yorkshire with . . .

'I've never been able to slake my thirst for falling in love, never found that lady reincarnated.' He added, meaningfully, 'Until now.'

I frowned, as much from the glare as to show my displeasure. I wasn't going to let him start off on that road again. To divert the conversation, I asked, 'Do you believe in reincarnation? What do you think you'd be in another life, if you weren't a writer?'

'Not an architect.' His answer was quick in coming.

We resumed walking among the beds of white and pink and lavender flowers. The sun was so bright I couldn't look very long at them for the glare, couldn't make out what varieties they were. The heat and light melted everything into something like the paintings of Mr Turner. I blinked and saw the full heads of the flowers were drooping in the heat, as if they were napping. The garden was so still the whole world seemed asleep. Except for the two of us, wrapped in light.

'I've got it,' he said, going on with the game of what-if. 'I'd be a West Country farmer with dirt under my nails.'

I glanced at Hardy's immaculate fingers covering my gloved hand on the sleeve of his linen suit in the parasol's shade. 'You're joking.'

'Perhaps,' he said earnestly, 'but I do understand farm folk. I know their frustrations and their longings, the lure and strength of the snares that catch and hold them.'

I tilted my head. 'Snares?'

'Early marriage, for one, motivated by economics and bio-logy, rather than by mutual affection. The anguish caused by such misbegotten and unbreakable unions is immeasurable.' His reply was becoming a tirade. 'If a marriage is only a sordid contract based on material convenience, for taxing and inherit-ance of land and money by children, making it necessary that the male parent should be known – which it appears to be – why, surely, a person may say when it grieves him.'

I couldn't do anything but listen. He was so upset I thought any response from me might be taken the wrong way. Inside my gloves, my palms were wet with perspiration.

'At Max Gate, I often pass the night in my study.'

This sounded like a *non sequitur*. I didn't understand. Nanny sounded in my head: *Don't be daft, girl. You know what he's getting at.*

I must have looked puzzled because Hardy began to explain. 'I can no longer bear . . .'

I pulled my arm free of his and turned on him. 'No! I shan't listen to this.' I could hear Nanny dictating what I was supposed to say: 'We two are friends. If you persist in making love to me, Thomas, our friendship must be ended.'

A white butterfly, like the tiniest of angels, flitted up from a flower-bed and through the silent space between us. I pictured the angel that drove the sinful couple from the Garden of Eden, an angel with a flaming sword. And Nanny's face.

Hardy's chuckle startled me. 'What a paradox you are,' he said, the corners of his eyes crinkling, 'unpredictable and passionate, yet possessed at times with such a sober and sensible way of talking.'

I was troubled and confused. I'd expected him to be put off, sulky, maybe offended, by my rebuff; instead, he found it tantalizing.

'My bright enigma,' he said, clasping my fingers again.

I tried, I told Nanny. *You can see it's done no good.*

Hardy fumbled out a gold watch from his vest pocket. 'I must apologize,' he said, 'but I'm expected shortly at a reception, guaranteed to be a deadly bore, but unavoidable. However, the next time I'm up in London, you must let me give you supper. I shan't tell anyone else I'm coming, I promise, so I may quietly enjoy myself, and you.'

'Yes, I'd like that,' I said impulsively, before Nanny could stop me.

He took my arm again and slipped it under his. As we moved on together across the sunny grass towards Sidmouth Street, Hardy lifted my hand from his sleeve, peeled back the edge of my glove, and inserted his middle finger along my moist palm. A shiver ran through me, and I was blushing, not with shame but with a strange, unnameable, painful pleasure.

There is but one for such as I
    To love, to hate, to hunger for;
I shall, perhaps, grow old and die,
    With one short day to spend and store,
One night, in all my life, no more.

from 'Pécheresse'

An autumn afternoon, after a day of undeclared sun, now grey and thickening towards evening. We rode in an open-fronted hansom cab – Hardy and I – to the jingle-jangle of harness brass. Ahead, the black horse's vision was blinkered, seeing only what suited the purpose of the cabby seated above and behind us, hidden by the roof. It occurred to me the horse must come to believe this was the only way of seeing, all there was to see, everything else simply unformed light and sound. My upbringing had been meant to blind me in much the same way. By entering this cab with Hardy today, I'd torn off the blinkers; I intended to be one who does not look away.

The cabby shouted something at the horse and cracked a whip in the air. A nervous twitch ran across the horse's glossy flank, and we lurched forward, melding into the slow-moving congestion of carriages and wagons in Southampton Row. Seated next to Hardy, famous man and ardent friend, I felt a deep, harmonious excitement.

We'd agreed, through a recent exchange of letters, to meet today at the British Museum and walk a bit, along the Embankment maybe, and take an early supper at a restaurant in the Strand that Hardy favoured. We'd set off from the museum and were well along Great Russell Street when the threat of rain prompted him to hail a cab because both of us had come

without umbrellas. It was still early, so he suggested we go first
to the place where he was staying, a borrowed flat in Tavistock
Place: Marchmont Mansions, a red-brick neo-gothic building
with terracotta pointed arches and acanthus capitals, and
leaded, faintly ecclesiastical windows.

Inside the flat, I hesitated in the doorway to the parlour,
feeling rash and wanting to retreat, my boldness already gone.
The room smelled of lemon oil and damp. 'Shall we have some
light?' Hardy asked rhetorically, as he struck a match and put
the flame to the wick of a lamp on a side-table. With its tinted
globe replaced, it gave off a vile green glow.

'May I?' Hardy asked, took my red shawl, and folded it over
the back of a nearby upholstered chair. I crossed the room and
lowered myself stiffly on to the edge of a sofa covered in
damask. I perched there, my handbag clutched in the lap of
my Sunday brown, incongruous as a sparrow on a satin
pillow.

Hardy removed his grey felt hat and tossed it into the chair.
His hair had receded further and gone greyer than I
remembered, making him even more venerable. And vulnerable.
The fragileness of his bare brow touched me, somehow. He
opened the doors of a cabinet and offered me madeira as he
poured a glass. I couldn't think what to say. My family had
gone teetotal since Henry went away; Mama had concluded
alcohol was the cause of his illness, and Nanny, a staunch
Methodist, had supported her in that.

Thinking of Nanny brought her into the room, where she
watched me from the corner by the drinks cabinet. Her Gorgon
stare petrified me for an instant. Hardy cleared his throat. He
was standing in front of me. I could see fine white hairs on the
back of his hand. I could see the surface of the wine ripple
from the tremor of his fingers. He was as nervous as I. An odd
consolation in that. I accepted the stemmed glass from him and
set it on the lamp table near by, changed my mind, retrieved
it and gulped a generous swallow. The wine lighted a fire in

my throat that spread upwards into my cheeks. I was dizzy for a moment or two. When I looked again, Nanny's scowling spectre had vanished.

Hardy gave a broad wave round him; I followed his gesture, noting the vine-leaf and Greek-key patterns stencilled on the walls, the Attic pottery, the copper bowls, the sandalwood boxes and, sharing the lamp table, two bronze figures – Venus and Apollo. He was saying, 'The worst thing about a furnished place is that the articles in the rooms are saturated with the thoughts and glances of others.'

With that, the parlour was all at once crowded with poignant objects and strangers' eyes. I fiddled with my handbag, and then laid it aside. I wished I had a cigarette to occupy myself, to cover the awkward moment. I'd never smoked outside my bedroom. Hardy, in any case, disapproved of women smoking and didn't know about my small vice. I was a creature of small vices. Maybe I didn't have the courage for sin on a larger scale. I drank the last of my wine.

Hardy refilled the glass, calling me his fidgety little thing when it wavered in my gloved fingers.

'I've got no choice,' I said quite honestly, 'but to be what I am.' He unbuttoned the coat of his ash-grey suit and seated himself close beside me on the sofa. I felt trembly. I drank some of the madeira and set the glass on the table so as not to spill it.

I turned back and was taken by surprise. Before I knew it, he had his arms round me, his lips touching my cheek, and he said, 'You know you're the dearest woman to me.' His ardour shook me; his whispering, half heard and half felt against my skin, filled me with dread. I'd thought I was free to do as I liked, but something bound me as tightly as a whalebone corset. I struggled from his arms and leant away into the corner of the sofa, shaken, flustered, a bit dizzy. My cheeks stung; my face must have gone bright red. 'I've renounced all physical love,' I blurted out.

'But why?' Hardy's face was the picture of astonishment and disbelief.

I might have pitied him more if I hadn't been so confused.

'I promise I shan't hurt you. Ever.' His tone, solemn and paternal, reminded me of Father.

I'm afraid of bearing a child, I told myself, afraid of passing on the germ of madness. But that was a matter I'd sworn never to speak of. Still, I had to say something. 'It was always impressed on me,' I told him, 'I oughtn't to marry. I belonged to a peculiar family, the wrong breed for marriage.'

'Marriage?'

No wonder he was puzzled, poor man; he hadn't even mentioned the word. I'd somehow muddled marriage with the marriage act. I knew the one is supposed to precede the other. I also knew it doesn't always. Sometimes, the act occurs outside marriage. It begins with a kiss and is followed by inescapable, dire consequences. I'd heard stories.

Hardy rose and drew himself up until he towered over me, but his voice was gentle, edged with hurt. 'Don't you care for me?'

'I care as much for you as for any man I've ever met.' I was utterly sincere in that.

He walked to the far end of the sofa, the twilight misty in the bay window behind him. He shifted round towards me. His face was changed, twisted. 'Charlotte, don't tease.'

'You've been so good and kind to me,' I said, getting to my feet. He came to me, expectantly taking my outstretched hands. 'I want the friendship between the two of us to continue,' I told him. 'I want to meet and talk with you, to exchange endearments, to touch' – I nodded at his fingers clutching mine – 'but nothing more.' His features collapsed into a sullen frown. 'If you want to love me, Thomas, you may,' I said, placating, 'but please show me this further kindness. Love me as friends love.'

'Damn it, Charlotte, what you want is impossible!' His grip

tightened. 'We've come this far. Good God, you can't mean to go on as if we were merely casual acquaintances.'

I wrenched my hands from his. 'I've never yielded myself to any lover.'

I went as far from him as I could, looking out the window at the street below, where rain was falling, lights reflected and shattered in the dappled pools on the black pavement.

I continued, my back to him so I didn't have to watch the pain I was inflicting: 'My liking for you isn't the same as some women's perhaps. But it's a delight in being with you, of a delicate sort, and for myself, I don't want to go further and risk it by . . . any attempt to intensify it.'

'You're a sort of fay, or sprite – not a woman!'

I faced him and tried again to explain: 'I'm sorry if I've treated you cruelly. I admit I'm flattered by your making love to me.' I stepped nearer to him. 'I don't dislike you, Thomas,' I said, imploring. 'Only, I oughtn't to love you.'

'You understand how you've tortured me?' he said in reproach. 'That doesn't seem to disturb you.'

'But it does!' I cried. Tears made Hardy and the hideous green light run together. 'God knows it does.'

'You're beyond me.' His words became harsh. 'I frighten you, and you make me, somehow, half a fool and half a brute. The man that's left can't reach the woman in you.'

Was I simply so wicked I wilfully gave us both pain? What sort of perversity was this?

'I'm utterly confounded by your double nature,' he said, sounding miserable, dejected. 'I think you're incapable of real love.'

'Oh, no! That's not so!'

'Then, what is it? Are you innocent of your own sexual nature? Or are you simply afraid of it?'

What *was* it I was truly afraid of? My ignorance? What was the cure for that? I must swallow the fear, I decided, before it swallowed me.

'Oh, Thomas' – I went to him and laid my forehead on the rough weave of his suit jacket – 'you mustn't think I'm completely cold-natured and heartless.'

He clasped his arm round me, his hand gripping the in-curve of my waist, and said, with firmness and warmth, 'Come with me.' Although I thought fleetingly I should offer some resistance, I didn't. If he cared to, he could easily have lifted and carried me under his arm, the way he'd joked about the day we met. He led me across the parlour to an adjoining room, continuing to talk: 'Do you know the term *mariage blanc*, Charlotte?'

I couldn't answer. I understood the individual words, and I could guess at their joined meaning, a reference to his own loveless marriage.

He brought me into a shadowy room, where a large bed with its head against the far wall was lighted by the greenish glow from the parlour. I went hot all along my spine. Together, we sat on the side of the bed.

Hardy took my left hand and began, with infinite care, to remove the glove. Lightly, he caressed each finger through the thin black leather, for several tantalizing moments.

I was having trouble breathing. Heat was rising to my throat.

Then, ever so slowly, he drew off the glove, dropping the empty kidskin to the carpet.

My cheeks were scorching. I was on fire, inside and out.

He went on, stroking each finger, undressing my right hand.

I waited for my fingertips to burst into flame.

The second glove fell to the floor.

Repelled and attracted, I was burning in bewildered equilibrium.

Finally, he took both my hands and brought his prickling moustache and soft lips down upon my bare palms.

This was carnal lust. Sin had never been so concretely present for me. I was caught in blazing tension between desire and renunciation.

Hardy raised his head and regarded me at length, his pupils hugely dilated, his stare like a corner I couldn't get out of. He folded my hands together and pressed them deep into my lap.

I watched, paralysed, as he undid the buttons on his waistcoat and the laces of his shoes, removing them and his black stockings. He dropped the stockings, one by one, on top of my gloves where they lay on the carpet. His bare feet shone white in the half-dark. Veined, sensual, evocative. With a shock of recognition, I saw they were Henry's feet, and I was appalled. I shrank back. 'Don't touch me. *Please.*'

'Charlotte . . . .' he said, broken, pleading.

I leapt up and retreated a manageable distance away. My stomach was churning. I was terrified of being sick, the final humiliation. 'You think I'm indifferent as stone,' I said, gasping, 'but you're wrong. I'm in agony, too. I'm trapped between a longing for love and an invisible something that forbids it.'

Hardy leant forward, his head hung between his shoulders, his hands dangling impotently between his knees. He groaned.

I turned away.

Out into the black street and into a chilling rain I stumbled, ragged and burnt, incoherent with revulsion and grief. In loving and refusing to love, I'd leapt, and I knew the rest of my life would be one long plummet, an inevitable, unalterable succession of consequences.

1894

Oh! Sorrow, Sorrow, is my bed
    So wide and warm that you must lie
Upon it; toss your weary head
    And stir my slumber with your sigh?
I left my love at your behest,
    I waved your little boughs of yew,
But Sorrow, Sorrow, let me rest,
    For oh! I cannot sleep with you!

from 'Song'

I rushed up the stairs and shut my bedroom door. I leant against it, shaking, soaked through; my breathing was hoarse and heavy, as if I'd been chased. Hardy's behaviour had caused me surprising and unpleasant sensations: dizziness, nausea, an inability to get my breath. And a sadness, an utter sadness that shadowed my thinking for days afterwards. The handkerchief I carried in my skirt pocket was wet and crumpled. My unhappiness climaxed with the arrival in the post of a parcel containing the gloves, handbag and red paisley shawl I'd left behind.

Marchmont Mansions had begun to seem like the product of a perverse imagination. Now, unwrapping and fingering my restored belongings, my shame was complete. I was mortified by what I'd done. And deeply remorseful. I'd been contrary and cowardly. I'd been afraid. And ashamed of my fear, too ashamed, even now, to examine its deeper causes. Given our shared oath and her own lack of experience, Anne wasn't the one with whom I could talk about any of this. My innocence was an ignorance I'd have to live with; I swore I'd never risk such anguish and humiliation again.

With the arrival of the new year, 1894, I was feeling diminished, flat, lifeless. My friendship with Hardy was dead, dead as a leaf in a lump of coal. I was again in deep mourning, all in black, watched over by a melancholy angel, the sort of thing one sees carved in marble, bending over the graves of those who died young.

Only the red thread of my writing ran through the dull weave of tedious days. I sorted through the manuscripts I'd stored in my travel trunk, those written since I'd burnt everything and made a fresh start. I found a sketch I considered promising, one based on what I'd watched on an afternoon walk along the Grand Union Canal: several young boys fishing and their indifference when the smallest fell in and came close to drowning.

When I was satisfied with the rewritten story, titled 'The Minnow Fishers', I sent my scribbled pages out to a female typewriter, a distressed gentlewoman whose name I'd got from a card posted at the tobacconist's. A short time later, the typescript came back, wrapped in brown paper and tied with string. It only wanted return postage enclosed, and I could mail the story out. But to whom?

Anne and I were readers of several journals and magazines that published fiction – weeklies, monthlies, quarterlies – so I went through the back numbers in Father's study next to his office on the ground floor. I decided on the *Illustrated London News*, in which we'd read Hardy's *Well-Beloved*. I liked the idea of my story in such a place, already sanctified by his earlier presence. I posted the story and waited.

In the days that followed, winter warming into spring, I spent many afternoons and evenings with Anne. At twenty-two, she was pretty and vivacious, a bit taller and more social than I. She wore her long brown hair pulled up and cascading down between her shoulder-blades, with a fluffy fringe in front. She was fond of blue and most often wore a frock of that colour; it made her lavender eyes startling and memorable. If our family condition had been different, if she hadn't been bound by our vow of celibacy, she should have had a dozen suitors.

Anne had made a friend at art school, Elsie Millard, whose sister Evelyn was an aspiring actress; we went together to wherever she performed. We called and were called on by the Chick sisters and the Olivers, Ethel and Winifred. Anne and I took long walks when the weather was fine; we recommenced our reading aloud in the parlour. The old blue and yellow parrot, with his lids closed, muttered on his stand by the window, sounding a malcontented bass note as we read. No more Hardy. Instead, we shared George Du Maurier's novel *Peter Ibbetson*, and after that, we began his *Trilby*, as it appeared in serial. We waited for each new episode as if it were Christmas.

I didn't tell anyone about having submitted 'The Minnow Fishers'. Sustained by a secret, almost giddy hope, I had daydreams of seeing it in print with my name in large, heavily seriffed type. And I imagined Hardy reading it – and doing what? I wouldn't allow my fantasy to go any further. The fantasies ended with the reappearance of the brown-paper package. Up in my room, with anxious fingers, I undid the string, parted the wrappings, and took out a letter from the Fiction Editor of the *Illustrated London News*. I steadied myself against the writing table. I was thanked for my submission. I was complimented on the promising quality of my work. I was encouraged to continue developing my talent. And, finally, I was told, 'We regret that your little story is most difficult to categorize, unlike anything we have read before, and does not meet our needs.'

I'd been rejected!

If the letter had been a knife, I'd have slashed my wrists right then, without a moment's hesitation. My life as a writer was over, ended; the rest of it might as well be ended, too.

What threat of old imaginings,
Half-haunted joy, enchanted pain,
Or dread of unfamiliar things
Should ever trouble you again?

from 'Requiescat'

Anger is a great cathartic. I raged against despotic editors and
a publishing establishment that was obviously conspiring to
prevent me from entering the charmed circle of authors in print.
I had great difficulty hiding my anger. Mama insisted I was
moody because I missed Nanny Elizabeth. One of Mama's
acquaintances, a recent widow, had got involved in spiritualism
and recommended I attend a seance with her medium in Scala
Street.

'You must go, Charlotte,' Mama said, 'and find out if she's
a Christian spiritualist. If not, Nanny won't respond. Oh, I do
so want to speak to her and hear from her again.' I poured
Mama another cup of tea, sugared it well and placated her
as best I could, while stoutly refusing to become involved in
summoning ghosts, Christian or otherwise.

Anne was more sympathetic. Every day, she suggested some
agreeable distraction to jolly me out of my furious sulks. But
in the privacy of my room, I continued to stride up and down
and curse the *ILN*'s Fiction Editor the best, or worst, I knew
how, even after I'd torn the man's letter into indignant bits and
scattered them in the fire. 'The Minnow Fishers', in some way
spoiled, went into the travel trunk. Then, I woke one morning
after a string of restless nights, determined to prove that he'd
been badly mistaken to reject me.

Soon after that, I learnt a new and daring quarterly had just started up, calling itself *The Yellow Book*. Its cover was a bright lemon with a sensuous black drawing of an androgynous person by the young artist Aubrey Beardsley. The journal's declared purpose was to give authors a freer hand in what they wrote and to specialize in publishing courageously modern short stories. I read the first issue eagerly, liking in particular 'Irremediable', a piece by a woman named Ella D'Arcy. It was about a married couple bound together by a hatred stronger than love, and it changed my idea about what stories involving men and women might be. It also changed any idea I might have had about abandoning my writing. Something that had been dormant in me stirred and stretched and reached for my pen.

The spring was unseasonably warm and dry, the city hot and dirty. I wanted to get away by writing about the country, the happiness and freedom I'd had there on holiday as a child, to escape from pavement dreams – those thoughts that come sometimes in cities of the weary length or terrible brevity of life. And yet Hardy had once counselled me to write from what I knew best, and what I knew best was London and my own experience of it.

So I decided to try again to write about the night I'd gone searching for Henry. I scratched through draft after draft, trying not to let too much of the private and personal show through – another of Hardy's recommendations. He'd taught me more than I'd realized at the time.

When I finally got it to suit me, my story began with evening in a part of the city where the main character is a stranger, the way I'd been, but I couldn't tell about Henry, not ever. Instead, a narrator evolved, a young woman who's lost and led through an unlighted slum to the bedside of a dying harlot. Where did this come from? Was she a part of me, too? In the story, the narrator is terrified and flees; later she suffers great guilt at her failure of nerve, at not being able to save the dead woman's younger sister from similar degradation.

I'd first called the piece 'Violets', for the flowers at the harlot's bedside, but by the time I had it ready for the typewriter, I'd retitled it 'Passed'. I sent it off to the new journal, this time with totally unsupported hope, ready to forget about it and get on with the next story, already beginning to form in my mind.

One afternoon, coming in from a walk with Anne, I found an envelope addressed to me on the table in the front hall. I opened it and began reading before it occurred to me what the letter might be.

> 144 Cromwell Road, SW
> April 29, 1894

Dear Madam,

I think your story, 'Passed', is in many ways highly remarkable, and I shall be very glad to print it in the *Yellow Book*, provided your price for it be within our income and provided also you will agree to make one or two very trifling changes in the text. Can you call upon me here at about three o'clock tomorrow afternoon?

It was signed *H. Harland, Ed., Yellow Book*. I swayed, close to fainting.

Anne gripped my elbow and said, 'Is it bad news?'

Grinning, I shook my head and reached round to hug her. I told her about my good fortune, and she let out a squeal of delight. The door to Father's offices was shut; Mama was somewhere on the floor above. I didn't want them to hear about the acceptance yet, certain neither of them would approve. I held a finger to my lips and whispered, 'Upstairs, my room,' and hugged her again and kissed her on the cheek. How good it was to have someone to share my happiness!

In a bold daze, I presented myself to Mr H. Harland at his flat in Cromwell Road, promptly at three. My self-assurance, my boldness sprang from my new-found status as a very nearly professional writer. When he opened the door, I wavered a bit at the sight of him: a thin, stoop-shouldered man with a moustache, the ends curled up in a hirsute smile, and a goatee trimmed to a point; his longish hair badly wanted combing. He was wearing an unbelted burgundy dressing-gown over a collarless shirt and rumpled trousers.

His accent was jarringly American, but his words as he ushered me in were reassuring. 'Dear beautiful little lady, welcome,' he said, squinting short-sightedly, eyeglasses dangling from a cord round his neck. He shook my hand and introduced himself as Henry Harland. In spite of the hearty Yankee manner, something about his pallor suggested he might be ill.

Harland shut the door behind me and directed me into the parlour of the flat, to a rather large upholstered chair, its arms worn the colour of dried moss. The room had the feel of one let furnished, everything dark and fusty and nondescript. I imagined that if I were to check round, I'd find the whole place covered in a fine sooty dust. I decided, instead, to focus on my host, who was going on about how pleased he was I'd come. He offered me tea or sherry. I declined, too nonplussed to manage either. His energy was daunting. All I could do was watch, fascinated, and try not to stare while he did all the talking, which appeared to suit him completely.

'As I said in my letter, Miss Mew,' he continued, seating himself opposite in the equally worn mate to my chair, 'I think your story is a highly remarkable piece of literature, and for that reason, I think it's destined to meet with scant recognition from newspaper reviewers. I think it's destined to be violently abused, and *The Yellow Book* will be abused for printing it.'

Oh, dear, I thought, suddenly distressed. Harland didn't seem to notice my reaction even though it must have been plainly painted on my face. Oh, dear. I hadn't considered the possibility of a negative response to my story once it got past the guardians at the gates of publication. Then I remembered the pillorying Hardy had taken over his *Tess*, and I shrank deeper into the upholstery.

Harland spoke on in a lively, good-natured manner, as if he positively relished unsettling the reading public. 'Directly a writer goes out of his way to get at close quarters with his thought, directly he casts aside the ordinary, the banal and approximate word, and uses the surprising one, the right one, he may count infallibly upon abuse from the dear old reviewers. They do so love the ready-made phrase, and they do so hate the fresh one, the one that fits, being made to measure.'

I nodded knowingly, having already met with that species of reception from the *ILN* editor. I was waiting for Harland to say exactly what changes he wanted me to make in my 'remarkable piece of literature', which was soon to bring the wrath of the critics down on both of us.

'I have mountains of manuscripts to read every day' – he waved a hand in the direction of stacks of papers and packages forming a sort of alpine range across a table at the far end of the room – 'and nine hundred and ninety-nine thousandths of it is hopeless rubbish. So when I pick up a manuscript, it's with a foregone conclusion that it will be worthless. Now, here's a question for you: why is it that when I picked up yours, and before I read a line of it, I had a presentiment that it would prove a treasure? I turned to a friend who was seated near me and said, "I feel that this is going to be a *find*, a new discovery."'

He waited as if he expected something from me. 'Thank you,' I croaked, surprised at the sound of my own voice, so long unused. I cleared my throat. 'You mentioned revisions?'

'Yes, yes.' He stroked his goatee as if his fingers needed something to do for the moment. He got up and, speaking as he went, went to a large desk near a window curtained with yellowing net, and came back with my typescript. 'There are priceless bits of very subtle observation, of very subtle imagining, and of very subtle wording in "Passed".' Seated again, he leafed through it. 'However . . .' He paused long enough for my heart to shrink with apprehension. 'I read your story out to my sub-editor and he – whose judgement in these matters is of the best – admired it as much as I did, but agreed with me that the description of your horror in the presence of the

dead was almost too painfully strong, that it might be shortened, condensed a little, made more suggestive and less explicit.'

'Yes, I understand,' I said, not understanding at all. Chagrin
at the deficiencies in my writing had made my ears go hot and
muffled. What was it he wanted me to do? Rewrite the entire
thing and take out the dead woman? For a minute, I could only
bob my head. 'Thank you,' I said as he handed me the typescript. I stood up to leave. 'Thank you,' I said again, feeling
idiotic.

I chewed my favourite penholder nearly through. I scribbled a
dozen and more versions of 'Passed', with and without the
deathbed scene, and discarded them all. I was too much a
novice to know what was wanted to satisfy the loquacious Mr
Harland. I lighted another cigarette and, made frank by my
desperation, composed a note to him, confessing my confusion
and offering to withdraw my unsatisfactory story altogether.

His reply came the following day:

I am afraid I have not made myself clear on the subject of the
modification I suggested. I don't mean in the least that you should
change the *substance* of the part in question. On the contrary, I
think that is wholly admirable, and I should be sorry to see it
touched. The psychology, the sequence of ideas and emotions, the
interaction of ideas, emotions and sensual impressions – all are of
the highest value. What I mean is that I think your *method* of
presenting these might conceivably be improved. I mean that a subject in itself of the most poignant ought to be treated as lightly, as
easily, as possible. Such a subject speaks in great measure for itself,
and makes its own appeal to the reader's emotions; it seems to me
that the author should by his style endeavour to soften, rather than
to accentuate the effect of pain. He does not need to insist, to
emphasize, to raise his voice.

Finally, I grasped what it was I must do with my story and set
to work doing it.

*

Thanks to Henry Harland I'd been instructed in simplicity and restraint in writing. And I had a simple, unrestrained need to rush the repaired story to him with my sincerest thanks. The instant it came from the typewriter, I hurried off to Cromwell Road.

My knock at the door to his flat was answered by a handsome woman of about forty, her black hair knotted casually on top of her head. Her costume – white shirtwaist with fashionably full leg-of-mutton sleeves, taupe gored skirt in the newer length, some three inches from the floor – made me feel incredibly dowdy in my old schoolgirl tartan and black jacket. I took a half step backwards, ready to hand her my typescript and flee.

'Miss Mew?' she said, with an appealing lilt.

'Why, yes,' I replied, baffled. 'Have we met?'

She laughed lightly. 'No, no, but Henry's description drew you for me as clearly as a Whistler portrait. He said you were a tiny young woman with short curly hair and parenthetical eyebrows permanently elevated in shock or bemusement. He wasn't sure which.'

I wasn't sure myself how to react. Was I being made fun of? Her expression told me not.

'Forgive my rudeness, please, for keeping you standing here,' she said, 'and do come in.' I followed her into the parlour and took my earlier chair. The flat was brighter than before, as if the light had found another way indoors instead of being strained through net curtains. The woman pulled up a low footstool. She was tall seated in front of me, and her eyes – jet and glittery – met mine on a level. Her face was narrow, rather triangular, with a prominent nose that gave her an air of importance.

'Mrs Harland –' I began.

Another light laugh. 'No, no. I seem to go from one blunder to another. All my fault. I should've introduced myself at once' – her hand shot towards me – 'Ella D'Arcy.'

'Oh, Miss D'Arcy,' I stammered, pumping her hand, 'your "Irremediable" was brilliant.'

'Thank you,' she replied. 'I thought it quite good myself.'

What an extraordinary woman, with no demurring or false modesty. I might have envied her talent and success if she hadn't been so obviously worthy of them. Instead, I was awed. I was mute, gawking, with a fatuous grin stretching my face.

'You must call me Ella. Everyone does. And you're Charlotte, is that right?' I nodded. 'Mrs Harland, by the way, is still in New York. I stop at the flat occasionally to, well, to help Henry.' Something in my expression must have caused her to add, with a faint smile, 'With the magazine.'

'Are you the sub-editor Mr Harland mentioned to me?'

'Nothing so grand as that. More an unofficial assistant. I merely tidy up a bit and see that the letters and returns get posted.' Ella rose and stood looking down at me. 'I'd offer you tea, but I'm sorry to say there is none. Henry's neglected to get things in. I suppose I shall have to go out to the shops.'

I got to my feet, protesting that I didn't deserve tea, dropping by uninvited as I'd done.

'No, no. You must come often – perhaps to one of Henry's Saturday nights – so we may all become better acquainted.'

I followed Ella D'Arcy back across the parlour, noticing how strands of her hair had come loose and curled at the nape of her neck.

She was saying, 'Henry speaks so highly of your story. I'm looking forward to reading it.'

At the door, I handed it to her, having all but forgotten what I'd come for. And then I remembered the second part of my impulsive mission, to ask for the money due me. I reasoned that Father might accept the publication of my writing if it were understood to be a business transaction. I'd given up on devising a way to make it acceptable to Mama, who'd find my appearance in public print shameless behaviour, unbecoming to a lady and a disgrace to her family.

Ella said, 'Our mode of payment is like that of all other magazines.'

Puzzlement must have been clear from the tilt of my head.

'We pay on publication, not on acceptance,' she explained. 'Henry says when we are older and stronger, he hopes we may be the pioneers of a better system. In the meantime, you may expect a cheque shortly after the next issue.'

I thanked her, and as I prepared to leave, she took my hand and shook it warmly.

I carried that pleasant warmth through the weeks following. It was enlarged and intensified into the purest, rarest elation – reserved for new authors and other recipients of minor miracles – at the publication in July of 'Passed' in Volume II of *The Yellow Book*. My work was in the exalted company of several Beardsley drawings, and short stories by Henry James, Netta Syrett and Dauphin Meunier – and a second brilliant one by the admirable Ella D'Arcy.

1895

Sometimes in the over-heated house, but not for long,
                Smirking and speaking rather loud,
        I see myself among the crowd,
Where no one fits the singer to his song,
Or sifts the unpainted from the painted faces . . .

from 'Fame'

A moment ago, I was walking the grit and glare of afternoon pavement along Russell Square. Now, here I was in a foreign country.

Or what seemed to be.

I'd hurried out of the house and off down Gordon Street without bothering with hat, gloves or handbag. Presently, I stood in the lobby of the Midland Bank, gazing at the cream and black marble pillars and the polished brass. I realized I was panting, out of breath, as if I'd been running, and maybe I had. I'd been in such a state I might well have skipped along the pavement, like a gay little girl. I couldn't recall.

The space round me echoed solemnly with the murmurs of men transacting business at the grilles; I was the lone woman. The decor – shadowed and weighty with masculine fiduciary seriousness – implied I might be the only woman who'd ever ventured on to the premises. Inside one of the brass cages, a clerk in a stiff collar adjusted his wire spectacles and peered at me. His shoulders bent, his hair slicked back and spiky, he reminded me of a hedgehog. He said, 'May I be of assistance, miss?' His voice was high and reedy, as if his collar were too small for his neck or his glasses pinched, too tight on his pointy nose. My first impulse was to laugh at this wheezing, clerical hedgehog. But I *did* need his assistance.

I glanced at the piece of paper I'd been clutching in my bare fingers, until it was bent and wrinkled, and up again at the clerk. I laid the paper on the marble counter, not sure how to phrase my request. This was the cheque from *The Yellow Book*, only just arrived in the post, payment, at long last, for my story. It was the first cheque I'd ever received, the first money I'd ever earned, in fact, the first money I'd ever had that was all my own, mine alone. Not a gift nor requested from my father and doled out in dour silence.

'You wish to cash this cheque?' the clerk asked, solicitous. And cautious.

'Yes,' I said and shoved it towards him.

He smoothed it out with a pass of his hand and picked it up and turned it over. 'You haven't endorsed it, miss.' He regarded me as if I were mentally deficient. 'You must sign your name' – he indicated the narrow end of the piece of paper – 'here,' and slid it towards me.

I had no pen and could find none in either direction along the counter. The clerk handed me one dipped freshly into his own ink pot. I signed and gave both cheque and pen back to him with a sigh of satisfaction. At last, I'd have my money.

But, no. He examined the front of the cheque and again the back. 'Do you have an account with us, miss?'

I'd no account with any bank. I struggled to remember where Father did his banking and took a wild stab. 'My father, Mr Frederick Mew,' I said, with much *gravitas*, 'is one of your depositors, I believe.'

'Excuse me, please, miss,' the clerk said, with a slight bow, and walked away, taking my cheque, my precious money, with him.

I could see him conferring with an older, stouter gentleman in a black suit, who looked at the cheque, at me and again at the cheque, speaking all the while words I couldn't hear, first shaking and then nodding his head.

The clerk returned, the hint of a smile – or was it a sneer?

– on his lips, and counted out my money in pound notes. When, at long last, he pushed it to me, I snatched it up, shoved it into the pocket of my skirt, and strode out of the bank as fast as decorum and my short legs would allow.

I'd got my money. I'd passed some further, unexpected test. I was truly a professional writer.

At home again, I fished the notes from my pocket and tucked them under the manuscripts in the travel trunk at the foot of my bed. While I might have got a humiliating lesson in cheque-cashing, I understood next to nothing about financial matters; Father managed all that.

With the death of Nanny Elizabeth, I'd been forced to take on many of her domestic responsibilities. A new maid called Sarah, a raw ginger-haired girl from the Isle of Dogs, had recently been engaged and trained by me, but she'd fallen far short of what Nanny would have made of her. Altogether too much of my time was taken up with answering Mama's complaints. 'This simply will not do, Charlotte,' she'd say about the temperature of the tea water or the quality of shine on the fireplace fender or the way the parlour curtains had been pulled back. I had to call Sarah in to redo whatever hadn't been done to Mama's satisfaction.

And when it came to Cook's green baize account book with its cryptic entries – those not smeared were too crabbed to be legible – I was at a complete loss. I'd no idea whether the charges at the butcher's and the greengrocer's and the fishmonger's and the like were reasonable or even accurate. Mama was as helpless as I was, maybe worse. She seemed unaware that the food on the table had come from anywhere more remote than the kitchen in our basement. Nanny had taken care of checking all the household bills. I simply handed them on, unexamined, to Father, and he paid them. I was a perfect goose about money. How would I ever learn without Nanny to teach me?

But I had room for only one ghost. Nanny had got elbowed out; it was Hardy who bent over my shoulder when I wrote. I was working on a short story I called 'The China Bowl', set in the West Country, in a Cornish fishing village visited years ago on holiday, where the sky was all over flinty and the sea dark and quarrelsome. A local legend, some overheard bit of gossip spoken in a remembered dialect, something set the drama going in my head, with its three characters – an older woman and a younger one, in conflict over the love of a man.

Nothing I was writing satisfied my Hardy. I set aside the story and made myself a cigarette. These days, the tobacconist sold them ready-made, ten a penny, but I preferred to roll my own, to perpetuate the finger-dance Henry had taught me, to earn each smoke by crafting it myself.

I lighted my cigarette and sat for a few minutes, watching the smoke rise, coil and vanish.

I knew no way to exorcise Hardy, so I decided instead to appease him. Hadn't he said I was a born poet? I took a fresh sheet of writing-paper and began again. I started sketching out a poem. After several weeks' work, I called it 'The Farmer's Bride'. As atonement for my behaviour at our last – our *last* – meeting, I allowed Hardy, in the character of the Dorset farmer he might have become, to speak his suffering at the fearful shyness of the young girl he'd taken to wife but not to his bed. Part of my penance was to write from the man's point of view, without completely losing sight of my own, that is, the girl's. I found all this surprisingly easy, wearing the masks of both personae, the male and the female, at the same time, one over the other.

What was difficult were the feelings, to have them come pounding back again, at once more clearly and more confusedly. I had problems, too, with the mechanics of the thing. I calculated the lines by syllables, not certain if that was correct – how I wished I could remember what dear Miss Harrison had taught us about iambic pentameters – hunting for a form, a rhyme scheme, to shape mutual suffering into art.

In the meantime, I attended Henry Harland's Saturday nights.

In spite of dust in the corners and ashes spilling from the fireplace, candlelight made the parlour and its pink walls and weary furnishing less forlorn; the figure in the oriental carpet was changed into something intricate and exotic, like a Persian miniature. Wrapped in the red shawl over my drab Sunday frock, I spoke rarely and in a voice gruff with shyness and too much smoking. Because of my small stature, I could move round the room without being much noticed; some mistook me for a child, an error soon corrected as I lighted a cigarette or accepted a glass of sherry from our host.

I met Netta Syrett and Evelyn Sharp and other female writers who, like Ella D'Arcy, embodied the qualities of what was coming to be called the New Woman: one who lived independently, making her own decisions in personal and business matters. The very sort of person I intended to be.

I met, or more often simply watched across the chattery room, Henry James – portly, avuncular, with the appearance of someone slumming – and Aubrey Beardsley – dark fringe over long, pallid boy's face – and a number of other contributors to the magazine and some of their artistic friends – women in harlot's make-up, men in velvet trousers, and occasionally, men in make-up and women in trousers. A fug of pagan sensuality hung round them like the cigarette smoke.

And there was a slight, weaselly man in thick spectacles, who called himself Baron Corvo. Ella said, 'He's no more a baron than I am. He leaves fleas in the armchair, so avoid it until it can be treated with insect powder.' Another man, bearded and heavy-lidded, she kept under polite surveillance as he had a habit of pilfering the spoons and selling them for laudanum.

I listened. There were rare moments of raised voices, sotted and adamant, and rarer moments of hushed waiting for the next literary pronouncement. Mostly, I listened to gossip about the famous and notorious I knew only by name. I listened to talk about exhibitions opening and plays closing and books forthcoming, about suffrage and politics, and about art and aesthetics. Any question I might have asked – 'Can anyone explain to me iambic pentameter?' – would have sounded so puerile that I remained a member of the audience and said very little.

And because I said so little, the others assumed I was more knowledgeable than I was. Most of the discussion, of such subjects as French Symbolist poetry, was conducted in some code I couldn't decipher. A gnomic *hmmm*, a toss of the head at a crucial point, these were my responses. Harland thought I was a young genius – 'Darling of my heart!' he called me. 'Child of my editing!' I was flattered and felt a great fraud all the same.

Within this bizarre circle, though, I was protected from any criticism of the magazine or my story. Harland's prediction was half right. Negative reviews of *The Yellow Book* appeared in the newspapers because of its blatant modernity. Thank God, 'Passed' was never specifically mentioned. Nor was there any mention of it within my family. For the first few weeks after publication of my story, as critics of the magazine raged, I waited to be found out. All my apprehension proved to have been for nothing. Anne alone in the family knew about my story because I'd shown it her, and, of course, she was pleased for me. Not surprisingly, no word from Hardy down at Max Gate. About the lack of recognition, I had mixed feelings, like a naughty child wanting and not wanting to be caught.

On those Saturday evenings, Ella was especially kind to me. With eyes that seemed to swallow light, she saw my bewilderment. She leant near me, smelling of attar of roses. Her manner was passionate as she explained the work of the most frequently mentioned French authors – Verlaine, Huysmans, Mallarmé – and lent me a volume of Rimbaud's poems. I read them with something like fascinated horror.

And Ella inspired me by her example to adopt a new uniform. I had tailor-made a suit of iron-grey serge: an Eton jacket with the fashionably full sleeves, and a skirt in the shorter length. I bought myself one of the popular trilby hats, a smaller version of the man's creased felt hat named in honour of Mr Du Maurier's heroine, and handed in the bills to Father with the rest of the household expenditures.

Ella and I were becoming acquainted, not quite close friends, when she simply disappeared from Harland's literary gatherings. 'Little lady,' he replied to my asking after her, 'when the cable arrived from New York with the news that my wife was sailing for England, our Ella conveniently took herself off to somewhere in the Channel Islands, I believe, or perhaps she's gone to Paris.' I was confused, wondering why Mrs Harland's coming would send Ella out of London. I asked for an address where I might write to her. 'So very like that dear gypsy spirit,' he said, 'she left none. I fear we've seen the last of her.'

At that, there came a stirring of some earlier loss, unforgotten deep in my bones.

I finished my Cornish story, 'The China Bowl', and sent it out to the typewriter. One Saturday evening, I arrived at Harland's flat early and gave the manuscript to him, and he thanked me profusely. I left that night with the unspoken assumption he'd include it in the next issue of *The Yellow Book*. In the weeks following, I heard nothing further. I began to think he'd lost it, not unknown in the shambles that was the editorial organization, or lack of it, after Ella's departure.

I was going less often to his evenings by the time I found Harland's letter on the front-hall table with the rest of the post.

Dear Miss Mew,

I cannot tell you in a letter how very fine, how splendid, I think your story. The humour, the wit, the supreme emotion, the grasp of life, of life in its tragedy, its relentlessness, and the rich beautiful 'cello-voice in which it is intoned – these, and a hundred other qualities, lift it above all praise. There is no living writer of English fiction who can touch you.

My feet scarcely reached the floor as I read. I was aware Harland was given to hyperbole, but I did so want to savour his words for a minute before I discounted them to the value of ordinary speech.

I have a million things to say about it. Can you make another pilgrimage to the Cromwell Road? I would not ask you, but I am seldom well enough to leave the house . . .

Poor Harland. I knew he'd been unwell, but I'd no idea it had got so serious. As I was sympathizing with him, I read the next sentence:

I am afraid the tale is too long for the *YB* . . .

Caught unawares, I didn't understand. I reread it. He was rejecting 'The China Bowl'! Too long? Not true! It was no longer than some stories that had already been published in the magazine. Maybe he thought the fulsome praise and the mention of his poor health would soften the blow. It didn't. I was hurt, terribly hurt. Too hurt, in fact, to be angry. That came later, after I'd got back my manuscript, which I tossed into the travel trunk. I sat a long while at my work table, paralysed with fury and frustration.

The Saturday evenings came to an end for me then. I'd have left off going soon in any case. They were less enjoyable without Ella, and by the spring of 1895, the scandal surrounding the magazine was too offputting. 'ARREST OF OSCAR WILDE, YELLOW BOOK UNDER HIS ARM', screamed the headline. With the trial of Wilde and his unnatural affection for Lord Alfred Douglas, the newspapers railed against those wicked creative people known as the Decadents. *The Yellow Book*, with Beardsley's sensuous and sardonic drawings, they said was an example of that sallow corruption. It came out later that the 'Yellow Book' under Wilde's arm was actually a paperback French novel. Even so, the magazine would soon fail, and I heard the Harlands had gone to live abroad.

At the same time, as if the two were linked unnatural phenomena, the newspapers instigated a backlash against the New Woman. I'd come to consider myself a New Woman: unmarried, independent-minded, going about without a chaperon in defiance of Mama's – and Nanny's – antiquated standards. I was amazed that so many of the general public seemed still to share them, equally amazed to be told I was a freak and an abomination, and constituted a public menace. As if such a woman, as if I were the very devil roaming the earth like a ravening lion, searching for someone to devour. The whole notion was laughable. And daunting.

I wouldn't, couldn't, change my nature, and yet I needn't be a fool, either, and put myself in the way of trouble.

So, when the ship of *The Yellow Book* was sinking, I, who'd always considered myself no more than a stowaway, leapt into the first lifeboat and rowed back to the safe harbour of my family. Over cups of tea in the parlour, while Mama fed bits of biscuit to the parrot, I sometimes thought about the people I'd met at Harland's flat. I now considered them louche, jaded, self-indulgent. With the single exception of Ella D'Arcy. One was well out of it all, I assured myself as I read about the scandal from the safe and respectable distance of Gordon Square.

'Not near, not near!' her eyes beseech
When one of us comes within reach.
    The women say that beasts in stall
    Look round like children at her call.
    I've hardly heard her speak at all.

Shy as a leveret, swift as he,
Straight and slight as a young larch tree,
Sweet as the first wild violet, she,
To her wild self. But what to me?

The short days shorten and the oaks are brown,
    The blue smoke rises to the low grey sky,
One leaf in the still air falls slowly down,
    A magpie's spotted feathers lie
On the black earth spread white with rime,
The berries redden up to Christmas-time.
    What's Christmas-time without there be
    Some other in the house than we!

    She sleeps up in the attic there
    Alone, poor maid. 'Tis but a stair
Betwixt us. Oh! my God! the down,
The soft young down of her, the brown,
The brown of her – her eyes, her hair, her hair!

from 'The Farmer's Bride'

Some time in November 1895 I received in the post a copy of
Hardy's new novel, *Jude the Obscure*, sent by the publisher,
Osgood, McIlvaine. A printed card accompanied it: 'With the
compliments of the author'. I tumbled the grey-green volume
over and over in my hands, weighing the solidity of it, unwilling
to open the cover, as if Hardy were waiting for me inside; my

feelings for him were still far too muddied and complex. I laid the book on the side of my work table. I looked at it each day but couldn't bear to open it and hear his voice in his words. There it stayed for several weeks until I saw a letter in the newspaper from the Bishop of Wakefield, who insisted *Jude* was so iniquitous and indecent he'd thrown it into the fire. I had to smile at the picture that conjured up. Such a book, bound between covers of heavy pasteboard, with all those thick hundreds of pages, simply tossed into the grate, would be difficult to burn. His Eminence must have had jolly work, trying to destroy the thing. If the novel could inspire such a laboured conflagration on an episcopal hearth, I decided it was time I read it.

I chose to begin on a wet afternoon when I was virtually alone in the house, Mama gone calling and Anne at her studio. I pulled my chair up to the bedroom window; to the accompaniment of the rhythmic splash of raindrops on the pane, I entered the book and commenced reading.

Here was Hardy's 'story of young man who couldn't go to Oxford, his struggles and ultimate failure', which he'd mentioned on our Sunday walk to Regent's Park a few years ago. Jude Fawley, the title character, bore many of the marks of Hardy himself: prevented by poverty from gaining the university education he wanted, largely self-taught through wide reading; pious in his youth, aspiring to the clergy, later disillusioned and disgruntled with religion; attracted into a marriage that proved unhappy; fatalistic and wounded, crippled by Fate. Hadn't Hardy said as much to me more than once? My pity was enormous for the boy Jude, scaring away the crows from the farmer's field, climbing a ladder to a rooftop in order to glimpse the far-off towers and spires of the university glittering at sundown. I couldn't help but think of him as the young Hardy. And I wondered, was the character of Arabella – the tawdry, common country girl, the fleshy, coarse woman – a reflection of his own wife? Poor man.

As I read on, I met the novel's heroine, Sue Bridehead. My heart shrivelled, and my compassion leaked away. Dazed, I closed the book and stared out the window at the sycamore in the back garden, leaves black with rain. With dusk darkening round me, the startle and numbness passed, and I felt stabbed by the sharp edge of betrayal.

How dare he!

Hardy had given Sue Bridehead my self and my very nature. Resentment was a lump in my throat: 'mocked', 'exploited', 'cannibalized', these words formed and stuck there. He'd been so unkind as to expose me to the entire reading public. Scandal was a cry in the street, and I was in terror of it.

I spent the evening in troubled, solitary reflection; outside my door Anne worried I was ill. She wanted to fetch the doctor. 'Nothing to be concerned about, a cold coming on,' I told her from across the room and sent her away. I sat in blue quiet beside the window on the night.

I'm stripped naked for the world to see, I wailed inwardly. On the other hand, my rational self said, Who will know? Just he and I, and hadn't we already a good many secrets between us? What evidence existed that might connect the two of us? Hardy had told me long ago that, prudently, regretfully, he destroyed my letters after reading them and, he swore, committing them to memory. His to me lay buried under manuscripts in my travel trunk, kept locked, the key with me always, on a red ribbon round my neck. Some day, I would – I must – dispose of them, too, but not yet. Not yet.

If his use of me to create Sue were an injury to my person, it was a blow, however hurtful, that leaves no trace others might see. The scar was on the inside of my skin.

Finally, at the collapse of night, a sort of equanimity settled over me, a pleasant fatigue, and I forgave him everything. Everything. Only then did I see, in choosing me to be the model of his heroine, Hardy had paid me a rare honour. And, too, it was a link between us, Hardy and me; it would last as long as

Jude the Obscure was read in the years to come, beyond his lifetime and mine. A species of immortality.

When I took up reading the novel again, on another rainy day in a month of weeping skies, I met my own soul in Sue – sceptical and at the same time yearning for something in which to believe, palely sexed, wary of the physical act, given to boldness and flight, tossed by contradictory impulses. Sue was called, as I'd been, disembodied and hardly flesh, and yet we were both so conscious of the flesh as to be cruelly governed by it, mortified by it, unable to help ourselves.

And it occurred to me that part of our temperament was shared by a third person – the brown, brown farmer's bride of my poem. Hadn't I transformed Hardy into its rustic narrator? How, then, could I fault him for using me in his characterization of Sue Bridehead? Her agnosticism, while more intellectually developed than mine, was another quality we two had in common, but when I read further, I was dismayed as Sue became more religiously orthodox. Was that the future Hardy saw for me?

Reading about Sue was an eerie experience, like meeting one's ghost, like coming upon one's reflection in a pier glass set at the end of a dimly lighted hallway.

Here in the novel were the tragic consequences of mismarriage; here was the sorrowful outcome of sexual union for those like us: Sue, the farmer's bride, and I. No wonder the Bishop of Wakefield was so upset. Again and again the church and other social institutions were examined in the novel, their value questioned, and most often found wanting. Jude's charges against marriage as an insensate civil contract I'd heard before from the author himself.

Here – wrenching to read – was our parting; here were my words, our words, as best I could remember, even though Hardy had embellished them in such a way that I cried as I read until I was sobbing and couldn't read any more that day. He'd taken my very thoughts and let Sue think them and speak them aloud.

How well he understood me, after all, riddle that I was, even to myself. Especially to myself.

As I closed the book, still thinking about Sue, I felt inside and outside myself at the same time, the way I'd done as a child looking at the nursery in the doll's house, in the nursery of our house.

At the end of Sue and Jude's story, I was again in tears, for something of Hardy had been dying, too, like Jude, and surviving in a living death, like Sue. I closed the book, feeling oddly protective of Hardy now, defensive on his behalf in the face of the scathing reviews of the novel, resentful of his being abused by the press. I was perturbed at the critics' response to *Jude*; it was a great book, powerfully written, and they were blind and priggish not to recognize it.

A new boldness surged through me, and I broke my long silence and composed a note to Hardy, congratulating and commiserating, without any mention of finding my self-spectre in Sue Bridehead. He replied:

My dearest C.,

How strange that one may write a book without knowing what one puts in it – or rather, the reader reads into it. The detractor, I mean. The critical response has been painful in the extreme. The experience has cured me completely of further interest in novel-writing. A man must be a fool to deliberately stand up to be shot at.

T.

No mention of our disastrous parting, but on a separate page:

P. S. Without you, I am a dead man walking.

I bit my underlip, folded the letter into its envelope, and slid it underneath the manuscripts in my trunk.

*

Some reviewers attacked not just Hardy and the novel – the *Pall Mall Gazette* called it 'Jude the Obscene' – but also attacked Sue Bridehead, as if she were a dangerous, flesh-and-blood person, plotting, like Satan, the ruination of innocent folk. She was censured for her advanced ideas, for her independence of mind, for her resistance to marriage, for those qualities she shared with that dread creature, the New Woman. After reading so much vituperation directed at her, I had a fantasy that one evening I'd answer the bell, open the street door, and find myself on the threshold, seeking sanctuary from the scrutiny of public eyes.

1899

While Father watches from his chair
Day follows day
The same, or now and then, a different grey,
Till, like his hair,
Which Mother said was wavy once and bright,
They will all turn white.

from 'The Quiet House'

In those last days, his had been a kind of animal grief, profoundly felt but never expressed. Poor Father died of cancer on 13 September 1898, sixty-six years of age. When his eyelids closed for the last time in the darkened room – gone like Nanny to the country of all-white things – I was the one who sat by his bedside. The air chilled with the breath of the dead, and it remained for me to fold his tallow-coloured hands on his chest. I couldn't. I'd touched and been touched by him so rarely in my lifetime that I was shy, reluctant to touch him now. Not because he was dead but because he was my father.

I rose, without tears, and went to tell my mother and sister, who waited in the parlour. The fingertips of Mama's ringed hand touched her temple. 'What will become of me!' she cried, followed by huge, wrenching sobs. A startled Wek flapped and squawked loudly on his stand. The commotion brought the maid running, and she was sent to fetch the doctor, for Mama. Anne bent over her, murmuring comfort. 'You must be the man of the family, Charlotte,' Mama said and dabbed at her cheeks with a sodden handkerchief. 'You must see to the arrangements, make certain that standards are upheld. A large wreath for the street door. A carved marble headstone. Draped urns and a weeping willow, I think.'

Like the old Queen, she was prepared to wear black for the rest of her life. This tiny, frail woman gazed out at her circumscribed world with a vision that protected her from tragedy by focusing on bathos, her faded eyes ever ready for tears. What she held fast to was her expectation that, no matter what became of the rest of us, she'd for ever be cared for. By me.

After the funeral, complications began to arise. Mama was greatly upset because Father's death certificate was erroneously filed by the registrar in the name of 'Maw'. In death, he'd lost everything of this world; now even his name had been taken from him. After a pointless exchange of letters with indifferent officials, I decided I'd have to ask my cousin, Walter Mew Barnes, who was our solicitor, to remedy the situation. Why is it one must be a man to be taken seriously?

Walter came to meet Anne and me to talk about the disposition of Father's estate. He was a tall, satisfied-looking man with tidy hair and moustache, inclined to heaviness, with the promise of a double chin. He seated himself behind Father's broad mahogany desk, oddly bare of clutter. The drawings on the walls were old, familiar renderings of the 1878 Hampstead Vestry Hall, Father's favourite commission. When had I last been in this place? Nine years ago. Little Freda newly imprisoned by her childish madness and Father's cuffs beginning to fray.

Walter gestured my sister and me to the chairs opposite and opened his leather case of legal papers. 'I'll be as brief as possible, ladies, but in all honesty, mine is not a happy task.'

I didn't care for the sound of that and hoped Walter was simply speaking rhetorically.

He wasn't. Father's final bequest to us was a worthless business: the architectural firm of Kendall and Mew was an illusion, having not had a client in more years than the family could have suspected. Not since our older brother's departure had they been truly busy. Father's days, until his final illness, had been a charade. We'd been living in prudent yet comfortable circumstances, and although Mama had often complained about Father's lack of generosity, it wasn't a character flaw but an economic necessity. According to Walter, we'd been surviving on capital; there was no life insurance, only a large overdraft at the bank. No wonder the manager was so hesitant about my cheque from *The Yellow Book* when I went in to cash it.

'Damn!' I exploded, forgetting myself. 'Why didn't he tell us?' I demanded of Walter.

'Your father, like most men, believed that members of your gender should never be troubled with the details about money.'

I groaned. He promised. Father said we'd never know want. I wavered between outrage and alarm. 'Is there nothing at all?'

'Just your mother's small income from investments, an annuity of £300 a year. That's barely sufficient to cover fixed expenses: the lease payment on this house and the nursing care of . . .' Walter ducked his head and shuffled together the paper in front of him.

'Henry and Freda,' Anne said, sitting rigidly straight beside me. I reached across and took her hand.

'What shall we do?' I wailed, sounding distressingly like Mama.

'You're both of an age to marry, you know,' he answered brightly, as if that would solve all our problems.

I was unwilling to explain why it was impossible, so I simply asked, 'And until then?'

Cousin Walter waved his hand around. 'You might get yourself, say, £100 a year if you let the upper half of this house.'

The idea wasn't particularly appealing to Anne and me as we discussed it later, after his departure, but we were certain it would appal Mama. To have to take in boarders was the mark of a fall from respectability. But what alternative did we have?

Together, we laid out the necessity and advantages to Mama: 'By sharing the house,' I told her, 'we can keep our furniture and retain a good address.'

'And you'll be able to call on your friends, Mama, and continue to give them tea here in the parlour,' Anne added, with sham enthusiasm.

After a series of lachrymose tantrums, Mama at last agreed. With the assistance of Cook and Sarah, the maid, Anne and I shifted our bedrooms down to the ground floor, to what had been Father's offices. We settled in, I in the front room, Anne in the rear. I had difficulty sleeping at first because of the street noises – the carriages and the horse-drawn cabs, the tradesmen's wagons and the pedlars' cries – right outside, just beyond the iron railings. And I missed my old view of the sycamore in the back garden. I missed the stir of light and leaf, the cool shadow it cast across my window on summer days, the golden way it shed its leaves each autumn, the black tangle of its branches against the winter sky.

In time, the top two floors were let to a shapeless, quiet-spoken Scots widow, a Mrs Caroline *McHardy*. I couldn't escape the echo each time her name was mentioned. But we soon left off mentioning her at all and pretended to Mama's family and our callers – and to ourselves – that we were the only ones residing at 9 Gordon Street.

I assumed the complete responsibility for overseeing the family's finances, and it became clear Anne and I were going to have to find some way to get more money if we were to keep up appearances for Mama's sake and afford to pay Cook and Sarah, both absolute necessities. To Mama, for a lady to be seen to earn a living, even if circumstances dictated she must, was the ultimate fall from grace. She'd never have agreed to either of us seeking employment. So Anne told her each morning that she was off to the studio she shared with some school-friends, to pursue her art. She had, in fact, given up her portion of the space and been engaged by a company that restored antiques, to touch up decorative painting on pieces of furniture, fire-screens, tea trays and the like, specializing in birds and flowers.

I sat at my work table, chewing the end of my pen, stymied. I knew some women made a profession of writing, but I was unsure how and where to begin. Like a gift from the gods, a letter arrived from Ella D'Arcy in France. She'd read the notice of Father's death in an old copy of *The Times* and wished to extend her belated sympathies.

Here was a woman who earned her living with words, writing, editing, translating. Almost shyly, I composed a note asking how one went about it. My first efforts sounded all wrong; by the third draft I got the right tone, friendly, chatty, not too serious or anxious.

A reply came within the week, giving me some most useful advice: 'Write essays, reviews, short stories. There's no money to speak of from poetry unless you make a name for yourself and put together a book.' She suggested some magazines and journals where I could send my pieces and the names of several editors from whom I might solicit review work. She concluded her letter with a warm invitation: 'If you should come to France on holiday, I would so much enjoy seeing you again.' It was signed, 'Warmly, Ella.' My heart plumped with gratitude and revived affection.

I gave up writing poems and studied the market for essays and stories. I read to dissect and wrote in imitation of what I found in print, just as Anne, while a student, had imitated the Old Masters to learn the craft under the polished skin of the art. I needed to be calculating and single-minded if I were to earn money through my writing. I considered a *nom de plume* to avoid embarrassing Mama, and tried a few on my sister – Charlie Cat, Charles Catty – plays on my name that made us both laugh, for the first time in ages. Anne said, 'Whatever you call yourself, I know you'll do great things.' We clung to each other in our black mourning frocks, for a minute's reassurance.

Occasionally, I went to the British Museum to work on literary essays, half hoping, half afraid to meet Hardy. One day as I passed along Bedford Place, I saw a woman in trousers – *à la* George Sand – going in at number 8 and remembered my father's dress suit hanging unused at home. As Mama said, I was the man of the house, so next day I took the suit to a tailor and had the trousers and tailcoat cut down to fit. Also father's long double-breasted topcoat of grey tweed with a black velvet collar, too warm and serviceable to go unused. The topcoat was most welcome as winter was setting in, yet when it came to wearing the black suit, the starch went out of me, and I shoved it to the rear of my wardrobe.

I'd got, as well, Father's signet ring, gold with an engraved Old English M; I had it sized to fit the little finger of my right hand, where I took to twisting it round when I was agitated. A suit, a coat and a ring. The whole of Father's legacy to me!

Daily I wrote, converting my anger at my father's perfidy into creative energy. In recent years, I'd neglected my family in favour of my writing; now I had to double my efforts and divide myself equally between the two. I'd no time for social calls and saw few of my old schoolfriends and none of my former literary acquaintances. I was smoking ceaselessly, and my nerves were as raw as red meat, but I persisted. An essay, 'The Governess in Fiction', was published in the August 1899 edition of *The Academy*; it was much reduced in length and otherwise altered by the editor, so I'd chosen to sign it simply M. But there was a cheque to soothe me for having my work tampered with, as well as the satisfaction of opening my own account at the bank. And soon after, 'The China Bowl', my Cornish short story – too long for *The Yellow Book* indeed! – was serialized in the September and October issues of the magazine *Temple Bar*.

1901

Leave him: he's quiet enough: and what matter
  Out of his body or in, you can scatter
The frozen breath of his silenced soul, of his outraged soul to the
  winds that rave:
Quieter now than he used to be, but listening still to the magpie
  chatter
        Over his grave.

'Here Lies a Prisoner'

Church bells tolled for hours in the evening, marking the death of Queen Victoria, twenty-two days into the new year, 1901. All London put on mourning so deep it blotted out the winter sun, and Mama insisted a funeral wreath be hung on the street door so that we might be seen to be a part of the general sorrow and solemnity.

The wreaths round Gordon Square had scarcely come down when ours went up again. A message came from Peckham Hospital that Henry had died of pneumonia on 22 March, aged thirty-five. Mama received the news as if she were made of frozen snow. None of her usual hysterics: for her, Henry had died thirteen years earlier. Forbidden by Father, bound as if by hoops of steel even after he was dead, neither Anne nor I had seen our brother in all that time. Not since he'd run howling and barefoot from the breakfast room. I was overwhelmed now with regretful yearning, aware of the final, irreversible loss of Henry, whom I'd adored since nursery days. Anne was so stricken she had to be put to bed. I was left to deal with the arrangements. No religious service, no funeral as such, he was to be quietly buried in Nunhead Cemetery not far from the hospital. Mama wouldn't allow me to let any of the Mews or

Kendalls know about the burial. She refused to attend herself, sitting mute and withered in her parlour chair.

Some consolation: at last, at least, he was free, no longer a prisoner of the sooty brick asylum, the solitary chair of his madness. Anne and I stood at the open grave. A perpetual, melancholy rain was falling on the black umbrella I held over us, falling with a sound like the flutter of birds' wings, pigeons' wings. It came to me, then, how much Henry, the gay, dashing Henry of my girlhood, had loved the lions in Trafalgar Square and the legend – had he made it up? – that they'd get to their feet and speak on Judgment Day. We'd all be reunited on that day, wasn't that how it went? All the dead souls would be raised, and we'd meet our dear ones again. How I wished I could truly believe in all that.

God! What *is* God? Maybe Henry finally knew the answers to all my most troubling questions, but his silenced soul was beyond speech, over there, on the other side of – what?

A gust of chilly wind, cold as iron, threatened to pull the umbrella from my hand, but I gripped it all the tighter. I moved half a step forward and dropped a single red rose down on to the pine coffin. A stooped old man, grizzled and toothless, looking like Death himself, waited across the way from us, his cap held respectfully against his chest. With a curt nod, he settled the cap on his head, lifted his shovel, and started to fill in the hole with muddy clods. They made a hollow thud when they hit the bottom, the most grotesque sound I'd ever heard. Water puddled brown at our feet and ran down the sides of the grave as he worked. Anne sobbed and stepped away and began walking towards the cemetery gate, her shoulders shaking and her black frock getting darker and heavier from the wet. After a last glance at the shattered, disappearing rose, I followed, hurrying to catch her up and bring her what little protection I could with the umbrella.

Anne and I, we were right not to marry and not to explain why. How frail are the dead who can't define or defend themselves. They, too, must be protected. Henry's madness and Freda's – such cruelty, such waste – marked a degeneration of the family and, even though we might try to deny it, of our lives. The new century had been welcomed with such hope and promise for better times, but it hadn't halted or even slowed the deterioration and dismantling of all I saw round me. The city had never been so dinning and dirty, so morose and fretful, the people more ragged and despairing. The churches were empty. Great buildings were falling down, or being pulled down, whole streets become gaping ditches. The dark houses leant in over the pavement, blocking out the light. This was no new beginning. All that was left was for the three of us – Mama, Anne, and I – to huddle together, wrapped in the tattered black remnants of our lives, and go on.

The stillness of the sunshine lies
    Upon her spirit: silence seems
    To look out from its place of dreams
When suddenly she lifts her eyes
    To waken, for a little space,
    The smile asleep upon her face.

      .   .   .

That is her window, by the gate.
    Now and again her figure flits
    Across the wall. Long hours she sits
Within: on all who come to wait.
    Her Saviour too is hanging there
    A foot or so above her chair.

            from 'The Little Portress'

Summer 1901 brought the coronation of a new king and the optimistic light of a new age, to be called Edwardian. I'd been living on the edge of my nerves, writing unsigned essays and book reviews to earn whatever money I could, when Cousin Walter informed us we were richer by some £120 per annum because, as his letter said, 'the obligation to Peckham Hospital has ended'. Anne insisted, rightly, that we both needed to get away from black frocks and funeral wreaths. The King, as Prince of Wales, had created something of a vogue for going abroad on holiday. Anne and I and some of our old school-friends decided to do the same. We planned a fortnight's holiday in France. At last! I was going to the land of Lucy Harrison's memories. Ella D'Arcy was there, too, in Paris. We were going only as far as the Brittany coast, though, to a Roman Catholic convent that took paying guests.

So it was that Ethel Oliver, Maggie Browne, Florence

Hughes, Margaret Chick, Anne and I – a party of six unmated females – started from Southampton in an August rainstorm. In spite of the wind and the waves tossing the boat, we sang and joked. I was so happy to be on my way that I lifted my skirts in something like a cancan and capered round our cabin in my directoire knickers, behaving like the schoolgirl who'd made them laugh so many years ago. They clapped their hands. 'Oh, Lottie!' Ethel said, grinning. Florence giggled, and Margaret called me a jolly scamp, and they all joined in, dancing and high-kicking along with me.

We six and our numerous valises disembarked at St Malo and reached the convent by cart at a starry, belated hour. The air was thick with seaweed smell, and the sound of the ceaseless tide came to us from out of the dark. We found the gate in the grey wall locked. The rusty chain was pulled, and a bell resounded with a startling clangour. A pale face behind the grille examined us and in a soft Gallic voice welcomed us to the Convent of St Gildas de Rhuys. By lantern-light we were shown to our rooms, cells really, with whitewashed walls, a crucifix, a narrow bed, a haven, a heaven, a paradise in miniature! Exhausted, I staggered in, shut the door and slept.

The morning was like the first day of the freshly created world. The convent's sunny gardens blossomed and tangled edenically, all green and gold. Beds of herbs, clumps of carnations, their scents heavy and insistent. In the quiet cloisters, between the stone arches, huge pink bushes of hydrangea. Above them, white roses climbed up to the windows of the nuns' corridor. Through the open casements, I glimpsed the faded doors where their black habits hung. Now and again, a figure moved against the bare white wall. Above the long uneven slate roof, the tower of the convent chapel stood high and square. A cracked bell jangled from it, above a broken balustrade, telling of storms that blew in from the winter sea.

I carried my journal notebook out to a bench in a corner of the courtyard and began writing. Anne soon appeared with her paintbox, intending to do some watercolours, and before long, our group was assembled in white lawn shirtwaists and white linen skirts. As was the fashion, the others' hair was piled up and rolled round thick pads and topped with large beribboned hats. How smart and pretty they all were – Anne, too – but for myself, I still preferred short curls and a plain straw boater.

Our days, bright and hot, filled with pearly-gold light, were passed in reading, letter-writing, and sea-bathing. We took evening strolls along the quay in the village near by, watching fishermen mend the nets they cast into the sea for *langoustines* and *crevettes*, or set out for night-fishing in small lamp-lighted boats. We took walks through the surrounding countryside away from the sea cliffs under a sky unknown in London, a great dome of a blue Anne called cerulean. We met grey stone farmhouses with haystacks like plump loaves of bread. Apple orchards of ancient, gnarled trees. Dogcarts and horsecarts rattling along rutted lanes. Breton peasant women in shawls and starched white caps and sabots, knitting even as they drove the cows home for milking. And wayside shrines: crucifixes, weather-beaten, lichen-covered, with bunches of wilted wild flowers left at His feet. I remembered Hardy's desire to die a peasant's death and thought warmly of him, so far away in time and distance.

For myself, I cherished the quiet times of meditation in the convent chapel. I'd been struck from the first with the great serenity and sweetness of the sisters, whose life – not lives but seemingly a single communal life – centred on daily Mass, supplemented by sessions of ritual prayer. How I envied such peace, such certainty.

I attended Mass each morning. Above the nuns' black-veiled heads, high in the chapel arches, like a flock of sea birds, hung models of full-rigged ships, frail and all white, ghostly little ships of dreams. I joined in the recitation of litanies to the '*patronne des Bretons, mère des veuves et arche de Noé, refuge des pêcheurs, et protecteur des pêcheurs en pleine mer*', voices

most fervent in their prayers for the safe return of those gone
to sea. As the old priest stood mumbling Latin with his back
to the congregation, I realized the plain cross I wore on a
chain round my neck, silver or gold, was merely jewellery. The
crucifix above the altar – and in the country lane, in my cell, in
the refectory, in the common room, everywhere in the convent –
was not simply decoration but a suffering man, stripped
and scourged. He was, in that instant, alive for me, so hurt, so
hurt.

When His suffering became too harrowing, His blood too
painfully red, I dropped my gaze, resting it on the painted
plaster figure of St Anthony of Padua on a side altar of the
chapel. He wore a tarnished halo, fallen across his forehead
like a pantomime crown. He was the one the sisters petitioned
for small favours, such as the blessing of clear, cloudless
weather during our stay. I came to hold quite an affection for
this saint of little things. I liked to see him stationed in his dim
niche, down here with us poor, imperfect human beings.

In the convent garden one evening, I was reading in the dusk
when I sensed someone coming and looked up, and over my
page I saw a black-habited figure with a soundless step, walking
towards me with that sober swiftness the nuns had. She came
across the darkened grass in the vague shadows of the trees,
stopped in front of me and motioned me to shut my book. I
put it down.

'But you will ruin the eyes,' she said. 'There is not light
enough.'

'They're quite strong,' I said. 'Up to this moment one could
see well enough.'

'Today perhaps – but later, when you are as old as I am,
then, *mon enfant*!' And she made a little groping gesture.

'As old,' I echoed, laughing. 'None of us are half so young.
We never shall be, I imagine. You have the secret of *jeunesse
perpétuelle*, of perpetual youth. *N'est-ce pas la vérité?*'

'*Peut-être.*' She smiled. '*C'est possible.* Truly it is the world which ages, that world out there' – she waved her hand – 'in which there is much of sin, of suffering, of illusion. And is it not itself the Great Illusion, your sad, brilliant, rebellious world?'

'This place, too,' I answered, 'seems unreal, illusory, at times, in its serenity. We of the world, as you would say, we sometimes wonder how it could be possible, your world, your life.'

'*Vous n'êtes pas catholique*,' she said, with certainty, and went on. 'It is the blessed, the protected life. And it is possible, in part perhaps, because we do not question. It is not permitted. We accept. Is it not this insistence of the world to question – *questionner la vie, questionner la souffrance, questionner Dieu, questionner tout*, which ages, brings the lines about the face, the weariness of heart?'

The light had failed. She was an outline, a murmur in the twilight. We walked across in the darkness to the convent door.

'*Je prierai pour vous*,' she said, her habit making her invisible. '*Bon soir.*'

Each time I came and went through the convent gate, I was struck by the beauty, a finer kind of beauty, of the portress whose ageless face I could see through the grille, a face thin and sensitive, but lovely with its appearance of all worries discarded – all questioning abandoned, as my twilight *soeur* had explained – along the way to some diviner reality. She sat framed in the slit of window, reading her prayer-book, the black profile of her veil with its white rim so still under the crucifix behind her on the wall. As I passed, although she didn't raise her head, I sensed a sort of benediction and a smile, faint and a bit sad, like starlight.

One afternoon in the last week of our holiday, she did lift her eyes as I passed, and I recognized a resemblance, a reminder of someone I knew. With a start, I saw her again, the face rather triangular, with a straight, prominent nose. And all at once, I wanted to speak to her, to be with her. I walked out through the gate again, clutching my handbag. Under a sky scalding white, I hurried to the railway station in the nearby village. Like one possessed, I rushed up to buy a ticket just as the train for Paris puffed into the station. My mind was confused by the pounding and roaring of the engine: I couldn't hear what the man in the station master's cap was saying nor could I remember how to say in French what I wanted. What was it I *did* want? The engine hissed a burst of steam. The man's eyes went round and glassy. His mouth opened and closed like a fish under water.

I'd gone oddly deaf and dumb. I turned away, retreated out through the door of the station. I ran along the dusty lane towards the convent until I was gasping and close to stumbling. I dropped, panting, by a hedgerow on the verge, my vision black from the sun in my eyes. The broken stalks crushed under me smelled warm and green and sour-sharp. I pressed my forehead hard against the ground until the pain brought tears. I pictured the little plaster St Anthony, my poor saint with his tin-pot crown.

I tried to reconstruct the links in the chain of thought and feeling that had taken me from the face of the nun at the grille of the gatehouse to a longing to be with Ella D'Arcy. The discipline of the nuns and their dedication to Christ, their Bridegroom, attracted me. Renouncing the marriage bed was no obstacle. That I was committed to already. But what was it I wanted? Sisterhood? Peace? Certainty? Love? The kind of bliss acceptance brings, which lighted the face of the portress?

From somewhere behind me came the high-pitched shriek of the train whistle as it prepared to depart for Paris. I covered my ears to stop out the Siren call.

If one could accept authority, renounce individuality, cease to question, and surrender control as the nuns did, why, all else would follow. It would be easy then to be a Roman Catholic or anything else orthodox. Something in me revolted, though, revolted at every turn. A creature of impulse and renunciation, I had the cravings of a *religieuse* for order and tranquillity. But I wanted the fervent chaos of my self and the world, as well.

1902

... and though Christ stands
Still with scarred hands
Over my mouth, I must answer. So
I will come – He shall let me go!

from 'Absence'

When Anne and I returned from France, we found the house in a perfect shambles. Mama had sent Cook off to visit her family in Clapham, discharged the maid Sarah for incompetence, and apparently hadn't eaten anything in days. Dishes of spoilt food sat untouched on the dining-room table. Mama had attempted to make her own tea over the fire in the parlour, broken the best china teapot, the one painted with garlands and cherubs, by placing it directly on the hot coals, and soaked the carpet with the spilt water. Seed shells and shed feathers and bird droppings littered the floor under the parrot's stand.

Mama's white hair was dishevelled, her frock wrinkled, slept-in. All this was her childish way of punishing us, her faithless, negligent daughters. 'You went away,' she insisted, in tears, 'and forgot me entirely. I've not had a single word from you in all these months.' We'd written her letters almost daily during the two weeks we'd been abroad. I suspected she'd burnt them from what I found in the ashes on the parlour hearth.

I was so angry at first I couldn't trust myself to speak. It was useless to put forth any rational argument with Mama in any case. Finally, to placate her, Anne and I swore never to leave her alone in future, and she agreed to recall Cook and reinstate Sarah, who, because she'd nowhere else to go, had been cowering in her room in the basement since Mama's outburst.

135

Relative tranquillity descended on the household, and France seemed a mirage, a sort of distant place of eternal sunlight and foliage, hydrangeas and roses – with hidden thorns. Sometimes, I fancied I heard the sounds of the sea in the ebb and flow of city traffic or saw the cloistered blossoms in the flowers of our back garden. When the occasional letter came, bearing a Paris postmark and French stamps like miniature works of art, I longed to open it but forced myself instead to leave it on my work table for a day or two, where it cooled and became ordinary. Finally, I slid the envelope into my work table drawer, unopened. I mustn't be tempted. Ella D'Arcy was somehow the wickedly beautiful queen of that green and gold fairyland I'd glimpsed once and mustn't be enticed into entering.

I applied myself to my work. In addition to the unsigned reviews and articles that paid the rates and the butcher's bills, my writing appeared with some regularity in journals and magazines where I was pleased to see my name in print. In 1901, I published two poems and 'Some Ways of Love', a short story about renunciation and self-sacrifice, whose heroine is called Ella – my way of saying hello across the miles without the possible consequences of actual correspondence. There were also two essays, one about our long-ago Cockney seamstress, Miss Bolt. The second was a recollection of our holiday in Brittany, for the October issue of *Temple Bar*. The drafting of it was a kind of re-experiencing and an exorcism. I was quite certain that would be the end of it. But, of course, I was wrong.

Four poems and a short story were published in 1902, all in some way drawing on my experiences abroad. The story, called 'In the Curé's Garden', was about an Englishman, Mr Vidal, who meets Anita, a French priest's seventeen-year-old ward, falls in love, and is rebuffed. I simply couldn't shake myself free of France. In my wayward imagination, I kept revisiting those idyllic hours in the summer sun, and yet just when I felt most strongly cleansed, purified by memories of daily Mass and ritual prayers and the piety of the chaste nuns, the train whistle sounded again in my head, and I found myself having anxieties about my sex and my soul.

So I left off writing poems and stories altogether. Daydreams and nightdreams might come, bringing spectres to tempt and taunt me, but when they passed, when I woke to my responsibilities as the 'man' of the Mew family, they left no trace, no black marks on white paper to shame me.

Hardy stared back at me when I opened the newspaper one day. A murky photogravure of him and a story underneath said he'd been given some literary honour but was too ill to attend the ceremony and accept it. My heart smashed at my chest. Panicky and agitated, I left the house and walked along the sunny pavement. I wanted to go to him. Impossible. I crossed to Gordon Square and found a shaded park bench and sat, my mind tumbling over and over. Had I thought Hardy, unlike Father, was immortal, that he'd always be as I'd first met him, hale and robust? Knowing he was down in Dorset, perhaps reading my poems and stories when they were printed in the literary journals, had given me an audience for whom to write, a standard to attempt to reach. Without him . . . there was no thinking of a world without him.

To distract myself, I watched as a removal van was being unloaded at number 46, a reed-thin young woman in white on the doorstep directing the men as they unloaded boxes and trunks and twine-tied bundles of books. The woman had the face of a soulful saint and reminded me of the novitiates in the Convent of St Gildas de Rhuys, with their white habits and high, bird-like voices.

Why was it that no thing was content to be a thing unto itself? Why did everything remind one of something else? Why did everything that didn't resonate of Thomas Hardy evoke memories of France and all its splendour and sting?

*

In April 1902, after a lengthy interval of silence, a note from Ella D'Arcy came for me in the morning post. I couldn't ignore its message as it was written on a picture postcard – a view of the Seine, lamp-posts receding along the embankment towards a low, arched bridge:

Charlotte, dear friend –

I came upon your 'Notes on a Brittany Convent' in an old copy of *Temple Bar* – such a lovely, witty piece of writing – and wondered, again, why you have never answered my letters, why you came to France and did not let me know. What have I done to injure our friendship? Forgive me, whatever it may be.

Your penitent Ella

I tossed a few clothes and my sponge bag into a valise, dug out the money from my first story in *The Yellow Book*, so long hidden in the trunk at the foot of my bed, scribbled an inadequate note to Anne, and left to catch the next boat-train from Charing Cross Station.

I think my body was my soul,
And when we are made thus
Who shall control
Our hands, our eyes, the wandering passion of our feet . . . ?

from 'Madeleine in Church'

I stood at the kerb in front of the Gare du Nord, dazed, like a sleepwalker abruptly awakened. I discovered myself facing the evening streets of a strange city, famed for its wickedness and depravity. The warm, dusky air was loud with the clatter of horse-drawn carriages and the sputter and honk of motor cars. The pavement streamed with people, and I was invisible to all those who passed me, speaking too rapidly in a language I couldn't understand. I didn't exist for any of them. I hardly existed for myself. I was an insubstantial stranger set down in a dark, hostile place, with none of the blind certainty or thoughtless urgency that had brought me here.

Back in my bedroom in London, reading Ella's postcard, I'd come to the belated realization that so strong an emotion ought to be tested. But I'd begun to repent my rashness in coming.

The jolting squawk of a klaxon, and a motor-cab stopped in front of me. My hand reached out, without my willing it, and opened the door. I climbed in and fell back against the seat.

The cab put me down in the Rue Chateaubriand, in front of a grey stucco building with the address on Ella's card. I spoke to the concierge, a thick, sour woman. In the flickering light of a gas bracket, she eyed my valise and seemed deaf to my stumbling French. I repeated Ella's name two or three times until a glimmer of recognition crept over her suspicious face.

'*Ah, oui, l'Anglaise.*' She started up the hall stairs with me right behind. On the shadowy second-floor landing she bent her head towards a closed door. '*Ici,*' she said, '*mais pas de partage, pas de tapage, pas de fumer, et pas de cuisson.*' And she went away.

Puzzled, unable to catch her meaning, I raised a tentative fist and rapped on the door. It opened almost at once, before I could change my mind and follow the concierge back down the echoing stairs.

Ella's cry of 'Charlotte!' and her clasp of my hand in hers as she brought me into her room sent all my doubts flying. She was just as I'd remembered her, with her triangular face, her glittery jet eyes, and her bright way of speaking. But there was a new sharpness to her and new colour, a patch of red on each cheek, her lips scarlet with make-up. She was a mature woman now, handsome rather than pretty. She laughed lightly, as excited as I was about my unexpected appearance on her threshold. She welcomed me to Paris – my first time, I told her – and waved away my worry about finding accommodation. 'Later, we can find you a *pension* somewhere near by. For tonight, you must stop here, with me.' She waved her hand round the bed-sitting room.

Only then did I take in the smallness, the clutter, the disarray of the little space, lighted by a single gas fixture on the wall by the door. Books, masses of papers, unwashed plates and cups littering the top of a round table. Rumpled clothing draped over two straight-backed chairs. And an unmade bed against the far wall, two dented pillows, a tumble of sheets, over which Ella hastily tossed the counterpane she retrieved from the floor.

'Charlotte, dear, how long has it been? Ten years? We've so much to catch up on.' Ella took my valise and set it behind a curtain hung across the corner of the room, at the foot of the bed. With her back to me, I was aware of how the dark strands, strayed from the loose knot on top of her head, crinkled at the nape of her neck. Strangely, I wanted to touch Ella, to tidy that hair and, at the same instant, I wanted to escape the room suddenly too small for the two of us. But I would not, again, be one who turns away.

. . . You need not fear the touch,
Blindest of all the things that I cared for very much
In the whole gay, unbearable, amazing show.

from 'Ne Me Tangito'

I'd not shared a bed before with anyone but Anne and that not since we were young girls. Now, Ella lay there, asleep, her thighs, belly, breasts touching mine through our nightdresses. She smelled just the way I'd remembered, of attar of roses. Tonight, in the moist darkness, it became the scent of all the roses in the world. My fingers longed to move over her, my lips to kiss hers. And yet, I didn't dare, afraid I'd wake her.

A great shudder went through my body and out through my limbs. A mad wickedness had come over me such as I'd never known existed, and I was unexplainable to myself.

Overhead, the stars reeled. We slept face to face the whole night through, one breath, one throbbing stillness.

> . . . I shall never touch your hair
> Or hear the little tick behind your breast,
>   Still it is there,
>   And as a flying bird
> Brushes the branches where it may not rest
>   I have brushed your hand . . .
>
>   from 'On the Road to the Sea'

I should have been shocked and horrified by my midnight experience if it hadn't been so pleasant. No, I tell a lie. It was more than that – it was overwhelming, an incomparable rapture. And I coveted more, unmindful of the implications.

The next day, Ella led me to a *pension* in the Rue du Turin. I was given a nice room with a small balcony overhanging the cobbled street with shops opposite and a flower seller on the pavement below, her stall heaped with bunches of lilies-of-the-valley, pinks and lilacs. I should have been quite content, but all I wanted was to be with Ella. I thought of her constantly when we were apart: Ella, my co-conspirator, from the Latin *conspirare*, to breathe together. I spent the hours alone in my room, smoking and writing poems and unsent letters to her, filling my notebook, then locking it away in my valise.

We took our meals together, Ella and I, in modest restaurants and outdoor cafés. The concierge's '*pas de cuisson*' meant no cooking was allowed in Ella's room. I swung like a pendulum between terror and joy at the sight of her each time she rounded the street corner and came towards me. Our time together was charged and awkward on my part. Ella was as gay and unaffected as I'd always known her. We laughed and talked about the people from our *Yellow Book* days. I told myself, absurdly, not to stare. At the very least, not to be caught staring at her.

One wet, foggy day, she suggested we visit the Louvre after lunch. 'I want to show you the *Salle Grecque*,' she said. 'My friend Jules once pointed out to me that not all the fragments from the Parthenon are in the British Museum.' She laughed. 'He says the English aren't the only ones who knew how to loot Greece of its antiquities.' She pushed back her chair and began opening her umbrella.

'My friend Jules' echoed in my ears so that I barely heard what else she was saying.

When we climbed the steps of the great grey palace-museum, we found the galleries closed because the day was too overcast for one to be able to view the exhibitions. Ella slipped her arm through mine and said, 'Never mind. Come on, Charlotte. We'll walk along the Seine instead.'

The lamps were lighted early along the Quai du Louvre, fading off into the distance as if they were melting, as Lucy Harrison had said so long ago. It was indeed like being lost in a memory. Or a familiar dream. Or a work of art, a Monet or a Whistler. For the first time since lunch, I was calm, untroubled, the two of us alone, strolling along under a single grey umbrella.

The spell was broken when Ella checked the watch pinned to her bosom and announced, 'We must hurry. There's someone I want you to meet.'

As we stepped through the etched-glass door of the Café LePell, a tall man, bald, with a reddened nose and ginger moustache, stood up from behind a marble-topped table. He set his wineglass down and came to meet us, grinning like a fool, a damn silly clown. I disliked him, even before Ella said, with an equally idiotic grin, 'Charlotte, this is *mon cher ami* Jules, who's just got back from Switzerland.'

I remember rooms that have had their part
In the steady slowing down of the heart.
The room in Paris, the room at Geneva,
The little damp room with the seaweed smell,
And that ceaseless maddening sound of the tide –
Rooms where for good or ill – things died.

from 'Rooms'

I didn't go to Ella's room after the arrival of Jules. Nor did I see her for the next two days. Partly, my fault. We agreed to meet in a park halfway between my room and hers, but I chose at the last minute not to go. I didn't send an explanation. Instead, I started off by myself in the opposite direction. I toured the cathedral of Notre Dame, but I couldn't do justice to it. My head was stupid from lack of sleep, and my eyes achy and tired. I browsed about the Latin Quarter for an hour or so before taking one of the heavy, double-decker steam trams back to my *pension*.

But somehow, I got on the wrong one or failed to get down at the proper corner. I was soon lost in a part of the city where no one was about, and I couldn't locate any street signs. Unreadable posters peeling off walls. Narrow streets cut in five directions, sinking dimly in the distance. A three-legged dog, small, white, hobbling, sidling, scurrying away. Stone buildings soiled black round the doorways. Ghastly stretches of desolation, mean, dirty, sordid. I was in danger of slipping again into nebulous non-existence. In desperation, I began praying, bargaining with God. If He would lead me safely to the Rue du Turin, I'd go immediately and apologize to Ella for failing to meet her. I'd swallow my jealousy and think of her only as a friend, whose happiness was the dearest thing to me.

Like an answer to my prayer, a shop girl with a nimbus of white-blond hair came out from the door of a *boulangerie*. She'd noticed my distress, she said, thought I was '*un enfant perdu*', and offered herself as guide and guardian angel. Shortly, I was on my way to my *pension*.

I went next day to make amends to Ella but got no answer to my knocking, so I asked the scowling concierge to let me in to wait. The room's one window was open to the cloudy, breathless afternoon, but there was no view to distract me, only a row of similar unshuttered windows in the building opposite. I turned back to the room. It hurt too much to take notice of the two empty glasses on the table, the green wine bottles, the crushed stubs of French cigarettes, in spite of the concierge's '*pas de fumer*'. The petticoat abandoned over a chair back, the bedclothes spilling on to the floor made my throat ache with held-back tears. I paced the little room, twisting my signet ring, impatient, longing myself for a cigarette.

I was about to have one when a key rattled in the lock. Ella opened the door, and she was alone. Thank God. She didn't seem at all surprised to find me there. And yet not pleased either.

I was acutely aware of my body, its desire, its shame, its fear. My voice wavered like an adolescent boy's as I spoke first: 'I'm here to say how sorry I am that I failed to meet you yesterday.'

'Yes?' she said, waiting, I supposed, for an explanation.

What could I tell her? How self-torturing and perverse I was, how something in me made me run from the very thing I wanted most? With a flush of shame, I blurted out – 'I love you, Ella!'

'Yes? And I love you too, Charlotte, but is this how you treat a friend?'

'It's more than friendship. Much more.'

'When did you decide that?'

'It wasn't a decision I made,' I said. 'It was a decision that seemed made for me. I acted on some unthinking impulse in coming to you, responding to you.'

'Are you mad?' Her face twisted into an ugly frown. 'Did you imagine I haven't love enough and plenty?' There was a sneer in her words. 'That I'm not oversupplied? That I'm no longer attractive to men and must settle for anything I can get into my bed? Did you think I was that sort?'

Her tone, the way she glared at me made me feel shrivelled and grotesque.

'Surely you know my preference is for men. Couldn't you see I was Harland's mistress when you and I met? Why do you think I left London when Mrs H. so unexpectedly popped in?'

I hadn't understood any of that. How naïve I'd been. And was yet. What ever made me think . . . ? 'I was wrong,' I said, in a voice quite small.

'Yes, you were.' She hesitated. 'You may certainly love me, if you like,' she said, 'but from a distance, please. I'll be less inconvenienced.' She dropped her handbag on the cluttered table and went to sit on the edge of the bed. Her hands made star-shapes in the sheets as she leant back. 'Jules is returning to Switzerland tomorrow, and he's asked me to go with him.'

'But –' I stopped. I'd embarrassed myself enough. Where was my pride? I tossed my head and said, 'Are you two to be married, then?'

Ella simply laughed in that light way of hers. 'Oh, Charlotte.' She shook her head.

'How can you laugh,' I asked, with unshed tears, 'when you must know how I'm suffering?'

'One doesn't die because one suffers. Everything can kill but pain.' She rose and came to stand looking down at me with some of her old kindness. 'We can be friends, you and I, and only that.'

I heard an echo in those words. It was my turn to accept rebuke. 'You're right, of course,' I said, stiffening my spine. I extended my hand in a gesture of friendship, holding on to her warm fingers a moment too long before she pulled them away.

With Ella gone, I set off for London alone, chastened, weary and full of remorse. My dash to Paris had been an absurd mistake. On the Channel ferry, when I calculated we were equidistant between Calais and Dover, I tossed my journal notebook over the railing and watched it bob and float away, like a black sea bird. As I left the train at Charing Cross, dropping one shaky foot on the step below, then the other, I put my face in order so as to appear cynically indifferent. The fact was she'd torn my heart to rags.

1911

We knew no Eden and the poisoned fruit
We did not pluck, yet from the bitter root
We sprang, maimed branches of iniquity.

Have we who share the heritage accurst
Wrought nothing? Tainted to the end of time,
The last frail souls still suffer from the first
Blind victims of an everlasting crime.

from 'A Question'

What kind of God had I been trying to speak to, who answered my prayers with silence? What was it He wanted from me? If I possessed a self intricate and peculiar, quirky and individual-istic by all accounts, who made me this way? If I found myself attracted to a married man and an indifferent woman, longing always for what was out of my reach, who made me this way? What kind of God punishes one for being what one cannot help being? My Heavenly Father was very much like my earthly one, leaving me to be responsible for circumstances I didn't create. I felt estranged from both of them.

My solace was writing. Between 1904 and 1906, *Temple Bar* printed four of my signed essays. One of them, 'The Poems of Emily Brontë', I'd higher hopes for. I adored her – tragic, heroic, majestic – and her work. I felt a spiritual sistership with her in her isolation at Haworth Parsonage, with only her own dear Charlotte and Anne for company in the end. Emily was one of nature's outcasts – a self-determined outlaw. With the face of a pagan warrior, she confronted life and met death. It scarcely meant obscurity to a soul thrust back on itself for light. Some had called her genius masculine, but I thought it purely spiritual, severed from embodiment and freed from any accident of sex.

I boldly sent the essay off to the publisher Elkin Mathews, suggesting it form the introduction to a collection of Emily Brontë's poetry, since none was currently available. The poems, I wrote, 'have rested alone and almost unnoticed in the lumber room of literature: it is time the dust was shaken from them'.

Weeks passed. A letter came. I received a polite but firm rejection for my boldness. I abandoned the entire project. How terribly little it takes to shatter one's confidence as a writer. Mr Mathews's response sent me into a black mood of self-recrimination: if only I were better educated, more proficient at punctuation, a man – a thousand senseless ifs – *then* my work would be instantly accepted and I'd be spared such painful rebuffs.

For myself, what seemed almost perverse was that shortly I was back at my work table, dipping my pen into the ink pot, writing again.

During this same period, two of the poems I drafted were derived from my experiences in Paris. Those days and nights were a source of images and emotions to which I went over and over again without being able to use them up. Or rid myself of them. Ella inhabited both of the poems. In 'The Fête', she was as an enchanting bareback rider in a travelling circus, and the speaker of the poem was a moon-struck young man enamoured of her. But I couldn't bring myself to conceive an ending to what had become quite a long narrative piece. I put it away, unfinished.

In the second poem, 'Requiescat', Ella reappeared as the dead lover it was addressed to, although its composition didn't manage to lay to rest my feelings for her as I'd hoped it would. I held open the issue of *Living Age* where it was published, and considered the solid *there-ness* of the black letters on the white page. And I wondered whether she'd ever come across the verse in print. And if she did, would she be able to read its poignant message?

My domestic responsibilities kept multiplying. Mama,

coming across me in an apron with my sleeves rolled to the elbows, invariably said something like 'Charlotte, whatever are you doing? Go and change into a decent frock before someone sees you!' What I couldn't make her understand was that Sarah had got married and old Cook had retired, leaving only Jane, the maid-of-all-work, who interrupted my writing as much as Nanny ever had. Jane's skills in the kitchen were limited. But mine were practically non-existent, so we had to muddle on and make do.

Mama ate little and criticized a good deal: 'Really,' she said of Jane's first attempt at pudding, 'just look at the condition of that blancmange. It hasn't been properly unmoulded at all. I simply can't bear anything so misshapen!' Anne and I helped ourselves to servings of what actually tasted quite vanilla-y and delicious. Mama sat silent and disapproving, her table-napkin pressed to her lips. When the rest of the blancmange, looking like a ravaged igloo, appeared at dinner the next day, Mama insisted on sending it back. 'It's an insult, that's what it is! The very idea! Giving us the servants' leftovers!' Jane removed it from the table. After dinner, the three of us – Anne, Jane and I – gathered in the kitchen to finish it off, laughing and licking our spoons like mischievous children.

Anne gave what she was able to the upkeep of the household, but she had her restoration work to go to. I, who'd once scoffed at the invidious concept of Duty, did mine now without comment or complaint. No matter what, at times, seethed inside me. I carried coal and emptied ashes and swept hearths and re-swept them when Mama called me in and said, 'Send for Jane. See what a sloven she's become about her work.' I'd bite my tongue and reach for the broom while Mama turned away and stared out of the window.

Still, I managed to steal some time every day to escape into my writing. It was no longer possible to hide my professional employment, such as it was, from Mama. I didn't even try. She surely must have suspected something of it before now. Like so much within the shrinking circle of her life, she chose not to see what she chose not to see.

At my work table, I concentrated on the making of short stories, scribbling tale after tale of love and loss. I wasn't so blind to my darker self as not to see the pattern emerging. Each new story was somehow a variation on a single theme: into a household where two sisters lived in harmony came a man who shattered their lives. But it wasn't my sister Anne about whom I was writing. It was Ella. Invariably, the stories ended unhappily. The last and longest of them I tossed into my trunk unfinished, along with all the rest. I knew that none of them was publishable.

Dear, sweet Anne. She'd been so patient throughout my long twilight of sadness and never pressed for details of my sudden flight to Paris and my ignoble return. Her own creative work was beginning, at last, to receive some recognition. Thanks to a bequest in Aunt Mary Kendall's will, Anne was able to take space at the Hogarth Studios in Soho, where she could paint as well as do furniture restoration. All this, of course, was best kept from Mama, who would have disapproved, even when one of Anne's pictures, white roses in a crystal bowl, was accepted for exhibition by the Royal Academy.

That was the highlight of our 1909, an otherwise dreary year when I published nothing and passed my fortieth birthday. It rather took me by surprise. Forty. I wasn't any older than the girl who first met Hardy, twenty-two or -three on the inside, no matter how I appeared on the outside.

In 1910, our jolly King Edward died. His son, George V, brought to the monarchy a more serious, almost bourgeois mood. He reminded me of his grandmother. It was difficult for me to view the coronation as a shiny beginning, the start of a glorious new Georgian Age, not to be confused with the previous one, renowned for its periwigs, its silver and its architecture. Many people welcomed the return of what they called Victorian moral ideals, but this was a different century with quite different ways of looking and of seeing, and a diminished tolerance for hypocrisy.

I understood that, even though inside the house at 9 Gordon Street Mama still reigned with all her Victorian notions firmly intact. When Anne and I shortened old skirts a couple of inches above our insteps, Mama was adamant in her objection: 'You're simply flaunting yourselves.'

'I quite like not having to lift my skirt to climb a stair or step over a rain puddle,' I said. 'And I doubt seriously that any man will be driven mad by the sight of my ankles.'

Mama cried, 'You'll be mistaken for a common doxy, mark my word. You'll be ruined!'

Anne put her fist to her mouth to keep from laughing out loud. I bit my underlip. We promised to let down our hems. Although we didn't, Mama never mentioned them again. She found, instead, an endless number of other modern outrages to lament, sour with vexation.

I continued to treat myself to occasional afternoons in the library at the British Museum. There, I was sustained by the waking dream that is reading. As long as I hadn't read a book, it still potentially held the answer to all my most profound, unanswered questions. Waiting between closed covers, the words stood perfected, arranged in an expectant poetry. Opened, read, the book provided an orderly and satisfying drama, acted out for me alone.

One day in 1911, as I left the museum, I met some workmen felling a huge old plane tree, with all the instruments of butchery. They shouted and laughed and drove their team with whoops and whoas. I stood awhile, watching the hideous operation. The grate of the saw, the swish of the branches as they fell, the crash of the trunk, the rustle of trodden leaves, it all seemed to me a sort of sacrilege. Daphne, pursued by Apollo, became a laurel tree, and the classical tree nymph died with her tree. Who knew what might be dying with this one?

Why, primitive man, and civilized man until a few centuries ago, owed everything to the tree, his fire and his shelter, his gods and his devils – Satan began his serpentine pranks, after all, in a tree. I'd recently been reading that Man himself is descended from the ash tree and the elm, at least according to the Old Norse Edda. I thought about Constable's painted studies of the trees on Hampstead Heath, all long since cut down. I stomped off ferociously down Great Russell Street, determined to write a poem, no, better an essay, on men and trees before all of them – both so dependent on one another – vanished for ever.

I strode along, mulling over the murder of the plane tree, when my fretting was interrupted by something that caught my eye in the window of the bookseller's shop in Gower Street: on display were several copies of *Time's Laughing-stocks* by Thomas Hardy.

He'd been a silent shadow in a far corner of my mind all afternoon. Every time, in fact, I went to the museum. The sight of his name on the book's cover in the window brought him into full awareness. In that moment, I was alive with the sense he was trying to get in touch with me. I wanted, no, had to have, that new book of poetry in order to read the message to me I fancied he'd written. I opened my handbag and counted the coins. Jane had asked me to go to the shops on my way home and buy the kippers for our supper. If the book wasn't too dear, I might be able to afford both. At once impetuous and prudent, I opened the bookseller's door, a bell tinkling over my head, and went in.

In the yellowish light from a brass gaselier, the clerk, a harried young man with crooked tie and receding chin, was engaged with an older man, who sounded irate at not being able to find what he considered a satisfactory translation of Voltaire. 'You call this the King's English?' he sputtered, jabbing his finger at the open page of a book on the counter between them.

I idled in front of the table of poetry. The cost of the Hardy, I calculated, would take a goodly part of my money. What to do? Leave the book? Impossible. Steal it? I checked round furtively. The clerk's gaze met mine.

Again, what to do? Forgo my share of supper? Yes, of course. A small sacrifice to make. I purchased the book – lovely, weighty, pleading to be read – and, at the fishmongers, fewer kippers. I cried off supper for lack of appetite and took Hardy to my bedroom, stirred up the coal fire, pulled my chair up to the hearth, and propped my feet on the fender. In the faltering light, I read:

> They hail me as one living,
>   But don't they know
> That I have died of late years,
>   Untombed although?
>
> I am but a shape that stands here,
>   A pulseless mould,
> A pale past picture, screening
>   Ashes gone cold.

I could hear his voice, the harsh Dorset vowels, saying the words as if he were there in the room with me. The last three stanzas chilled me through:

> And when my Love's heart kindled
>   In hate of me,
> Wherefore I knew not, died I
>   One more degree.
>
> And if when I died fully
>   I cannot say,
> And changed into the corpse-thing
>   I am to-day;
>
> Yet is it that, though whiling
>   The time somehow
> In walking, talking, smiling,
>   I live not now.

I looked up at the poem's title – 'The Dead Man Walking'. It had a strange resonance. An odd familiarity. In his last letter to me, Hardy had added a postscript. I dug in my trunk, tossing aside manuscripts and old letters – none of them the one I was hunting for – and, finally, found the right envelope, addressed in his spiky scrawl. I took out the pages and unfolded them, and read the P.S. with a pang, sharp like the crack of breaking ice:

Without you, I am a dead man walking.

Three Summers since I chose a maid,
Too young maybe – but more's to do
At harvest time than bide and woo.
    When us was wed she turned afraid
Of love and me and all things human;
Like the shut of a winter's day
Her smile went out, and 'twasn't a woman –
    More like a little frightened fay.
        One night, in the Fall, she runned away.

from 'The Farmer's Bride'

The temptation to make too much of it was great. In the days following, I went about my work with half a mind. The other half was attempting to reason with my heart, wanting Hardy's poem to have been written to me. Poetry is the language of love, my heart insisted. What better way to speak of the consequences of loss? His Majesty's Royal Mail is quicker and more certain of finding the intended reader, my head answered.

Finally, I couldn't stand the bickering any longer. I went into my trunk and located the manuscript of the poem I'd written as penance for our parting so many years ago. Here, in 'The Farmer's Bride', I could show Hardy I was aware of what I'd made him suffer, for I'd since been made to suffer in the same way. I decided to send it out, to try to get it published in a journal where he might read it, to say to him that I knew – that we shared – the red shame of wanting and not being wanted.

1913

Please you, excuse me, good five-o'clock people,
    I've lost my last hatful of words,
And my heart's in the wood up above the church steeple,
    I'd rather have tea with the birds.

from 'Afternoon Tea'

If Hardy down in Dorset saw 'The Farmer's Bride' when it appeared in the February 1912 issue of *The Nation*, I got no response. But others saw it, read it and were affected by it. The poem became my *entrée* into an ever-widening circle: I was taken up by a most formidable personage, Mrs Dawson-Scott, called by her many acquaintances Sappho. I didn't much care to be taken up – by this plump, enthusing doctor's wife or by anyone else. But Mrs Sappho's patronage, I soon found, was useful and, once she'd made her mind up, nearly unavoidable.

In her house at Southall, one might hear the roar of any number of current literary lions, and according to our hostess, I was becoming one of them. Mrs Sappho asked me down one Saturday afternoon to read my poems to some of her dear friends. In addition to my prose writing, I'd been devoting some time to poetry. I'd things now in my head rather unmanageable and possibly too big to pull off, and I'd been experimenting with the sonnet form but hadn't got far. It placed too many restraints on me, and I chafed to be free to say what I must in a way that suited me. I'd found in my trunk a draft of a poem, 'A Quoi Bon Dire', begun in 1910, and had re-worked it.

When it came my turn to perform, I felt trapped and owned, like an organ-grinder's monkey, on display in her ornate drawing-room to amuse and astonish. I read 'The Farmer's Bride' and 'A Quoi Bon Dire' and 'In Nunhead Cemetery' and 'The Changeling' in a low, rough voice, constricted by embarrassment. When I finished, I sat petrified, waiting for some response. Silence. Next, a few murmured questions. I couldn't answer. Their words, dense and tinny, stuck in my ears. Then, I heard someone say, 'She's not here yet', as if I were a medium in a trance. Or I'd been away in the world of my poetry. Maybe I had. They were all staring at me. I tossed my head and bolted out of the house and took myself back to Bloomsbury, determined never to be subjected to such torture again.

I wrote rather impolitely, declining Mrs Sappho's next invitation to read. And, damn, if she didn't send me a note saying the Saturday tea was cancelled owing to her ill health and she'd not trouble me by writing again. I understood then how I'd offended her. Feeling guilty and ashamed, I immediately set out to find a cab to carry me to Paddington Station and the train for Southall.

There was now an Underground station at Russell Square, and I'd tried descending to the platform in a cage-like lift. But it was much too claustrophobic to suit me, like going down with the worms and the moles. And loud! The sound of the trains was monstrous. What was wanted was a new Dante to describe these subterranean horrors. For myself, I still preferred the horse-drawn omnibuses, although many of them had of late been replaced with the motorized sort.

When I arrived at the Dawson-Scott house outside London, it was near dusk. I found the ailing Mrs Sappho fit and spry, walking about in a long velvet tea gown and insisting I stop for dinner. Over the meal, candles bright in their silver branches, we talked literary shop, as if nothing had happened between the two of us. How my hostess knew so many publishers and editors I'd no idea. She was altogether a wonder, having given up her own writing to guide and assist others. Her face was pleasant enough in a maternal way. She wore her brown hair twisted up into a knot on top of her head, and her full cheeks glowed fervently as she suggested several possible venues for my work.

After the meat course was served, I explained my determination to do no more poetry readings. 'I'm not a public person. It's an agony for me.'

'Well then, you must gather your poems and arrange them into a manuscript, and together we shall find you a publisher,' Mrs Sappho said, with her customary zeal for organizing other people's lives.

I shook my head. 'No, no. I haven't nearly enough poems to make a book.' Eager to shift the conversation away from myself, I said, 'I've been reading May Sinclair's novel, *Kitty Tailleur*.'

Mrs Sappho made a rather cruel remark about it. 'I wonder at her taste,' she said, her gold bracelets clattering together as she worked her knife and fork, 'choosing the doings of a woman of that sort as her subject. Hardly the proper matter for literature, do you think? I mean, it's so immoral. And to make a demi-mondaine the heroine. It surely reflects badly on her own character that she's familiar with such creatures. One can't help but equate the writer with what she writes. If her women are loose, so must she be.'

At once, I became defensive. 'That's a thing one doesn't say.'

'But it's true,' she protested, her eyes wide.

To which I replied, 'Many things are true that only the commonest minds observe.' And, of course, I'd put my foot in it up to the knee and was immediately out of favour with my hostess again. Why couldn't I remember myself that there are numerous things one doesn't say, most especially to the goose that laid the golden egg?

Mrs Sappho's feelings, like her bodily health, showed amazingly rapid recuperative powers. Within a few weeks, another note arrived in the post, saying she missed my 'stimulating, irritating, interesting company' and inviting me to join her and her family at their summer cottage in Cornwall. I couldn't see my way to going. It was as if she were eventually going to present me with a heavy bill for something I never much wanted to buy, and I mightn't be able to pay for it after all.

In late November 1912, word *did* come, in a way, from Dorset. I opened *The Times* and read the obituary of Emma Gifford Hardy, wife of Thomas, dead after a brief illness at their home, Max Gate. I immediately drafted a note of sympathy. I sent it off, my heart filled with empathetic sorrow and guilty hope. I never received a reply.

> The buds begin to talk of May
> With learned rooks on city trees,
>   And if God please
>   With all of these
> We, too, shall see another Spring.

from 'Ken'

Since my ill-fated dinner conversation with Mrs Sappho, I'd thought often about May Sinclair's novels. And about the author. I'd recently finished reading her *The Combined Maze* – excellent, insightful, thrilling in its sensitivity to human suffering. It had completely got and kept hold of me. Then, to my surprise, Mrs Sappho wrote me in the early spring of 1913, extending an invitation to her next Saturday afternoon at Southall: I wouldn't be called on to read unless I chose to, and she held out the promise of an introduction to the writer whom I'd been so quick to defend.

May Sinclair was standing with her back to us when our hostess brought me across the busy, murmurous room to meet her. I saw first the mass of her auburn hair held up by tortoiseshell combs, the wisps of stray curl at the nape of her neck where her hair thinned to shiny, golden down, and the gold clasp of a string of amber beads. She turned at the sound of Mrs Sappho's speaking her name and looked at me with a level, gentle gaze, her eyes the colour of her beads. She was low-voiced, a bit prim, perhaps five years older than myself and nearly as small, though softer, more roundly feminine. As we talked, and we did so for the rest of the afternoon, I found we had a good deal in common. She'd stayed unmarried to care for an ailing, demanding mother. She wrote to support herself, having published an incredible eight books in the last seven years. She was largely self-educated, although she'd been allowed one year at Cheltenham Ladies' College. She had a fondness for the work and character of Emily Brontë. And all her life, she'd rebelled against the strictness of her Victorian upbringing. In spite of her womanly appearance, it was clear she was inwardly very strong, determined and boundlessly energetic in her good causes – suffrage and the reform of social practices that oppressed women, and often men, as well – such as marriage and sweated labour. Again and again, I heard echoes of Hardy in what she was saying.

I came away from Southall with my head whirling with new ideas and a high singing in my bones. By focusing so relentlessly in recent years on writing in order to help support my family, I'd become cynical and flippant about the problems of others. May Sinclair made me realize that in this world, we don't suffer alone. She and I had been immediately sympathetic to one another. I was once again the little girl I'd been when the doll's house was delivered to the nursery, feeling as if a great, unexpected gift had been presented to me.

By the time I reached Gordon Square that evening, I knew I couldn't let this marvellous woman slip away. So I dipped my pen in the ink pot and wrote to her:

March 15, 1913

Dear Miss Sinclair,

In the excitement of our meeting today at Mrs Dawson-Scott's, I neglected to tell you of my admiration for your novel, *The Combined Maze*. You demonstrate vividly how marriage can be intolerably burdensome, an iron yoke for two mis-mated. Such a heartless convention can weigh upon the spirit until it nearly squeezes the life out of one.

I wanted so much to invite her to call, but the state of things at home these days made that impossible. Mama would have made it extremely awkward and difficult. She dominated all conversation, complaining, detailing her every ache and pain: 'My head throbs unbearably. It's a brain tumour, I'm certain, and will kill me if the arthritis in my elbows doesn't carry me off first.' The doctor came frequently but found nothing serious to treat. And Mama repeatedly accused Anne and me of going off and leaving her alone for weeks at a time, even though neither of us had been on holiday in years.

An alternative occurred to me. I consulted Anne and finished my letter to May Sinclair:

> My fondest hope is that we may meet again soon to continue our discussion. Would you take tea with my sister and me at 6 Hogarth Studios, near Fitzroy Square, on Tuesday next?
>
> Yours sincerely,
> Charlotte Mary Mew

My writing had been, for the most part, going well. At Mrs Sappho's suggestion, I'd sent 'The Changeling' poem to Elisaveta Allen, the editor of *The Englishwoman*, where it was published in the February issue. Also, the long two-part essay, 'Men and Trees', prompted by the felling of the plane outside the British Museum, appeared in the February and March issues. A second poem was printed in the March *Living Age*. I was working on an essay about Nanny Elizabeth, based on the eulogy I'd begun at the time of her death. I wanted, finally, to lay that particular ghost. In revising the piece, I'd removed most of the personal pronouns and private references so it came more fully to focus on that exemplary old servant, Elizabeth Goodman.

One Monday, in the late afternoon, I'd just come in from taking the essay to be typed when I found a reply to my letter on the hall table:

> March 17, 1913
>
> Dear Miss Mew,
>
> How very kind of you. I would so much have liked to come to

you on Tuesday, but I'm booked with some American friends in Chelsea, whom I can't very well put off as they've not long in England. I'm so glad you liked *Combined Maze*. It was very nice of you to write to me.

Let me try my luck some other day.

Sincerely yours,
May Sinclair

Disappointment stopped my breath and blurred my sight. I swallowed, blinked, and only on second reading did I find the hope held out by the last sentence. But the prospect of another refusal left me shy. After my spirits were lifted by the acceptance of my essay about Nanny, to be printed in the October *New Statesman*, I found the courage to ask again.

The sun through the fog halfway up the sky glowed like a Blake watercolour of the risen Christ. The day was alive with promise. And apprehension. After a further exchange of letters, May Sinclair had written, asking me to call on her, adding:

Will you bring me any more poems that you have written? I'm told you've published several every bit as beautiful as 'The Farmer's Bride'. I want you to send something to the *English Review*.

Always very sincerely yours,
May Sinclair

I was on my way to her flat in Edwardes Square, where she'd lived alone since her mother's death. I strode along with all the nervousness of a schoolgirl. Under my arm was a small folder of poems as if I were going to deliver them to my teacher, as if I were back under the tutelage of Miss Harrison. At the corner of the Kensington High Street, on impulse, I bought a red rose from an old woman's flower cart at the edge of the pavement. I carried it before me like a ritual offering.

May Sinclair opened the front door moments after I tapped the brass knocker and, smiling, led me into her tidy ground-floor parlour. A morning-glory gramophone stood on a table next to the sofa, where a long-haired black cat lay curled, sleeping. May – she insisted on Christian names – introduced it as Tommy and spoke of him as if he were her child.

I waited, mute and happy, foolishly holding out the rose, unable to make a suitable presentation. May saw my dazed state and reached to take it from my hand at the instant I shoved it towards her. Our fingers stumbled into each other, and a jolt of red, like a galvanic shock, ran up my arm.

'Oh, Charlotte, how sweet of you.' She took the rose and went into the other room. I glanced round, trying to get my bearings. Books and papers were arranged neatly on the shelves of a glass-fronted case against the wall. Among the many photographs on the mantelpiece lay several ribbon rosettes of mauve and green, the colours of the Women's Social and Political Union. Lucy Harrison had been a suffragist, and I thought how much she'd have enjoyed meeting May.

By the time she reappeared with the flower in a white china vase and set it on her desk, between the front windows, I'd regained my power of speech and something of my composure. 'Thank you for inviting me,' I said and sat down in a chair opposite the sofa, resting my folder and handbag on my knees.

May was wearing a frock of a most becoming raspberry pink, and I complimented her on it. 'My favourite colour,' she said.

'I admire your sense of style. I wear the same clothes for years at a time without any clear idea of what's currently in vogue,' I said and smoothed the skirt of my grey suit.

'Oh, I'm rarely *au courant* myself. Fashion can be a terrible waste of time and energy, not to mention money. I think you dress quite sensibly, Charlotte. Did you ever notice that the more women have asserted their independence, the tighter the skirts designers have dictated? And now they've got women in hobble skirts so narrow at the ankles they literally prevent the wearer from walking in anything but mincing steps.'

'I'd not thought about it before. But it's true.'

May seated herself on the sofa, nudging the languorous cat aside. She'd brought a paper with her from the desk. 'Listen to this,' she said, already chuckling. 'One of my friends ran across it in a book published in 1870, called *Satan in Society*.' And she read aloud: '. . . if carried out in actual practice, this matter of "Woman's Rights" will speedily eventuate in the most prolific source of her wrongs. She will become rapidly unsexed, and degraded from her present exalted position to the level of man, without his advantages; she will cease to be a gentle mother, and become the Amazonian brawler.'

We both laughed out loud.

'I can't imagine either of us becoming Amazonian brawlers,' I said, laughing again.

'No, of course not. What's not funny about this is that after more than forty years many people still hold this fellow Cooke's opinion that if we'd simply stay up there on our pedestals in our hobble skirts and allow men to take care of us, the work of the world would go so much more smoothly. What they fail to take into account is that much of the world's work has always been done by women who'd never been near a pedestal in their lives.'

All of a sudden, she got up, causing Tommy to leap down and run under the sofa. 'The kettle!' she cried. 'I nearly forgot.' She went off to the other room and returned with a tea tray, setting it on a footstool between us.

I did so admire May's energy and commitment, and said as much. As she poured the tea and offered a plate of fairy cakes, she told me about how she'd participated in the famous Mud March from Hyde Park to Exeter Hall, in 1907. I, on the other hand, had rushed out on that wet February day to watch something like three thousand women with banners and sashes march by, women of all ages and classes, but I'd stood on the pavement, surrounded by the crude, vulgar hoots of men and shouts of 'Go home and do your washing.' The brave women marched on with stout heart through the drizzle, their boots and skirt hems sodden and muddy while I remained dry and silent under my black umbrella. A metaphor for our relative personalities, May's and mine, which didn't escape me. For all my occasional nervy bravado, I told her, as I'd told Mrs Sappho, 'I'm not a public person.'

'Nor am I, it seems,' May said. 'Later, the Pankhursts led my sister suffragettes to militancy: chaining themselves to fences and tossing bricks through windows and setting fire to letter-boxes. The Government were unmoved. The consequences for some of the sisters were prison and hunger strikes and forcible feeding. I chose to withdraw and support the cause through my writing. And I'm still at it, with pamphlets and essays and such for the Women Writers Suffrage League and the Society of Woman Authors and the WSPU. I'm planning a suffragist novel, too. Art can influence as well as arson.'

'Maybe better,' I offered.

'Art has already done a good deal to keep women in their place. What literature has done, I hope literature may have its part in undoing.' She took Tommy on to her lap and stroked his silky back. 'In Shakespeare's plays, you'll recall, women have to die so men can learn necessary lessons about their follies. Think of *Lear*, of *Othello*, of *Romeo and Juliet*.'

'Yes. Think of Emily Brontë's *Wuthering Heights*,' I said, suddenly seeing the novel in quite a new way.

May spoke with enthusiasm: 'We've become the sacrificial lambs in Western man's ritual for gaining self-knowledge. We've another lesson for them to learn, one we choose to teach them, that we're no longer willing to remain passive victims of the established political order.'

What power of intellect she had. And how marvellously she used it. I listened with awe and infatuation.

Another of May's interests, she admitted, was psychology. She wasn't simply interested in the psychological mystery of human behaviour, as any novelist in our time must be, but in the theories of Freud and Jung and the benefits of the clinical application of psychoanalysis to those who suffer from mental and emotional ailments. I couldn't help being reminded of Henry and Freda. Sadly, too late for either of them: my brother dead and my little sister irreparably mad after more than twenty-five years in care.

May mentioned her current attempts to raise funds for the new Medico-psychological Clinic of London. I offered to help in any way I could.

She shook her head and smiled generously. 'For you to address circulars would be a waste of poetic energy. Here,' she said, reaching out, 'let me see what you've brought.'

With a flutter of anxiety, I handed her the folder. I waited, twisting my fingers together as she read.

May raised her head. 'These are wonderful, Charlotte. They have such profound vitality. I especially like this one.' She held up 'The Fête', a long piece written in the persona of a young French boy who falls in love for the first time with the bareback rider he sees at the circus. I'd begun it years before with Ella D'Arcy in mind and had recently completed it, thinking of May, although I'd never tell her so. Still, I knew my words had touched her, and I was glad.

May had copies made of my poems by her typewriter, who lived in Hampstead, and in the next week sent them to Austin Harrison, editor of the *English Review*, and to her American friend, Ezra Pound, who was starting a new literary journal in the modern mode. After an involved correspondence, Harrison declined the poems. Pound, however, was most enthusiastic about my work, according to May. He, in turn, sent some of the poems off to an American journal, *Poetry*, which rejected them as well. I was dizzy and depressed by the Byzantine machinations of the literary business but delighted when 'The Fête' was published in the May 1914 issue of Pound's *The Egoist*, along with the serialized novel, *Portrait of the Artist as a Young Man*, by a new author, an Irishman called James Joyce.

On the whole, my poetry was finding, at last, a wider acceptance: 'The Pedlar' and 'On the Road to the Sea' in *The Englishwoman*, 'Fame' and 'Pécheresse' in *The New Weekly*. Also,
'The Hay-Market', an essay, appeared in the *New Statesman*,
and a short story, 'The Smile', in the *Theosophist*. The money
– such as it was, for *The Egoist* paid nothing – was needed to
pay Mama's doctor bills. Anne, too, had recently been ill, suffering a recurring backache from the strenuous work of antiques
restoration. Even Wek, Mama's ancient parrot, had been
unwell. I'd had to walk up and ask advice from the man in
charge of tropical birds at the Zoological Gardens in Regent's
Park. I thanked God for my continuing good health, though,
as May often reminded me, I smoked too much.

Who shall teach us
  To thrust the world out of our heart; to say, till perhaps in death,
    When the race is run,
  And it is forced from us with our last breath
    'Thy will be done'?

from 'Madeleine in Church'

That summer, May went off to Reeth, up in North Yorkshire, to finish her latest book. My fondness for her had recently led to misunderstandings between us. I was unable to moderate my emotions, to accept her friendship without being greedy for more, or fearing it might be abruptly withdrawn. Immediately after seeing her on to her train, I hurried home and, with crowding panic, dashed off a letter. She replied:

My dear,

I never dreamt you would take my 'good-bye and good luck' to mean 'good-bye for ever'. You must understand that I would invite you here to share this retreat with me, but I must have this brief period of solitude for my work. And you must attend to your poetry. We shall surprise each other with our mss. when we meet again in London.

Very affectionately yours,
May

I missed her terribly. I kept myself busy, drafting the longest poem I'd ever attempted. Inspired, made bold by the character of May's novel heroine, Kitty Tailleur, I wrote in the persona of a woman who'd had many lovers, an unrepentant magdalen. She kneels in an empty sanctuary and attempts to explain the confusion of her sex and her spirit to the crucified Christ hanging high above her – and to herself. Into her confession-prayer I poured my own forty-four years' confusions.

My magdalen wasn't a victim so much as one who's chosen her own path and goes on, defiant against all efforts to control her, even God's will as defined by the orthodox. Her body is ageing, but her need and her longing for sensation and for love remain undiminished:

> There must be someone. Christ! there must,
>   Tell me there *will* be someone. Who?
> If there were no one else, could it be You?

Having taken the poem this far, I was stymied. I'd entered into my own soul, a place tangled and terrifyingly dark, trackless, starless, where all light had gone out, with nothing to hear but my heart's beating, and I couldn't see where this was taking me. My hand shook so that I couldn't hold the pen.

A part of me was wicked and wanted to behave wickedly. And a part of me was weak and behaved timidly. To sin grandly requires more strength than I could bring to it. Instead, I wrote my desires into poetry. I doubted I'd be able to surprise May with my manuscript, as she'd suggested, or discuss any of this with her. Still, as I put the draft away, I knew I wouldn't be able to forget it and must face it again one day.

1914

Remember me and smile, as smiling too,
    I have remembered things that went their way –
    The dolls with which I grew too wise to play –
Or over-wise – and kissed, as children do,
And so dismissed them; yes, even as you
    Have done with this poor piece of painted clay –
    Not wantonly, but wisely, shall we say?
As one who, haply, tunes his heart anew.

from 'A Farewell'

Another message came by way of *The Times*: on 10 February
1914, Thomas Hardy was married to Miss Florence Emily Dug-
dale at Enfield Parish Church, London.

I sat for a long time in a kind of glazed trance, feeling the
terrible drag of remembrance, of vain hope and love. Presently,
I retrieved one of my earlier sonnets and forced myself to work
against the form and against my hurt and anger – like forcing
myself to hold my hand over a candle flame. The result of
this self-torture was 'A Farewell', a dark poem masked by a
light surface. After cursing and scribbling, after weeping and
smoking until my eyes and my throat were on fire, I decided
not to send my prothalamion to the new bridegroom. Instead,
the scratched-out and stained manuscript was interred at the
bottom of the trunk at the foot of my bed. *Requiescat in pace.*

For some of us there is a passion, I suppose,
So far from earthly cares and earthly fears
That in its stillness you can hardly stir
      Or in its nearness, lift your hand,
So great that you have simply got to stand
Looking at it through tears, through tears.

from 'Madeleine in Church'

On 4 August 1914, England declared war on Germany. On 25 September, May sailed for Belgium as a volunteer with the Motor Field Ambulance Corps. I couldn't write or eat or pray or sleep. My nerves were in tatters and shreds. I'd never known a time of such misery piled on misery, of such fear and despair. I felt as if I'd buried one lover and sent another off to war, never to return alive.

Not yet will those measureless fields be green again
Where only yesterday the wild, sweet, blood of wonderful youth
    was shed;
There is a grave whose earth must hold too long, too deep a
    strain,
Though for ever over it we may speak as proudly as we may
    tread.
But here, where the watchers by lonely hearths from the thrust of
    an inward sword have more slowly bled,
We shall build the Cenotaph . . .

                                        from 'The Cenotaph'

The lists of killed, wounded and missing started appearing in
the papers, posted in the window of the newsagent's shop. Some
days there were several thousand new names, almost more than
one could bear to read, searching for family members and old
friends. I lived in daily dread of finding 'Sinclair, Mary Amelia'
among them.

At first, we were distanced and safe here in London, but our
safety soon proved to be merely relative. In this new age of
airships and aeroplanes, the war came to us in the night, incendiary bombs falling on the city, starting great fires that lighted
the sky like false dawn.

Army huts were being constructed on the lawns of Russell
Square. The streets were less crowded than I'd ever seen them,
so many people off in the munitions factories or doing other
war work. Anne, sensible and uncomplaining as ever, knitted
socks and mufflers from skeins of wool the colour of over-
cooked spinach. I volunteered to assist wives and widows of
soldiers with filling in the forms to get their allowances and

pensions from the War Office. We met at the parish hall of St George the Martyr, Queen Square. In the beginning, I experienced the old pinch of shyness. It was difficult talking with strangers, asking them quite personal questions. But the women were so pathetically grateful. Compared to May, I felt a bit of a slacker, but I was needed at home. Jane had left us, gone to care for her ailing mother; she came in just one day a week to do laundry and help with the heavy cleaning. Food was becoming quite dear and in short supply; I often had to queue at the shops, spending more time some days shopping than writing, and what food there was tested my limited culinary skills.

Mama fussed about our meals: 'Cabbage? Charlotte, you must speak to Cook. We do *not* serve boiled cabbage in this house!' But she ate it all the same. As with so many subjects she found unpleasant, she forbade any discussion of the war in her presence. It simply wasn't happening. At night, street lamps went unlit, and all curtains were drawn shut. When warning sirens wailed and the gas in the fixtures dimmed and went out, Mama could no longer deny the war's existence. She became hysterical then, calling down the stairwell, whimpering pathetically for us to save her from the Kaiser. We huddled together on her bed. Anne and I, on either side of Mama, clutched her hands and, holding our breath, listened to the silence. Somewhere high overhead, deadly Zeppelins floated soundlessly, like huge silver sharks searching for their prey.

1915

I will not stare into the early world beyond the opening eyes,
  Or vex or scare what I love best.
But I want your life before mine bleeds away –
    Here – not in heavenly hereafters – soon,
    I want your smile this very afternoon,
  (The last of all my vices, pleasant people used to say,
    I wanted and I sometimes got – the Moon!)

from 'On the Road to the Sea'

After many nervous weeks with no word, a telegram came from May, saying she'd returned from Belgium, exhausted but unhurt. I was so elated I rushed off on foot, walking the entire distance to St John's Wood, where she'd taken a house in Blenheim Road before leaving for the front. The instant I arrived, trembly with joy, we fell tearfully into each other's arms, both talking at once, babbling really. I just wanted to hold her and feel the solidness of her sinew and bone, the pulse of life beating through her.

May walked me into her new parlour, furnished with all the old familiar pieces from the Edwardes Square flat, and we sat together on the sofa. She'd lost weight. Her plump cheeks were sunk and flattened. Their hollows caught and reflected a blush from her raspberry pink frock but had no colour of their own.

'How are you, really?' I said, taking her hand in mine.

'A bit ragged, that's all,' she said lightly, 'but I shall recover quickly now I've got my family of friends near me.'

Emotion took me over, and tears glazed my eyes, like when the organ burst out triumphant in church when I was a girl. I couldn't speak for a minute, only stare at her pale, lovely face until the spasm passed.

'You were very courageous to go off like that,' I finally managed in a watery voice.

She seemed dubious. 'Foolish more likely. That's what the men in charge over there would say. They resent the presence of women in war, you know. It's their own private game, like cricket at Lord's. Although I can tell you the Tommies in the trenches were happy enough to see a female face when they were injured.'

A new strength shone through her. 'Truly courageous women, splendid women were everywhere, Charlotte: the nurses, the refugees, the nuns who stayed in their convents, caring for the wounded and dying and keeping the Germans away by the sheer strength of their prayers. In Antwerp, Mrs St Clair Stobart set up a hospital in what had been a concert hall – run entirely by women, with women doctors, women surgeons, women orderlies.'

May's face had lighted with fervour as she spoke. She stopped, sighed. 'But, oh, I've had my share of blind obedience to orders, and I never want to feel the itch of wool khaki again. I've had my adventure. I won't deny there were exquisite moments of extreme danger – there's something sexual about war, Charlotte, that makes it easy to romanticize – but now, at a safe distance, I must write what I've seen, the blood and muck and futility of it all.'

I held her hand more tightly. 'Was it so terrible, then?'

'Yes, but I say that abstractly, as an intellectual conclusion. Memory has a way of softening experience, smoothing out the worst of it, hiding it away in your subconscious. I'll have to tease it out with the writing of it.' She needed to talk, apparently revived rather than tired by it. 'I haven't much. In the last week of the siege of Antwerp, when the wounded were being brought into Ghent by the hundreds and when the fighting came closer to the city, and at the end when the Germans were driving you from Ghent to Bruges and from Bruges to Ostend and from Ostend to Dunkirk, well, you couldn't sit down to write your impressions, even if you were cold-blooded enough to want to. It was as much as you could do to scribble the merest note of what happened in your day-book.'

We settled together against the sofa cushions, my shoulder pressing against hers, our hands clasped between us. 'Oh, Charlotte, I'm so glad to be here.' She squeezed my fingers and gave me a deep, thankful smile. For the present, there was nothing more to say beyond what her smile communicated. I, too, was glad we were here together, that she was safe and smiling and talking about her writing, a sure sign she'd soon be her old self again.

The weather turned cold and damp, and I took to wearing Father's cut-down topcoat on my outings to St John's Wood. May and I met often in her book-filled study. The magenta curtains lent the room a gay, rosy light. We sat by the fire, and the cat Tommy ringed my ankles with furry caresses and purred like a tiny machine of contentment. May had hired a house-keeper called Florrie, who served us biscuits and green China tea while we two exchanged snippets of gossip about our mutual acquaintances. These afternoons were idyllic, like those I'd spent so many years ago reading in our parlour with Anne before Father's death, before the world was at war. Here in this room with May, time wasn't marked by the tick of the clock but by the slow-moving passage of clouds across the sky. Here, at last, I found laughter, tranquillity, encouragement, and something more for which I had no name. Comfortable as an old married couple, we drank our tea and listened to gramo-phone records and shared drafts of our current writing.

May was reworking her few notes into a book. 'There's a ready market for what's called war-verse,' she said, 'those sentimental tokens about our brave boys dying or dead on the battlefield. But honestly, dear, I must simply voice a cry of disenchantment with the whole notion of *dulce et decorum est pro patria mori*.'

I lighted a cigarette and leant back in my chair to listen to her read from her rough draft:

When we got into the village of Lokeren, we were told to go back at once, for the Germans were coming in. It seemed that the wounded had been taken into houses in the village. We were given five minutes to get them out and go. I suppose we stayed in that village quite three quarters of an hour. We had to find the houses and the wounded men. The Commandant went into the first house and came out very quickly. The man inside was dead. We went on up the village. Down that quiet road and through the village, a battery of artillery came clattering in full retreat. The leader turned his horse violently into a side alley and plunged down it. I was close to the battery when it turned; I could see the faces of the men. There was no terror in them, only a sort of sullen annoyance and disgust. I was cut off from the Commandant as the men came on and on. There were gaps in the retreat, and I dashed through one of them (as you dash through the traffic in the Strand when you're in a hurry).

May regarded me over the paper. 'There's a bit more here about searching through the village and the others loading the ambulances and the stretcher-bearers walking on ahead of me that I've got to put in yet.' She went again to reading:

The man, horribly hurt, with a wound like a red pit below his shoulder-blades, was brought out and laid on the stretcher. He lay there, quietly, on his side, in a posture of utter resignation to anguish. He was clumsily built; he had a broad, rather ugly face, narrowing as the fringe of his whiskers became a little straggling beard. But to me he was the most beautiful thing I have ever seen. And I loved him. I do not think it is possible to love, to adore any creature more than I loved and adored that clumsy, ugly soldier. He was my first wounded man. We got him a few yards down the road. Then, to my horror, the bearers dumped him down on the paving-stones. They said he was too heavy. I didn't think it was exactly the moment for resting, and I told them so. The Germans were about due. But the bearers stood stolidly in the middle of the road and mopped their faces and puffed. The situation began to feel as absurd and as terrible as a nightmare.

'What did you do?' I cried, interrupting.

'Why, I shamed them into getting on with it. I grabbed one end of the stretcher and said I'd carry it myself. Maybe I wasn't very strong, but anyhow I'd try.'

She read on:

The ambulance had got its wounded in and was ready to go, but he had to have his wound dressed. He lay there on the stretcher in the street, stripped to the waist, with the great red pit of his wound yawning in his white flesh. I had always thought the dressing of a wound was a cautious and delicate process. But it isn't. The Commandant's hands worked rapidly as he rammed cyanide gauze into the red pit. It was as if he were stuffing an old crate with straw.

May looked up from her draft. 'Twenty-three wounded in all were taken from Lokeren that day. Hundreds had to be left behind the German lines.'

This was nothing like what we'd been given to read in the newspapers, none of the glory and the glamour of the accounts coming out of Whitehall. I thought her quite brave to tell the truth about the front-line experiences, almost as brave as her having gone out there herself in the first place.

'More an act of bravado,' she said. 'I shall likely never find a publisher. The critics will say a woman can't write about war, even when she's been blooded in the midst of it. No one wants to read the truth when it evokes such distress. All the same, the writing is necessary. It's simply what I must do for my own sanity.'

'I understand.'

May regarded me fondly. 'Yes, you of all people would understand the catharsis of writing.' She refilled our cups, set the teapot back on the tray, and said, 'Now, it's your turn.'

No, not today. Not after what she'd read. May and I were alike in so many ways, but she seemed able to direct her energies outwards while I could only turn mine inwards. And to what end? 'My poems are incredibly frivolous,' I insisted, 'by contrast with what you've written.'

'Oh, Charlotte,' she said, stroking my arms the way she might stroke her cat, 'your poetry will be read long after my journal of impressions has been lost and forgotten.'

I unfolded the single sheet of paper I'd brought in my handbag and cleared my throat self-consciously. In the week since our last meeting, I'd immersed myself in the poem spoken by my unrepentant magdalen. Somehow, she and I had blent our voices and our selves, and I did so want May to approve of us both. I glanced over at her, seated on the sofa, waiting, her fine brows lifted in anticipation. We'd drunk our tea, eaten the little sandwiches Florrie had made for us. No more excuses. No more delay. I cleared my throat a second time and shakily read the opening lines of poem, still untitled:

> Here, in the darkness, where this plaster saint
>   Stands nearer than God stands to our distress,
> And one small candle shines, but not so faint
>   As the far lights of everlastingness
> I'd rather kneel than over there, in open day
>   Where Christ is hanging, rather pray
>   To something more like my own clay,
>   Not too divine;
>   For, once, perhaps my little saint
>   Before he got his niche and crown,
> Had one short stroll about the town . . .

I left off reading. Silence. May stared at me as if I were a stranger. Too painful. I had to break the moment. 'It's still early days, of course,' I blathered. 'The form is so irregular there's no name for it. Or the rhyme scheme. Maybe I should give it up altogether.'

May looked truly alarmed. She waved my protestations

away. 'Oh, no. No. I was simply taken by surprise. You must go on working on it, no matter what.'

When we couldn't be together, May and I exchanged letters. The next day, she wrote:

My dear Charlotte,

Finish – finish your Courtesan. She's magnificent. The last verses are all there – coiled up in a lobe of your brain asleep and waiting to be waked – just like darling Tommy in his basket. Presently you'll hear them stirring in their sleep and soon after, the poem will finish itself.

I'm a little like you (in this) that I can't tell how fine a thing is till I've shut myself up alone with it – but even as you read the poem I could see how great it was. I shouldn't say 'even', for you read furiously well: I never knew anyone who could get out the passion of a thing as you can. But this time I felt that it was there – depths and depths of passion and of sheer beauty.

Love, always yours,
May

I could have flown like an acrobatic angel over the treetops and church spires of London on the wings her words had given me. I would never stop writing. Never.

One spring day, May took me to call on one of her acquaintances from the Lyceum Club, who was recovering in a nursing home after an operation on a gland in her neck. We'd only stop for a minute. 'Just long enough to inquire after her condition and leave her these,' May said, holding up a bunch of lion-faced pansies from her back garden.

The woman, about forty, lay propped up in the white metal bed. Her face was flat and pasty, her nose thin and pointy, like the gnomon on a sundial. Puffy lids dropped over large, wet eyes in dark sockets, like bruises. May introduced the patient: 'Charlotte Mew,' she said, gesturing, 'this is Florence Hardy.'

I fumbled for something to say. May knew nothing about my earlier connection with Thomas Hardy. I felt overwound and wanted nothing so much as to dash from the room and out into the street, running along the pavement and shrieking. The behaviour of a madwoman, surely.

I smiled weakly. I bobbed my head nervously. I said nothing.

I will not count the years – there are days too –
　　And to-night again I have said
　　'What if you should be lying dead?'
Well, if it were so, I could only lay my head
　　Quietly on the pillow of my bed
　　Thinking of Him on whom poor sufferers cried
　　Suffering Himself so much before He died . . .

from 'Friend, Wherefore – ?'

A season of ghosts. Another who'd been buried revived to walk again through the twilight of memory and then be reinterred once more. After some thirty years, I heard by post from Amy Greener – she of the large feet and stolen rosebud – who wrote to tell me of Lucy Harrison's death up in Yorkshire, in April 1915. 'I knew you would want to hear, Charlotte, having been one of her favourite pupils, whom she mentioned frequently.' I fingered the faint scar on my forehead, a talisman of remembered woe. Like Mama, I'd learnt to beguile myself into recalling only what was least likely to cause sorrow. And yet Miss Harrison had been with me all the time. Her madonna face had glowed often in my dreams, urging me to be what I was as she had to be what she was. I understood now, as I couldn't then, what it was she was trying to tell me: what was possible in a complete friendship between women. She'd found it with Miss Greener. And I was hopeful. And glad that even in the midst of sorrow I'd been remembered.

> . . . I think we shun
> The splendour of that everlasting glare,
>   The clamour of that never-ending song.
>   And if for anything we greatly long,
> It is for some remote and quiet stair
>   Which winds in silence and a space of sleep
>   Too sound for waking and for dreams too deep.
>
>   from 'Not for That City'

That damn poem again. Really, one would think I'd never written anything else. I'd nearly forgotten about it, moved on to other things, when quite out of nowhere, in November 1915, I received a note in the post:

Dear Miss Mew,

Three years ago, buying, as was my custom, a copy of the *Nation* one Saturday morning, I opened it eagerly to see if there might be a poem, and was electrified to find printed there 'The Farmer's Bride'. This poem I immediately committed to memory, and recently repeated it with enthusiasm to Harold Monro, who has opened the Poetry Bookstore in Devonshire Street, with the avowed intention of publishing the work of young poets and presenting them to a large audience. He has asked me to write to see if you might have other poems that could be got together to form a book. I look forward to hearing from you in the affirmative.

                                   Yours sincerely,
                                   Alida Klemantaski

The request made me all at once bashful. I replied immediately that I was neither young – having just passed my forty-sixth birthday, though I didn't say as much – nor the sort of poet readers of modern verse would be much interested in. I thanked Miss Klemantaski as kindly as I could for her offer, enclosed a copy of another of my poems, 'The Changeling', which I thought she might like, and believed that was the end of it.

Soon, she wrote again:

November 19, 1915

My dear Miss Mew,

Each Tuesday and Thursday evening at six o'clock, we hold poetry readings at the Bookshop. With your kind permission, on Tuesday next I shall read 'The Farmer's Bride' and 'The Changeling' – so very wonderful, thank you for sending it. There will be a number of other poets' new works read as well. Might you care to be present? I should so like to meet you.

With sincerest regards,
Alida Klemantaski

Through the following days, I debated with myself about attending the reading, but as a foggy dusk was settling in that Tuesday, I walked myself through Queen Square and into Devonshire Street. The neighbourhood wasn't at all what I'd expected, slummy and noisy with filthy children running and quarrelling in the street as well as on the pavement. I was glad I'd brought my horn-handled umbrella, which I carried like a weapon. At number 35, near Theobald's Road, I found the Poetry Bookshop, a refurbished three-storey pedimented build-ing pressed between its shabbier neighbours. On the ground floor, the mullioned shop-window was faced with books, and a ginger cat with a pink nose curled asleep against the bottom corner pane.

I hesitated with my fingers on the handle of the door. What was I letting myself in for? I'd consulted with May about Miss Klemantaski's first letter, and she'd said I must make the con-nections that would ensure a wider readership for my poetry.

And, of course, she was right. That didn't make it any easier, however.

I opened the door and went in. The shop was small and warm and lined with bookshelves. In the centre of the room stood a table spread with chap-books and broadsides – I recognized the names of Rupert Brooke, W. B. Yeats, the Sitwells – and chairs were scattered about for browsers to rest and read, to sample the poetry before buying. What a novel, clever idea.

A tall young woman of brunette Slavic beauty, with firm jaw and high cheekbones, came from behind the table, saying expectantly, 'Are you Charlotte Mew?'

'I'm sorry to say I am,' I responded, more self-deprecatingly than I'd intended. I cocked my head at a defiant angle intended to show I wasn't the pathetic creature I sounded.

'Alida Klemantaski,' the young woman said, shaking my hand with vigour. 'I'm delighted you could come.' Her smile shed all the warmth of a summer sun, and I relaxed and smiled in return. 'There's someone I want you to meet,' she said and steered me to the rear of the shop and into a minute office.

Seated behind a desk was a dark-eyed man in his mid-thirties, with short, thick hair, pronounced brows and a military moustache. He put down his pen and, smiling diffidently, got to his feet as we entered.

'Miss Mew, may I present Harold Monro?' We exchanged handshakes and pleasantries, and the two of them, Miss Klemantaski and Mr Monro, stood over me, talking about me and my poetry as if I were a child between two doting parents.

Shortly, I followed the brown serge hem of Miss Klemantaski's skirt up a steep and narrow staircase to a room above the shop. As we went, I explained that I preferred not to read myself. I'd got the chancy voice of an adolescent boy, I told her, liable to crack at any second and soar a full octave. I was, therefore, glad Miss Klemantaski – 'Alida, please,' she insisted – glad Alida was going to be the one in front of the audience, doing the reading.

'Miss Mew, it's my honour,' she said. In the dim room, its

white plaster walls crossed with diagonal black beams, she led me to a chair and sat down beside me. 'You'll excuse me for staring,' she said, 'but you're not at all what I expected from your poems.'

'And what was that?' I said, bristling a bit.

'I'm not sure. They contain such intense vitality, such rare individuality, such a striking mixture of womanly frailty and masculine severity. And the male persona of "The Farmer's Bride" seems to speak in a way that's your own, but not your own. I mean, you're most definitely not a West Country farmer, and yet . . .'

'It's what poets do,' I told her. 'We put on another's self like a mask, but behind it we remain ourselves. Beyond that, I can't enlighten you. It's not like a parlour trick one can do on demand. Or explain afterwards.'

As the hour of six neared, the rows of chairs were filling with men and women unknown to me. I was seated at the rear and glad of my anonymity: what they saw was merely a small woman in a man's topcoat and grey fedora, with a black umbrella laid across her lap. And a glimpse of red worsted stockings between shoe tops and skirt hem.

At six, Alida left me and walked confidently to the front of the room. A forest-green curtain covered the wall behind a table with a lighted candle on either side of the papers she spread out before her. After a brief pause, she commenced reading. I was so apprehensive about how these strangers were going to react to my poems that my ears were stuffed with cotton wool and I scarcely heard any of those preceding them. Only the names: John Masefield, James Joyce, D. H. Lawrence.

Then, Alida spoke my name and read the opening lines of 'The Farmer's Bride' in a deep, expressive contralto: 'Three Summers since I chose a maid . . .' And I was mesmerized. I'd never listened to my work read aloud by anyone other than myself. It was magical, like the wind passing over a field of long grasses, changing the colours as it goes.

After Alida read the last lines of 'The Changeling' – 'I shall grow up, but never grow old, / I shall always, always be very cold, / I shall never come back again!' – the crowd applauded appreciatively. It had been a grand performance. I slipped out of the shop and into the unlighted street, frightened by the intensity of the pleasure and excitement I was feeling.

May was angry with me. I'd not told her about the reading beforehand so that she might attend. I could only admit my horror of embarrassing myself in front of my dearest friend. 'Charlotte, I'd have liked so much to have been there to share your triumph,' she said, sounding truly disappointed.

I couldn't bear to have her upset with me. 'What you missed,' I told her, trying to divert and entertain her, 'was a gang of dirty boys in the street, playing war. They shouted and pummelled each other, and when one was taken prisoner by the others, he was shoved into a potato sack and dragged and bumped along over the rough paving while the others cheered.'

But she wouldn't be diverted. Over tea, she urged me again to consider Harold Monro's offer of publication of a chap-book of my poems. 'Dear, I don't think you understand how important this is. Monro is an influence, a figure in modern poetry, the editor of *The Poetry Review*, the publisher of the "Georgian Poetry" series and a good poet himself. An offer such as this may never come your way again.'

'It's merely a slim little paper volume that's planned, May. Not a book between hard covers.'

'But chap-books really are selling, as regulation books aren't. It's a ripping idea bringing out verses in this way, and it's justifying itself by its results. Monro has sold something like two hundred and fifty copies of Richard Aldington's *Images*, and Richard hasn't the strong human appeal that you have.'

May understood the publishing business well, of course, having published some sixteen books to date. I'd been naïve to imagine long ago that once in print, my writing – and I – would be immune from hurtful criticism. The truth was I was afraid of the sort of calumny and ridicule such as I'd watched being heaped on Hardy and his *Jude*. 'For myself,' I said, unwilling to admit my fears, 'I don't really care whether anyone beyond these four walls ever reads my work, dear. Yours is the single opinion I value.'

May's eyes pinched with reproach. She was no fool and recognized a bluff when she heard one. She answered with a restatement of her positivist philosophy: 'You know, Charlotte, the individual is under an obligation to develop to her utmost all the powers and latent capabilities of her nature.'

All the latent capabilities of my nature? Did May understand what she was saying to me?

We must arise and go:
The world is cold without
And dark and hedged about
With mystery and enmity and doubt,
But we must go
Though yet we do not know
Who called . . .

from 'The Call'

I'd committed myself. Through a series of letters, I'd agreed to let Harold Monro publish a collection – which of my poems I wasn't sure. I'd so few I thought complete. I was perhaps the least qualified to make a proper selection for a book. So I prevailed on Alida, who knew best what might satisfy Mr Monro, to help me.

In mid-January 1916, I invited Alida to the house in Gordon Street, where callers came so rarely any more. She arrived on a frosty afternoon right before teatime. I met her at the street door, took her wraps and brought her up the stairs to the parlour. I introduced her first to Mama, who behaved badly, waving her withered, claw-like hands about and saying over and over, 'Klemantaski? What sort of name is that? Foreign, I'll wager. Criminal, too, most likely. We know no one called Klemantaski!'

Over the din, I introduced Alida to Anne, whose expression showed we were equally appalled at our mother's rudeness. With a smile that begged indulgence, Anne shook Alida's hand and excused herself and hurried Mama from the room like a naughty child. Wek, on the other hand, took immediately to Alida. And she to him. She called him 'Willie', and he accepted bits of biscuit from her, with loud, raspy, greedy cries for more. I'd been mistaken to think we might conduct any sort of literary work in the parlour, so after Anne joined us again and we'd all finished our tea, I took Alida down to the ground floor and into my bedroom.

I seated her at my work table, and I sat on the bed, where I'd laid out the sheets of poems I considered worth her reading: all the ones that had previously been published in journals, a few others I thought worthy, and my newest one, the long unrepentant courtesan piece I'd finished at May's urging, now called 'Madeleine in Church'. I'd already decided not to include the poem about the old shepherd dying before a wayside crucifix and becoming a pile of dried leaves scattered by the wind. It was, after all, Hardy's story, told me so many years ago. Instead, I twisted that piece of paper into a spill and used it to light our cigarettes from the coal fire in the grate.

One by one, I handed the poems to her and watched her face as she read. The silence and the wait were excruciating. I was near to abandoning the entire project when she looked up, her eyes brimming, and said, 'Charlotte, this is brilliant.' She'd just finished reading 'Madeleine in Church', all two hundred or so lines of it. I knew then there was no turning away, no matter what difficulties might lie ahead.

And difficulties there were. After having persuaded me to agree to do the book, Harold Monro did a volte-face and decided it ought to be postponed indefinitely as men of his age were soon to be called up by the army and he mightn't be able to see it through the press. But he wasn't conscripted right away after all, and the project was on again.

As a novice author, I'd no idea how complex the publishing of even so small a chap-book such as mine could be. The next problem was paper. The war had made good stock of any kind scarce. Somewhere, enough was located. The dull green wasn't the colour I'd have chosen for the cover, if I'd had a choice. Its design, a pen-and-ink drawing of a thatched cottage with tiny windows, was done by C. Lovat Fraser and wasn't what I'd have chosen, either. 'I don't believe he even bothered to read the poems,' I lamented.

May, with her years of publishing experience, consoled and counselled me. 'That's most likely the only paper Harold could get, dear. And Fraser's just been invalided out and needs the work. There's a war on, you know.' She gave an ironic twist to the last, a current catch-phrase, lifting her fine brows and smiling slightly. 'You'd better accept what's available.' And, as usual, she was right.

I thought we'd got past all the major problems until one evening Alida offered me a chair in her bed-sitting room in Red Lion Square, lighted my cigarette, then her own, and said, 'Now, Charlotte, you're simply going to laugh when I tell you what happened today at the shop.'

Dubious, I cocked my head and said nothing.

'This morning, the printer's boy from Clerkenwell delivered the first batch of proofs. A sweet young man, rosy-cheeked, spectacled, diffident. He hemmed and hawed and beat about the bush for some time –'

'Just as you're doing?'

'Well, yes.' She tapped her cigarette in the ashtray. 'When he got his nerve up, he announced that their compositor, who's a Methodist, refuses to set the type for your "Madeleine in Church" because he says it's blasphemous.'

'What!' I jumped up out of my chair. 'Goddamn it!' I said, starting to curse, beginning truly to blaspheme, when our eyes met, and we both erupted into laughter.

'Oh, Charlotte, if you could see yourself. One would never guess to look at you that you even knew such words.'

'Oh, I know those and a few more if it comes to that.' I sat down again. 'Does this mean the book's off?'

'No, no. Harold says we'll have to find someone else to do the printing, which means more expense and more delay.'

And even after finding another printer, problems of margins, line lengths, the order of the poems, and minor typographical errors persisted throughout the setting and correcting of the proofs. I surrendered all responsibility for punctuation to Alida while I undertook to obtain the permissions to reprint from the editors of all the journals where the poems had previously appeared. In the end, at last, finally, the wretched little book was published in May 1916, forty pages containing seventeen poems, dedicated to Thomas Hardy without actually naming him

To ----

He asked life of thee, and thou gavest him a long life: even for ever and ever.

and titled, not surprisingly, *The Farmer's Bride*.

1916

But could I spare
In the blind Earth's great silences and spaces,
   The din, the scuffle, the long stare
   If I went back and it was not there?
Back to the old known things that are new,
The folded glory of the gorse, the sweet-briar air,
To the larks that cannot praise us, knowing nothing of what we
   do
      And the divine trees that do not care . . .

                                          from 'Fame'

A sort of fever took hold of me: a mixture of exuberance, anticipation and, yes, pride. And something like a sense of plenitude, as well. Although the usual chap-book edition ran to two hundred and fifty copies, Harold Monro had printed a thousand of *The Farmer's Bride*. I was to have six copies as an advance on royalties. The minute I had them in hand, I inscribed one to May: *'For my dearest friend: "Nothing is true that is not good . . ." C.M.M.'* I fairly danced along the pavement on my way to the bus and St John's Wood, a ludicrous sight, I'm sure, in a woman my age. But I didn't care. I was a poet with her first book in print!

May was as delighted as I. 'It's wonderful, Charlotte. I'm so glad you went ahead with this.' In her study, the light through the drawn silk curtains was rosy-pink, matching my mood exactly. May poured out two stemmed glasses of sherry and proposed a toast to the book's success. We raised our glasses. 'To *The Farmer's Bride*.' And, joyous, together, we drank.

We sat in facing chairs, smiling and sipping our wine. It made me warm and giddy, appropriate to the occasion. May smiled at me, her eyes honey flecked with gold, and a frisson passed through me, an echo of something at once rapturous and discomforting. She bent down and petted the successor to the late, lamented Tommy, another black Persian, called Jerry, who leant against her ankle and purred loudly. Right then, I wanted nothing so much as to be that cat.

May left off stroking him and said, 'I'm very proud of you.'

I stammered a thank-you and told May about going into the Poetry Bookshop that morning to collect my copies: 'There, on the centre table, was my book, and there was I, right next to Robert Graves and Yeats and Frances Cornford.'

'Some day,' she said, 'they'll brag about their work being on offer alongside Charlotte Mew's.'

A heady notion. Or was it the sherry?

May leant across, took my hand in hers, and said, 'Now, the serious work begins.'

I frowned. She'd seen me through all the pre-publication difficulties: the paper shortage, the typesetter's refusal, the numberless corrections of proofs: 'Surely you can't mean I've not worked hard enough already.'

'Of course you have, dear.' She was gentle, kindly. 'The next step is for you to get copies out to the reviewers. The right mentions in the right places are vitally important. It's a bit harder to get poetry reviewed at present unless it's written from the trenches, but it must be done.'

'I'm simply not the person to angle for notice. I know so few influential literary people and none well enough to ask . . .' My words shrank and disappeared.

She dropped my hand and gave me a stern look. 'Stop this instant. I won't have you undervaluing yourself like that. You know me, and I'm not shy about recommending your book to others. I shall send copies myself to Rebecca West, who reviews in the *Daily News*, and to W. L. Courtney and Clement Shorter and Mr Squire at the *New Statesman*. Hilda Doolittle will review it for *The Egoist*, I'm sure.'

'Maybe Evelyn Sharp' – an acquaintance from my *Yellow Book* days – 'might do something,' I added, catching some of May's optimism. She refilled our glasses, and we put our heads together and began making a list.

They stripped the very skin from my soul. In the next few weeks and into the summer, I read the reviewers with tears in my eyes. What May said were 'good, mixed reviews', I took as direct attacks on my profoundest and most personal self. A piece in the 21 September edition of *The Times Literary Supplement* was typical: 'These compositions, in an irregular but rhymed metre, will often strike the reader as unintelligible.'

May stopped me when I read that out loud. Together, we were sitting on a wooden bench in her back garden – lavender, lobelia, hydrangea, roses blooming in baroque abandon round us, mocking my feelings. The newspaper was spread over our laps, the shade of a bent apple tree lying across the print. 'But you mustn't take that out of context,' May said. 'Look here: it goes on to say, "When she is at her strangest there is something before you that is true and human . . . there is a meaning, a unifying thread, running through it all . . ."'

'And you mustn't stop there, either.' I took up reading where she'd left off: '"although you do not quite understand it".' I smashed my fist against the flimsy sheet of newsprint. 'What,' I wailed, 'is so damned hard to understand in any of the poems? Why doesn't he say?'

May took my fist in her hands and held it against her bosom. 'I know how frustrating it is, dear. You mustn't let it distress you.'

For a moment, I was distracted by her hair, freshly shampooed, spread across her shoulders and over the back of the bench, drying in the morning sun. I loved to see her with its thick length down, fascinated by its rich auburn colour and its sheen.

May brushed my knuckles lightly with her lips and unfisted my fingers. 'Now, read the next paragraph.'

' "An intense realization of the flow of sensuous impressions, hopes, reflections and recollections which go to make the inner drama of a single mind is the mark of most of these poems" – what does he mean "most"?' I was getting angry again.

'Go on, read the rest.'

'. . . "and it finds its medium in what seems to be a native unconscious gift of expression." That's supposed to be a compliment?'

'It is, and you should take it as such. Either that or leave off reading your reviews altogether.'

'Too late now. At least for this one. Here's what hurts most, what he said about "Madeleine in Church": "there is a true satiric force in this cry of rebellion" – satiric! There's nothing of ridicule or lampooning in it. It's a confession of spiritual doubt, agonizingly arrived at and deeply felt. It's me turned inside out, my very being exposed. How can he misread what I've so clearly written?' I wadded up the paper and tossed it to the ground. 'May, I mean it. This is pure torture.'

I dropped my head on her shoulder, and she stroked my bare arm lying across her lap, her words soft, soothing: 'I know, I know.'

My heart is lame with running after yours so fast
    Such a long way,
Shall we walk slowly home, looking at all the things we passed
    Perhaps to-day?

from 'My Heart is Lame'

The trees were undressing themselves, tossing their brown leaves away in the warm autumn wind. I let it blow me along the pavement as I strode along Wellington Road towards May's house. I'd passed the morning at the parish hall, filling in pension forms for new widows – there were so many, and more each day. For myself, I was weary of the war: the queues, the shortages, the sleepless dark while the sirens keened. Worst of all were the bandaged and limbless soldiers invalided out and sent home. They seemed to be everywhere these days. I hated the recruitment posters – 'Women of Britain Say "Go!"' I was untouched by the war's deadly glamour and could never have given out white feathers to young men, as some did. The hollow rhetoric of patriotism sustains one for a short time, but after that, hard reality can't be denied any longer, and with it comes a blend of grit and acceptance. I saw it in the faces of the young widows and those of the women who were bus conductors and trousered gravediggers and fire-fighters and farm and factory workers, taking the places of all the men who, indeed, had gone – and likely wouldn't return.

Though he was nearly forty, Harold Monro had been called up by the army after all, and Alida was operating the Poetry Bookshop almost single-handed. She fretted over Monro's safety. Ironically, it was the shop cat, Pinknose, who was the casualty, losing an eye in an incendiary raid.

After an initial rush, my chap-book was selling slowly. The runaway bestseller currently was, no surprise, Rupert Brooke's 'The Soldier'. May was having better success than I with her work. Hutchinson was publishing her *Journal of Impressions of Belgium*, with all royalties assigned to the Commission for War Relief. She'd set to work on a new novel, 'to pay the bills', as she said. It was to be about the nobility of those who sacrifice themselves in wartime. 'I may be giving the reviewers too many bad reasons for liking it,' she said, 'but you must sometimes write to buoy up the reader's courage.'

My letters to her went unanswered or brought brief notes of regret. For the present, she must give all her energies to her writing. Soon, very soon, we'd take tea together as we had before. Today, I decided, was soon enough. Even though I understood the necessity of solitude to the writer, I didn't like sharing her with her work to such an extent. While I'd never been jealous of the success of her writing, I *was* jealous of its total claim on her time.

I rang the bell at 1 Blenheim Road, and Florrie, the house-keeper in her starched white apron, answered. 'Miss Sinclair asks not to be disturbed, Miss Mew,' she said, peering round the half-open door. 'Sorry, ma'am.'

I waited on the steps after the door was shut, unable quite to take in what had happened. Where I'd always been so gladly welcomed, I'd been turned away. I staggered off along the pavement, stupefied. I couldn't get my mind to work. Where was I to go? How was I to get there? I loitered at the corner of the street, waiting for my confusion to pass. Behind me I heard voices. I came round in time to catch sight of a woman emerging from May's house – young, fair, wearing a stylish deep-crowned, wide-brimmed hat that hid her face above the eyes. Still, I could see enough to know she was very pretty. And she was smiling, smiling to herself as the street door closed behind her and she walked towards me, and on by.

A few world-cleaving seconds passed. I could taste anger's

coppery bitterness. I felt betrayed, ugly, all string and straw. I marched back to May's house and rang the bell again. When Florrie opened the door, I shoved on past her and into May's study, calling her name.

'Charlotte!' May said, getting up from her desk. 'What is it, dear? What's happened?'

'Oh, May, how could you?' I took a deep breath, labouring to compose myself.

May went to the study door, reassured Florrie, who was apologizing for my getting in. May closed the door and leant against it, as far from me as the room would allow. She spoke with a searching frown: 'Now, what's the meaning of all this uproar?'

'I saw her coming out, that young woman. If you've taken a new friend, if you no longer want to see me, why didn't you simply say so?' My voice cracked, but I rushed on: 'I could've saved myself the trip and the humiliation of being sent away.'

May looked sympathetic, then amused, then stern. 'I'm trying hard to sort this out, Charlotte. Something's been badly mis-understood. By you. And perhaps by me.' She gestured towards the chair by the fireplace. 'Sit down.'

I shook my head and stayed where I was, in the middle of the maroon oriental rug.

All business, May reseated herself at her desk. 'Let me try to explain what you think you saw. The young woman who just left is my new typist. Hers was no social call. She was delivering a manuscript.' May tapped a stack of pages in front of her.

The blood rushed to my face so quickly I felt faint. I moved to the empty chair and sank into it. 'I'm sorry,' I said, in a thin whisper. 'I restrain my emotions – I do, I know – and when they build up and force their way through and break down my defences – my intellectual defences – they overpower me. I mean, I simply burst out with it.'

'Yes,' May said, sounding reproachful, 'but what concerns

me is that you felt the need for such an outburst. Or that you had the right to it.'

Jerry, the black cat, hopped up into her lap and raised his haunches under her caressing fingers. And I remembered the run of electricity when she and I first touched.

I lighted a cigarette, my hand trembling, and tossed the match into the cold ashes spilled out on the hearth. As I faced her, a delicious thrill of danger went through me. 'I love you, May.'

'And I love you, dear. However, that doesn't mean I must account to you for what I do when it's none of your concern.'

'Don't criticize me, please, May. I can't bear it! I'm a pathetic creature. I know it. My behaviour was wrong, and I'm black with remorse.'

'Poor Charlotte. We've been through this before, haven't we? Remember the evening last spring when I said I'd like to walk you to Baker Street station, and you took it to mean I was eager to get you out of my house and be rid of you?'

'Yes, yes,' I said, contritely.

'Maybe I was wrong to allow you to form such a close attachment to me, dear. Maybe it was wrong, but it's one of the wrong things I'd do again tomorrow. I'm fond of you myself. But I will *not* be possessed. I had enough of that with my mother. Enough and to spare.'

I nodded. I understood completely.

'Now, you must leave. I've an engagement. I've got to change.' She stood up, and the cat leapt to the floor. He trotted after her as she crossed the room and opened the study door. 'Goodbye, Charlotte,' she said and went out into the hall.

I dropped my cigarette into the grate and followed up the stairs, saying to her retreating back, the nape of her neck, 'Whatever penance you prescribe, I'll do it – only, please, don't send me away.'

In her bedroom, May opened the door to the wardrobe and took out a frock of silk chiffon in a colour called ashes of roses.

She laid it out on the wide, white expanse of the bed between us.

'Goodbye, Charlotte,' she said, with crushing detachment.

'Oh, May,' I said, with a thrill of catastrophe, 'I've always loved you, loved even your shadow.'

'Really, this is too much.' Her face was disfigured by exasperation.

I was close to weeping, but I would not turn away.

'You mustn't go on like this.' Her expression and her tone softened. 'It's painful to both of us. Your affection has grown beyond natural bounds.'

'We are what we are,' I said, with a toss of my head, miming a composure I hardly felt.

'Yes, precisely. You are what you are. I'm not asking you to be anything else. Only allow me to be what I am.'

An alarmed defiance took hold of me. Wrathful and yearning, I was almost shouting: 'Oh God, do you imagine I'm attracted to you because I choose to be? Because I choose to suffer? As if being different from others weren't enough of a curse?'

She leant towards me, her spread fingers pressing asterisks into the white bedcover. She looked directly into my eyes and spoke with firmness and finality: 'You're simply wasting your perfectly good passion.'

I found my way out of the room and down the stairs and through the street door as if I were stumbling through the dark. I came out into the day and stopped, blinking, sun-blind. I'd made myself damn ridiculous, shamed myself, and destroyed my dearest, sweetest friendship. I *was* unnatural – May had said as much – defective and destructive. I stood now in the middle of the street, among fallen leaves and the littered corpses of my murdered joy.

1918

The world goes on the same outside,
> The sparrows fly across the Square,
> The children play as we four did there,
> The trees grow green and brown and bare,
The sun shines on the dead Church spire,
> And nothing lives here but the fire . . .

from 'The Quiet House'

When the first victory came, there were no parades, no shouting in the streets, no banners waving. On a chill grey-brown day in February 1918 the men of Parliament voted to pass the Representation of the People Act, and suffrage was granted to women – some women – namely, those over thirty who were wives of householders or householders themselves. This included Mama, who'd no inclination to vote. It didn't include me, of course, or the poor young soldiers' wives and widows I met through my pension work with the War Office.

I thought of May, dear May, marching bravely through the rain, in 1907, ignoring the nasty jeers of male bystanders. I missed her terribly, and yet I knew I'd exiled myself. I'd made myself ridiculous. I was appalled at my behaviour but unable to change my profoundest nature. I'd ruined it for both of us, and there was no chance of making it up.

One day, I came across a short story of May's in an issue of *Harper's* and read 'The Pinprick' with horror and fascination. She had me to the life in her description of the central character: a tiny woman – 'an exquisite person in spite of her queerness' – whose family was destroyed by insanity. In the end, she kills herself. I'd never mentioned Henry or Freda to May. Had I, then, been so transparent? Did she sense a strain of madness in me? Was I so pathetic she expected me to take my own life? Or was that her wish to be entirely rid of me? How cruel! How heartless! I was exposed and betrayed. And not for the first time.

I tossed the magazine to the floor and kicked it far away under the bed.

Harold Monro had been discharged from the army and was once more at the Poetry Bookshop. My chap-book continued to sell a few copies a week, and Monro nominated me to Eddie Marsh, who'd agreed to include a woman poet, one only, in his forthcoming anthology, *Georgian Poetry III*. Monro showed me the letter he'd written to Marsh, in which he'd detailed his reasons for suggesting my poem, 'The Farmer's Bride': 'The outline would have resolved itself in the mind of Mrs Browning into a poem of at least two thousand lines; Browning might have worked it up to six thousand. Charlotte Mew tells the whole touching story in forty-six lines.'

With no explanation, Marsh rejected me.

When the final victory came, this time there were parades, shouting in the streets and banners waving. On 11 November 1918 the Armistice was signed. At eleven o'clock that Monday morning, the sirens started wailing as they'd never done before in broad daylight. Outside my bedroom window, people were stopping one another on the pavement and staring up at the sky. I was coming out through the street door to look up myself when I heard someone call out, 'The war's over!'

Thank God! I ran up the stairs to tell Mama and Anne. My sister and I hugged each other and polka-ed round the parlour, singing 'God Save the King' in three-quarter time. And Mama sat *tsk-tsk*ing. 'Girls,' she said, when we'd collapsed out of breath on the sofa, 'remember who you are!' Right then, I was too excited and elated by half to want to be reminded of who I was.

Shortly, the whole of London seemed to have gone mad, church bells ringing, buses and lorries and motor cars honking, people dancing and singing through the streets. Children added to the din by banging after their elders with heavy spoons on cooking pots. Soldiers in their khaki uniforms went along the pavement, grabbing women and kissing them, laughing and walking on.

Mama, watching all this from the parlour window, cautioned Anne and me: 'Don't either one of you leave this house today. Those men are rampaging barbarians. No woman is safe from them. Your reputations would be spoilt for ever.'

'But why?' Anne asked, turning from the spectacle on the other side of the pane. 'Surely a little kiss . . .'

'Far worse than kisses would follow, mark my word! That's all I can say. When you're older, you'll understand.'

Anne, forty-six, and I, forty-nine in a few days – we peered sideways at each other and ducked our heads to hide our silent laughter.

An afternoon drizzle didn't dampen the city's spirits, and the racketing and rejoicing continued long after dark. The undersides of the low clouds shone pink, not from incendiary bombs but from victory bonfires. Mama retired early with a sick headache from the noise and confusion outside our house. 'I don't know what's become of manners and knowing one's place. Riff-raff, all of them,' she sniffed, 'with no thought for decent people's well-being.'

Anne and I sat late in the parlour over glasses of Father's brandy that had stood in a decanter in the dining-room sideboard all these years. I raised my glass in a toast: 'Brighter days.'

Anne responded, 'Heart's desire.'

Here we were, two ageing females with no prospects, but that night we shared the youthful optimism and high hopes of an entire nation. A nation that woke, not the next morning but some morning soon after, to the full realization of what the victory had cost: altogether nine million dead, some 750,000 of them British. We'd been left a country of spinsters, widows, cripples and old men.

His heart, to me, was a place of palaces and pinnacles and shining
　　towers;
I saw it then as we see things in dreams, – I do not remember how
　　long I slept;
I remember the trees, and the high, white walls, and how the sun
　　was always on the towers . . .

　　　　　　　　　　　　　from 'I Have Been Through the Gates'

Alida Klemantaski insisted I send a copy of *The Farmer's Bride*
to Sydney Cockerell, Director of the Fitzwilliam Museum at
Cambridge. 'He knows everyone literary,' she said. 'He's a great
letter-writer, and if he cares to, he can be most helpful in
publicizing your work.' So I posted the chap-book with a short
note and forgot about it. When I heard from him, Mr Cockerell's response was in the nature of a critique of the title poem
– that damn poem again – stating ways I might improve it
through revision. Really!

As the poem was already in print, any chance for improving
it along the lines he suggested – had I even agreed with his
appraisal, which I did not – was long past. I told him I was
really incapable of going back over anything once written, to
rewrite a line of it. Despite his arrogance and my petulant reply,
a correspondence was begun between the two of us.

One of Cockerell's subsequent letters mentioned having sent
a copy of my chap-book to his friend Thomas Hardy, who very
much admired it. Hardy *had* seen it after all! I was gratified
and exultant. And curious. Had he recognized our predicament,
his and mine, in the title poem? Would I ever know for certain?

Shortly, another letter arrived:

Max Gate
Dorchester
September 24, 1918

Dear Miss Mew,

I believe that you have heard from our friend Mr Sydney Cockerell of the immense pleasure your poems have given my husband. It is long since I have known him so engrossed by a book as by *The Farmer's Bride*. It now lies by him on his study table, and I have read all the poems to him – some of them many times – and shall probably read them to him many times more.

He is, as you know, not a young man, and he cares to see but few people nowadays, but he has expressed a wish to meet you if that should be possible.

My knees turned to custard. I went into my bedroom to sit down. Had I read the last paragraph right? He wanted to see me? He wanted to see me!

It is a tedious journey to Dorchester from London, and not the time of year one cares to go into the country – but if you should ever be near us – or indeed if you thought it worthwhile to come that distance to see him, we should be most delighted to put you up for the night.

Yours very truly,
Florence Hardy

If I thought it worthwhile! I wrote immediately, accepting her gracious invitation and naming a possible date. Letters went to and fro, postponing my visit because of difficulties at Max Gate: domestic problems – their cook had taken to drink – unpleasant weather, illness and so on. I was beginning to feel ill myself from the swooping up to the heavens and the dashing to earth of my hopes, again and again. Did Mrs Hardy know about my previous friendship with her husband? Was this some sort of epistolary revenge?

In the end, 4 December was agreed upon for my visit. I took the train to Dorchester and, as directed by Mrs Hardy's letter, took the waiting fly, an old-fashioned one-horse hackney car-riage, and arrived at Max Gate late in the overcast afternoon. I was set down outside a brick wall backed by thick evergreen foliage. Carrying my small suitcase, I walked through the open gate and up the narrow, chalky-grey drive that circled round a clump of leafless trees. The house of reddish brick was solid, mock-monumental, more like a vicarage than the grand country house I'd somehow been expecting. The crowds of trees ringing the property sighed when the wind blew in the gloomy cold, smelling of pine needles and possible snow.

The fly had gone. I was alone. For the first time since I'd got Mrs Hardy's invitation, I began to doubt whether I should have come. For reassurance, I thought of – could even feel against my skin – the key to the trunk of Hardy's letters in my bedroom, which I still wore on a thin red ribbon round my neck.

I hunched my shoulders against the chill, gripped my suitcase and strode up to the enclosed porch and the front door. I knocked and waited.

The door opened, and a great hairy grey and white dog dashed out, barking and circling. Mrs Hardy said loudly, 'Miss Mew, how nice.'

'Charlotte, please,' I said above the yapping.

'And I'm Florence.' She was nearly shouting. 'Do come in. You mustn't mind Wessex. He barks at everyone.' She took my case and set it on the floor by a tall, glowering grandfather clock. 'We have to close him in the box-room at night, or he goes about the house, barking at every shadow that moves. It's so annoying.' She waved me into the parlour where a wood fire burned feebly in the grate. The panting dog ambled after us, brushing roughly against my hostess and nearly knocking me over. I gripped the back of a sturdy armchair and, when the animal had got past, seated myself and unbuttoned but didn't remove Father's old cut-down topcoat. The room wasn't much warmer than outdoors. Mrs Hardy was wearing a thick lady's suit jacket herself and a woollen skirt. Otherwise, she was much as she had been when I'd first met her in the nursing home: pale, thin-lipped, her round eyes set in shadowed hollows. All the while, though she smiled and played the welcoming hostess, she seemed profoundly unhappy.

She sat on a sofa near me. The dog plodded over to the hearth, took a small log from the wood basket, and settled down to chew on it. 'Do you recall our silent meeting when May Sinclair introduced us?' she asked. I nodded. 'I promise this time I shall keep up my end of the conversation.' She got to her feet again. 'You haven't had your tea,' she said apologetically. 'We dine early here, but you need something to sustain you.'

'Really, just a cup of tea would be fine.'

'Yes, yes,' she said and left the room, shutting the door to the hall behind her.

For myself, I was glad for a minute or two to take in my surroundings. The parlour wasn't as large or as well-furnished as I'd expected. Although the front window was unusually large, letting in the icy, grey-white daylight, everything within was heavy, dark, old, not antique so much as old-fashioned. At opposite ends of the mantelpiece sat a pair of white Staffordshire spaniels and a second, smaller pair of china dogs, rusty-red whippets. Cushions, tassels, fringes everywhere. I suspected the dowdy furnishings had been chosen by the first Mrs Hardy, whose large portrait dominated the far wall. I recognized her, glaring, dumpy, chinless. What torture to live under the disapproving glare of a dead woman. My feelings softened a bit towards Florence, who returned, bearing a tea tray with two cups, leaving the hall door ajar. Where was Hardy?

'You've noticed Emma's picture,' she said, putting the tray on a low table. She swept her hand round. 'My husband won't allow anything to be changed in this house. It remains as it was when she died.'

'How awful for you,' I said. She poured out the tea. I took a cup from her, blue and white with bunches of pink flowers on it, and warmed my hands on it.

Her voice was low and confidential. 'You've no idea. She was a dreadful person. I came here first as his secretary, you know. I had to deal with her.' Once begun, Florence was unable to stop the gushing forth of what must have been long-held resentment. 'Emma was spoilt, wilful, childishly impulsive. And in her last years, she was mad, the mad daughter of a mad father, whose brother and sister went mad, too. Her brother died in an asylum.'

I was struck by the similarity to my own family, but I certainly wasn't going to tell Florence, who appeared obsessed with Emma's madness in order to justify her position as the better wife. The second Mrs Hardy went on: 'Emma kept a suitcase packed with food and clothes, ready to leave at any instant. She was terrified the French would invade along the south coast and overrun the countryside and force everyone to engage in worshipping the Pope and other Romish practices. She lived in horror of them for years.'

As she spoke, Florence seemed to be listening for something elsewhere in the house. Hardy? 'You know, she fancied herself a writer. Can you imagine? Living with one of the world's greatest writers and she considered herself his equal. She actually tried to get herself an agent on the strength of his name. Without any success, of course. I found boxes full of her poetry in the room in the attic where she died. Utter schoolgirlish tosh.'

I listened to all this while watching a white cat stroll into the parlour, leap up into an empty chair near the fireplace, arrange itself for comfort and go to sleep. Still no Hardy.

'I can't get rid of a thing. Nor can he, apparently. I believe he feels guilty that she died unloved by him or anyone else. His latest verses are all mourning the loss many years ago of an idealized girl – who never existed, I'm certain, except in his mind.'

I got a tingle along my arms. Could she be mistaken? Were the poems not about Emma but about me? Or at least some of them?

Her voice dropped even lower, to an exhausted whisper. 'I'm like a mother whose child never grew up. He's seventy-eight, you know. I'm thirty-nine. Sometimes, I feel eighty.'

I made suitably reassuring sounds – although it was difficult for me to believe this woman was ten years my junior – and for a time Florence was silent as we drank our tea.

'Forgive me,' she said, settling her cup in its saucer with a nervous rattle of china on china. 'I see so few people, and you seem so sympathetic. I didn't mean to burden you with my troubles.'

'Not at all.'

'It's your poetry that brought you to us. Let's talk about it. I must say again how very much my husband and I admire it. "The dreams upon the eyes of white geraniums in the dusk" – I was so inspired by that line in your "Madeleine in Church" that I planted white geraniums in the conservatory. You must see them before you leave. They're blooming now.'

The poem was about much more than white geraniums. Didn't she know that? No, she appeared to think she was complimenting me. I sipped from my steaming cup and swallowed my annoyance along with the tea. Where was Hardy? I was getting edgy. I wanted a cigarette badly but had been warned beforehand that smoking wasn't allowed because of Florence's respiratory ailments.

The room had become quite dark as we'd sat there, winter's evening coming on. Florence got up, struck a match and lighted an oil-lamp with it. A bit of an improvement but not much. 'We've no electricity,' she explained. 'My husband won't have it.' She came to stand over the tea tray and went on: 'This place is too depressing for words in the winter, when the dead leaves stick on the window-panes and the wind moans and the sky is grey and you can't even see as far as the road.'

She began clearing away the cups and saucers. The dog left off gnawing and raised his shaggy head. I looked up and saw Hardy framed in the open parlour door. He was completely white-haired, even to his eyebrows and drooping moustache. His face was thinner, more lined than I remembered, but his eyes still lifted at the corners, the familiar glint was in them yet, and his smile was as beguiling as it'd ever been.

What was *he* seeing? Certainly not the young girl he'd met at the British Museum more than twenty years ago. Although inside myself I felt her stir.

We looked at one another across the room for several seconds until Florence realized he was there.

'Thomas,' she said, 'this is Miss Mew.'

'How do you do,' he said, coming no nearer.

'Would you like some tea, dear?' she said to him.

'No.' His reply was quick and harsh. His eyes hadn't moved from mine.

'Very well, then,' Florence said. 'I'll take these things to the kitchen and speak to Cook about dinner.'

'Would you care to see my study upstairs?' Hardy asked me as his wife went past him and along the hall. 'You must overlook the books and papers scattered about. It's most untidy.'

I followed him up the stairs, my heart in my throat. He was chatting on about the hundreds and hundreds of Austrian pines he'd set out on the property years ago. 'My brother used to call the woods near where we were born the birds' bedroom. I've tried to create a suitable bedroom for them here.' Something in the way he said it gave the word 'bedroom' a wry, suggestive twist, like a wink. Was he making private fun of me while his wife might hear?

He held the door to his study open wide, closing it after me. I'd entered a square room lined with bookcases, the walls a rich Venetian red, like stepping into the heart of a rose. A work table littered with papers stood to one side. And there, there lay my grey-green chap-book. Facing the scant light of the window, a large desk with stained blotter was cluttered with penholders and inkpots and spectacles and magnifying glasses and paper-knives and the usual writer's debris. At the desk, a wooden armchair with worn leather seat. The oil-lamps were unlit. Shadow gathered in the corners. After the chatter in the parlour, this room was stiff with silence.

'Hello, old friend,' he said, at last, his expression gentle and uncertain. 'You looked so small and slender when I first saw you down there, it seemed as if you might be crushed in the intensity of a too-passionate embrace, but I yearned to do just that.' He held his arms out to me, and I stepped into them. Without words, we held each other for a quiet, comforting minute. I could feel the thinness of his bones through the wool of his jacket.

As we moved apart, he took my hand, pressing my cold fingers to his warm lips. 'Come over by the fire. You must be chilled right through.'

Hardy poked up the embers until flames leapt along the charred logs. I spread my fingers to the heat. 'Thank you,' I said, my voice ragged from disuse. We looked at one another again for a few warming moments.

How to begin after so long? I didn't want, this time, to be the one who turned away. 'I may be wrong,' I said, plunging into the murkiest depths, 'but reading some of your recent poems, I got the notion you were speaking to me. Especially in "The Dead Man Walking".'

He smiled. 'Poetry is an incomplete soliloquy. I'm so glad, my dear, you were able to complete the poems as I intended. Those for whom the message isn't intended rarely understand it. Or they overlook it altogether.' A chuckle of satisfaction. 'If Galileo had said in verse that the earth revolves around the sun, the Inquisition might've left him alone.'

It was wonderful to find him so well, in such high spirits.

'You know yourself when you meet her in print,' he went on. 'You knew yourself in Sue Bridehead, didn't you? And yet you didn't criticize me for it.'

'How could I object when you've made me immortal?'

'As you've done for me, in your "Farmer's Bride".'

'You understood, then?'

The firelight shone in his face. 'Of course. And I was pleased, even flattered.'

'But what about that poem and the others in West Country dialect? Wasn't that presumptuous of me?'

'No, no. In fact, to be honest, I was a bit jealous.' His shoulders drooping, he seemed sad for the first time since our meeting again. 'I'm getting old, Charlotte. I'm losing my salt. You'll outdo me if you continue.' His words were deep and earnest. 'No one writes of passion unfulfilled with the intensity you bring to it. In that, I envy you.'

'Now who's flattering?'

The amusement lighted his face.

Cautiously, I brought up our last meeting. 'Has it really been twenty-five years? I'm still ashamed, running off like that. My experiences since have taught me what you must've suffered.' I felt a rush of fondness, a new tenderness towards him. 'I was a bewildered child,' I said.

'You couldn't help yourself any more than I could. You were right to protect your virtue.'

What could I say that was true without its being the whole truth? 'Initially, I resist any act that's compelled, so I can hardly count myself virtuous, even when I act in a right manner. I've no capacity for surrender,' I insisted, 'either to God or to love. I've never yielded myself to any lover.'

That pleased him.

'Do you ever think about this old fool?' he said, with a wry smile.

'Yes, of course,' I admitted. 'More often than I'd like.'

He was eyeing me fully, searching behind the mask of years. 'What I recall most vividly is your tiny thumb cocked up against the handle of your sunshade.' His words sounded raspy with emotion: 'Like a series of cinematographic images, I see your face glowing in the suffused light of the white cotton parasol, its radiating spokes like rays of a halo behind your head.'

A patch of rosy colour had come on to his cheeks. 'And every time I visit the British Museum, I stand on the spot where I gave you that first kiss. As if it were possible that no one has passed there since, I stare at the floor and sigh. I convince myself I can just discern in the faint dust the imprints of our feet as we stood that afternoon.'

The poignancy of his remembering was enough to break the heart right open. 'In those days, I felt a sort of bliss in doing what was erratic and unexpected. And if I made you unhappy, I've been unhappy, too. It's all been my fault, the result of a wickedness in me.'

He shook his head, disagreeing. 'You were an ethereal, fine-nerved, sensitive girl, quite unfitted by temperament for physical relations. With any man.'

'I was ignorant of my own deepest self. Put it down to ignorance and timidity,' I said, with hurried evasiveness. So much I couldn't tell him, could never tell anyone. My burden, mine entirely.

He clasped my hands in his. 'I can see you through your feathers, my poor little bird. You were fearless as a thinker, and you deserved more tender consideration than I gave.'

'What I needed was humility and a chastened mind. I've not got either yet.'

He lowered his chin. 'What a monster you must've imagined me. You must still dislike me.'

'I don't dislike you, Thomas,' I said, imploring. 'Seeing you again, I realize I love you as much as ever. Only, I oughtn't to love you.' I took my hands from his.

'Because I'm married? Oh, Charlotte, haven't we discussed this often enough in the past? You must understand that, having for a second time based a permanent contract on a temporary feeling, I wish the weakness of the moment could've ended with the moment.' He sounded fiercely grave. 'Love is a terrible thing: sweet for a space, and then all mourning, mourning.

Time cures hearts, my dear, but I am always, always your loving friend.'

Just then, a knock sounded on the study door, and Florence came in, holding a wavering candle. We stepped apart, Hardy and I, as if we'd been caught out. She blinked, glanced from one of us to the other. 'Perhaps, Thomas, Charlotte would like to go to her room and rest a bit before dinner.' She gestured into the corridor, prepared to show me the way.

'Yes, thank you,' I said, with some reluctance.

Hardy leant towards me and whispered, 'You must meet me in the conservatory at midnight.'

I had to laugh inwardly at the shop-girl romance of it. But it was the sort of thing I'd come hoping to hear, wasn't it?

The guest room was the next one along. Florence told me it'd been Hardy's study before the original house was expanded. 'This,' she said solemnly, 'is where he wrote *Tess* and *Jude the Obscure*.' The room all at once took on great significance and became warmer, more intimate. Now, reflected light through the windows across one wall gave a moony glow to the white china pitcher and basin on the washstand and made this birth-place of Sue Bridehead eerily disquieting. The only other furniture in the room was a chest of drawers and a bed, where I lay, fully clothed, wrapped in Father's topcoat.

Dinner had been an ordeal, with conversation starting and stopping like a clogged spigot. Hardy was petulant and exacting. Florence touchy, with snapping replies. And I was tense and withdrawn, pushing the food from one side of my plate to the other in a pantomime of decorous eating. Florence and I took our coffee in the parlour. Hardy excused himself and went up the stairs. To bed or to work, he didn't say. I listened to another recital of the failings of the first Mrs Hardy until the grandfather clock chimed ten. Pleading fatigue, I'd taken a candle and gone to my room.

There, I lay on the bed, thinking about Hardy's whispered

instructions: 'You must meet me . . .' For nearly two hours, I drifted in the space between longing and refusing, desire and guilt, unable to decide what to do. A phrase from an Emily Brontë poem kept running through my mind: *The old clock in the gloomy hall* . . . When I heard the chimes striking twelve, I was roused by the lure of the necessary transgression. I got up and made my way down the stairs and through the shadowy parlour, stumbling soundlessly against the unfamiliar furnishings, to the small glass-roofed conservatory at the side of the house.

I opened the door, latched it carefully behind me and inhaled the humid, musty-sharp air. Black foliage cut an intricate silhouette against the moon-whitened grass outside. A stone urn in the middle of the lawn dropped a squat black shadow round its foot. Overhead, a sky silver-sprinkled with stars. Stepping between ferns and ivies, I went to where I could make out the pots of white geraniums, great snowballs of petals against the dark. I waited. Anxious. Joyous and terrified at the same time.

Minutes passed. My heated excitement, the thrill of a clandestine tryst, cooled to impatience. I wanted a cigarette, but my handbag was upstairs in the guest room. I paced back and forth in the narrow space like a disgruntled sentry. Damn it. I fisted my hands in my coat pockets. Where was he? He'd said midnight, hadn't he?

When I heard the clock strike again – the half hour, one o'clock, I couldn't be sure – I hurried back through the house and up to my room, shut the door, and threw myself across the bed and lay there, arms folded round myself in sad embrace.

I woke to a mockingly bright day, the sun high. I packed quickly, resolved to make my escape by the first available train. I found Florence at the head of the table in the dining-room. 'Good morning, Charlotte,' she said, warmly. She stood. 'Let me get you some breakfast.'

'Just tea, please,' I said, taking the chair where I'd sat at dinner.

She poured me a cup. 'I hope you had a good rest.' She sounded sincere. My pointless wandering through the midnight house apparently had gone unnoticed. 'My husband had a very restless night, I'm sorry to say, awake until nearly midnight. I fixed him a glass of warm milk with a bit of sedative in it. That always helps to settle him, although he'd protest loudly if he knew about the drug. Still, the doctor says he must have his sleep.'

I examined her expression for any hint of irony in what she was saying. Her face was plain as plain, her gaze innocently round, her tone level and friendly. 'You mustn't blame yourself, Charlotte. This often happens when we have a guest.' Was that the hint of a rueful smile?

Florence and Hardy walked me to the railway bridge near Max Gate. The afternoon was warm and clear and windless, the birds thick and noisy in the pines along the road. Fleet crow shadows passed in silence across the chalky road in front of us, then the headlong crows themselves followed, and we were at the bridge. Hardy explained, pointing, 'Follow the path along the tracks. It's only a short distance to the station.'

I shook Florence's hand and thanked her for her kind hospitality. Hardy removed his hat, pressing it against his chest. I shook his hand, watching for some sign, some gesture of apology. He'd come in to lunch, said little during the meal, and behaved as if nothing had gone awry last night. I'd had no opportunity to speak to him alone, to sort it out. 'Thank you for coming,' he said, with a polite, watery smile.

'Thank *you*,' I said. I walked away, determined not to look back.

In reply to my note of thanks, Florence wrote me a most cordial letter that spoke of our meeting again and concluded:

His Arms are Full of Broken Things

My husband insisted on waiting on the bridge until your train had passed. If you had known, you could not have seen us, and he knew that we could not see you. It was a curious act of sentiment on his part – I suppose the same feeling that prompts some people to wait to see a ship out of sight when it has borne a friend away.

1921

In Saturday Market there's eggs a plenty
    And dead-alive ducks with their legs tied down,
Grey old gaffers and boys of twenty –
    Girls and the women of the town –
Pitchers and sugar-sticks, ribbons and laces,
    Posies and whips and dicky-birds' seed,
Silver pieces and smiling faces,
    In Saturday Market they've all they need.

from 'Saturday Market'

Desperate gaiety. That's how the decade of the twenties began. The war was the past, consigned to the dustbin of history. Ragtime prosperity was the future, the Peace Boom promised to all. Spirits and women's hemlines were on the rise. So were prices, but our income at 9 Gordon Street wasn't. We couldn't afford even Jane's occasional service. Bric-à-brac went undusted and carpets unswept while Anne and I tried to earn what we could to add to the modest sum from Mama's trust fund, nearly half of which now went for poor Freda's care, far away on the Isle of Wight. Not to be begrudged. Nor dwelt on.

The only practical solution was to let out the ground and first floors of the house to more lodgers. I steeled myself for protests from Mama, but she behaved as if she were blind and deaf to the whole situation. While Anne and I packed up her things, Mama talked blithely about the grand holiday at Brighton she fancied we were all going on. 'My papa bought the house when I was a girl, you know. It's right near the sea. We used to spend part of every summer there and called on all the best people. You girls must have new frocks. White muslin, I think, with ruffled eyelet.'

'Oh, Mama,' I said, gathering off the parlour mantelpiece a dozen or so yellowed invitation cards, some of them more than thirty years old, 'putting me in ruffled eyelet would be like putting a pig in a peruke.'

'Don't be coarse, Charlotte,' she snapped. 'It isn't becoming.'

'That's exactly my point,' I said, but she wasn't listening.

We settled into the basement, Anne and I in one windowless room, Mama in a room with a narrow casement opening on to the steps to the back garden. The kitchen became our parlour and dining-room, too. Wek sat on his perch between the two front windows, his feathers dusty shades of their former jungle blue and yellow. Mama sat next to him in her worn brocade chair. The two of them were unusually quiet, looking out on the basement area, the outside stairs, the iron railings and the legs of people passing on the pavement up above. They'd watch until they dozed off and napped where they sat, dreaming, no doubt, of the better days they'd shared together.

Our dungeon, as I came to think of it, was dim and cramped and not suitable for entertaining callers. Except dear, sweet Alida, of course. As fond as I was of her, though, I knew my romantic nature, given to affectionate rashness and retreat, and vowed never again to allow myself to fall in love. With anybody. Such misery was secret, subtle and absolutely relentless.

Alida was married now to Harold Monro, and brought smiles into our dreary days and kept me writing poetry. As a result, I published several new poems in *The Monthly Chapbook*, in fine company with Edna St Vincent Millay and Edith Sitwell. 'The Cenotaph' appeared in the September *Westminster Gazette*, and 'Song' in the October *Athenaeum*.

Harold Monro again recommended me to Eddie Marsh for his anthology, *Georgian Poetry IV*, and again I was rejected. I never got used to rejection and always took it personally, each instance as painful as the first. It was ever thus. Any writer who says otherwise is lying.

However, at the same time as Marsh, Harold had been at

work on his own book: Leonard Parsons published Harold's
Some Contemporary Poets, in 1920, and I was delighted to be
included.

One afternoon on my way to the greengrocer, I dropped by
the Poetry Bookshop, and Harold, seeing me enter, called me
into his office. He'd been writing columns of figures in an
account ledger. He laid the pen in the gutter between the pages
and stood up. What now? I wondered. Harold must have caught
my worried frown because he smiled down at me his gentlest
smile and said, 'I think, Charlotte, a second edition of *The
Farmer's Bride* should be brought out.'

I was too surprised and delighted to trust myself to speak. I
simply nodded my head. The poet in me capered invisibly round
the little room. The practical me silently said, Considering how
much we need the money, this might prove a godsend.

'I suggest you include some new poems to make it more
marketable.' His black brows lifted expectantly. 'What do you
say?'

Pushing aside the memory of all the strain and difficulties in
getting out the first edition, I happily agreed.

My face is against the grass – the moorland grass is wet –
  My eyes are shut against the grass, against my lips there are
the little blades,
       Over my head the curlews call,
  And now there is the night wind in my hair;
My heart is against the grass and the sweet earth; – it has gone
still, at last.
              It does not want to beat any more,
                And why should it beat?
              This is the end of the journey;
                The Thing is found.

from 'Moorland Night'

If I'd inherited anything from Mama, it was a tendency to be
difficult once offended. Sydney Cockerell and I continued to
correspond, even after his irritating, unsolicited advice for revising 'The Farmer's Bride'. Following one of her poetry readings
at the bookshop, Alida had introduced the two of us, and
shortly after, Cockerell invited me to visit him and his family
at Cambridge. I refused, rather nastily, I'm afraid, in a letter
full of French phrases and literary allusions.

In early 1919, he'd written again, asking me to contribute to
a group of forty or so poems to be bound and presented to
Thomas Hardy on the occasion of his seventy-ninth birthday,
on 2 June. Among others to be included were Kipling, Bridges,
Graves, D. H. Lawrence, Yeats, Chesterton and Siegfried Sassoon. Of course, I couldn't refuse such an honour – or a chance
to 'speak' to him – and sent off a handwritten copy of a lyric
about the transience of romantic love. It began, 'Love, Love
to-day, my dear, / Love is not always here . . .' I hoped he'd
read it and understand. I later received a short letter:

Max Gate, Dorchester
Oct. 28, 1919

Dear Miss Mew,

I am sending a brief line to thank you for the beautiful poem you wrote in the volume made up by my poet friends, without my knowledge, which reached me about 10 days ago, having been delayed I believe by the binder. I shall always value the MS. & keep it for your sake, as will my wife also.

Believe me

Ever yours sincerely

It had been typed by Florence and signed by Hardy. I'd have liked to offer more personal good wishes but knew I couldn't, convinced they'd never actually reach him. Still, I cherished the note that probably went out to all the contributors. I ran a slow fingertip over the spidery *T. Hardy*, touched it to my lips and then tucked the letter away with the others in the bottom of my travel trunk.

In 1920, Cockerell again wrote – 'Do you feel like coming to Cambridge for the weekend? It would be so nice if you could . . .' He insisted no evening clothes were needed, simply pack a toothbrush and catch the train at King's Cross and come.

I consulted Anne, who urged me to go. 'You need to get away, Charlotte. You've had no proper holiday in years, and I can manage Mama for a day or two. If the truth be told, she may not even notice you're gone.'

The visit gave me an opportunity to know my famous letter-writing acquaintance at closer range. He was a dapper, bearded, balding man of about my own age, a gold watch chain draped across the front of his waistcoat. His name – Cockerell – suited him right down to the ground: he was cocksure in all he did and said. He could be tiresome in his certainty, and yet he possessed an undeniable charisma and an old-fashioned courtliness. He was an active admirer and advocate of my poetry. And yet . . .

Cockerell tended to lecture one on how best to be oneself. I'd told him once it was too late – I was past fifty, after all – too late for the poor clay that was me to be further moulded, even by the most skilful Pygmalion. Perfection wasn't possible. As far as I could see, it wasn't even desirable.

'I understand you went down to Max Gate a few years ago,' he said as we left the Cambridge railway station in a motor taxi. 'Florence wrote that you talked incessantly.'

I simply stared at him, unbelieving. If Florence had, in fact, said that, what other lies might she have fabricated about me? I resolved to say as little as I possibly could while in Cambridge, to show how false she'd played me.

The Cockerell house in Shaftesbury Road was a little museum of his treasures: Blake watercolours and first editions of Barrie and Shaw and medieval illuminated manuscripts and so much more. Even if I hadn't taken a vow of near-silence, I'd have been awed speechless. In his study, he showed me an exquisite Roxburghe book of Henry VIII songs. Then, from his desk, Cockerell took out Florence's letter and gave it me to read:

> Max Gate, Dorchester
> Dec. 6th, 1918

Dear Mr Cockerell,

Miss Mew has just left us. I think I never met anyone who was so different from the picture my fancy had made. What a pathetic little creature!

Pathetic little creature! It was she who was pathetic.

One longed to be kind to her and look after her. And she was not silent – talked all the time. We never have had anyone here who talked so . . .

This was too much! I nearly handed the page of calumny back to my host, but curiosity kept me reading.

T.H. talked very kindly to her, and read her some of his poems. But she is not his type of woman at all . . .

So that was it. Simple jealousy. I folded the sheet of paper and thrust it at Cockerell. 'Why did you show me this? It's dreadful and untrue.'

'I meant only for you to take note of the last sentence.'

I tossed my head. 'I didn't get that far.'

Cockerell took the letter from me and unfolded it. 'Listen to this – "She has genius, I think." Florence is sincere in that. I'm certain of it. As for the rest, I've been a frequent guest at Max Gate. I know she takes things very seriously, sometimes worries about what doesn't matter, and naturally feels protective of her husband.' He shut the letter away in a desk drawer. 'Let us be kind to her in her isolation and remember only her generous assessment of your talent.'

Having smoothed my ruffled feelings, Cockerell continued to show me round his collections, expounding upon everything, exhibiting his considerable knowledge. I said almost nothing, determined still to prove Florence Hardy wrong.

We ended our tour in the garden, where his wife, a thin woman in a large straw hat, her eyes shut, was reclining in a wicker chaise near a bloomy bed of roses. A little breeze lifted everything – flower petals, the leaves of the enclosing trees, the brim of her straw hat – and lowered them gently. Kate Cockerell, her husband explained to me as we crossed the lawn, had been an artist, an illustrator of considerable skill, and suffered now from a degenerative nerve disease. He introduced us, and we exchanged smiles as he went on talking. He was a bit of a domestic tyrant, I could tell. During my short stay, I saw that Kate was forbearing of his lectures but showed, on occasion, remarkable spirit in facing him down, of which he seemed to be completely unaware. I liked her at once, a familiar combination of the shy and the forceful.

After a quiet lunch, Cockerell hurried me off for a stroll

round the Fitzwilliam Museum, a large pale-grey limestone building fronted by a row of Corinthian columns and a classical pediment. 'When I came here to be director, in 1908, I found it a pigsty, and I turned it into a palace,' he said as we climbed a flight of side steps between two white lions couchant. And palace it was. Inside, I was overwhelmed by the scale and luxury of the foyer: medallioned and gilded ceilings, mosaics underfoot, coloured marble columns and panelled walls, and two grand marble staircases leading to the first-floor galleries. All the smooth, rich surfaces reflected the ambient light, and fine white sculpture – goddesses and busts of famous men – stared eyeless from pedestals and niches.

Taking my elbow, Cockerell guided me firmly through a series of high-ceilinged rooms, stopping at a display of porcelain here, a suit of armour there, to explain its history or aesthetic value. The picture galleries were hung in the new style – Cockerell wasn't shy about taking credit for having started it – a single row of paintings round the room, an oriental rug on the floor, and chairs for visitors to sit and contemplate the individual works of art. I admired a misty Turner watercolour, and Cockerell explained, 'Constable said Turner seemed to paint with tinted steam.'

I liked that. 'Very apt.'

We paused next in front of an elegant gold-framed Gainsborough, a double portrait in a country setting, a lake like a round mirror and a country house or church in the background. The subjects were a girl and boy in eighteenth-century dress, their faces sweet and untroubled. 'Who are they?' I asked.

'Difficult to say for certain,' Sydney answered, frowning. 'We're calling it "Heneage Lloyd and His Sister," but the identification is questionable. The provenance isn't, however. It was a bequest to the museum from Charles Fairfax Murray, who died last year.'

For all his arrogance, Cockerell did have a rare ability to charm or command money from the rich, art and precious *objets* from collectors, and manuscripts from writers. 'I've been accused of haunting deathbeds,' he said, clearly amused. 'Not true, of course. That's much too late.'

We both chuckled, and I said, 'You remind me of the old joke about the undertaker's cart returning empty from the graveyard when it ran over a crossing sweeper and killed him, and a passerby shouted, "Greedy!"'

He enjoyed that, throwing his head back and laughing out loud.

An elderly couple at the far end of the gallery glared at us with disapproval. Cockerell apparently didn't care. It was, after all, his museum, created by him for people's enjoyment, which included laughter.

Shortly, we arrived at the room housing cases of valuable manuscripts. There behind glass was the first draft of Keats's 'Ode to a Nightingale' and a lock of his hair. We began speaking in tones of reverent hush. 'If I remember rightly,' Cockerell said, 'you have an interest in Emily Brontë.'

'Some years ago, I did publish an essay about her, yes.' I didn't say I'd also written a short story and a poem, 'Moorland Night', under her influence. Both had gone unpublished.

'It's here on approval, and we hope to acquire this,' Cockerell said, with a curling smile. He took a key from his waistcoat pocket and unlocked a long, shallow drawer. He opened it, folded back a sheet of tissue paper, and solemnly lifted out a page of runes, a sort of secret-code calligraphy, minute printing that at first glance wasn't English at all but another, more ancient, bardic language. Between one heartbeat and the next, all came clear. I made out the first line: 'Cold in the earth, and the deep snow piled above thee . . .' I recognized that verse. It was called 'Remembrance'. Here, right in front of me, was a poem by Emily Brontë. In her own hand. I was quite shaken. A holy relic. With almost talismanic power. She, who'd died before I was born, who'd seemed distant as the moon, was here, now. I didn't dare touch the page, except with my eyes.

'She should have been a man,' Cockerell said, breaking the spell.

What was he saying? I blinked once or twice before asking, 'Why is that?'

'She wrote like a man,' he stated, with characteristic certainty. 'By all accounts, she very much resembled a man and behaved in a masculine manner.'

I cocked my head. Did he mean she was an invert? Why was he telling me? Did he see some similarities between Emily and me? 'What do you mean?'

'Simply that she was a superior kind of woman. No offence intended, Charlotte, but in the arts, as elsewhere, women are to some degree inferior to men.'

My gorge was on the rise. 'A woman cannot write with the power, the force of a man, do you mean, unless she's somehow not in fact a woman at all?' I was speaking much too loudly, but I didn't care. I meant to make my point without interruption. 'You say her genius was masculine, but surely it was purely spiritual, quite apart from any accident of sex.'

'She used a male-sounding pen name, Ellis Bell, right to the end,' he answered, with a *non sequitur*.

'And in the end, at age thirty, she committed suicide,' I tossed back.

'Never!' Now, he was the one incensed. 'She died from complications of a cold caught at her brother Branwell's funeral. It's a matter of record.'

'It's also a matter of record that she continued with her household duties and refused all medical attention. She willed herself to die rather than go on with her unhappy life.' I began quoting from Emily's 'At Castle Wood', memorized long ago under Lucy Harrison's tutelage:

> Dark falls the fear of this despair
>   On spirits born of happiness;
> But I was bred the mate of care,
>   The foster-child of sore distress.

No sigh for me, no sympathy,
　　No wish to keep my soul below;
The heart is dead in infancy,
　　Unwept-for let the body go . . .

I was inflamed on Emily's behalf, my memory buzzing with stray lines from I didn't know where:

Sleep brings no wish to knit
My harassed heart beneath
My only wish is to forget
In the sleep of death.

Cockerell dropped the manuscript into the drawer and slammed it shut. The echo rolled through the room like thunder. 'You're wrong, Charlotte. I'll grant you she was a wild and melancholy soul, but suicide? She'd never have been so weak as to do such a cowardly thing.'

He started to turn away, to end the disagreement with his final statement. I wheeled round and spoke harshly so as to make him listen: 'Isn't bearing great pain without flinching brave? Isn't choosing the time of one's own death and facing it without retreating brave?'

Cockerell walked away, his grey-worsted back his only response.

Now, if I look, I see you walking down the years,
Young, and through August fields – a face, a thought, a swinging
    dream perched on a stile –;
I would have liked (so vile we are!) to have taught you tears
        But most to have made you smile.

                                        from 'On the Road to the Sea'

After the customary struggles over punctuation and line lengths
and galley corrections, the second edition of *The Farmer's Bride*
was published in the spring of 1921. I'd expanded the original
seventeen poems with eleven new ones, and through Harold
Monro's efforts, an American edition, called *Saturday Market*,
was published at the same time by Macmillan in New York.
That my poems had crossed an ocean, gone where I'd never
been, would never myself go – to exotic-sounding places like
Sioux City and New Orleans and North Carolina – that they'd
be read by who knew what strangers, thrilled and pleased me.

   The book's dedication to Hardy, still unnamed, was the same,
and I included a new poem, 'I Have Been Through the Gates', I'd
written after my stay at Max Gate. It was built from bits of Jude
Fawley's – that is, Hardy's – vision of the city of Christminster/
Oxford in his last novel, my way of sending him my love and
admiration. I couldn't trust my feelings to a letter. And I was
quite certain Florence read everything that arrived at Max Gate
by post and destroyed what she didn't want him to see.

We were in the basement kitchen, having tea, Mama dozing in
her chair, Wek napping on his stand by the area window. 'In
order to publicize the new book,' Alida said to me, 'you have
got to go to a studio and have your photograph made.'

My innate shyness made me argue against it. 'I've no idea how to present myself,' I said and resorted to the ultimate female excuse: 'I've nothing decent to wear.'

Alida wasn't to be put off. She marched me along the corridor and into our bedroom, Anne's and mine. Alida sorted through my wardrobe, shaking her head. My few serviceable clothes were hopelessly out of fashion. Pulling out a hanger from far at the end, she said, 'What's this?'

I explained it was my father's Victorian dress suit.

'Yes, of course,' she said, 'absolutely brilliant.' She insisted I should appear in the cut-down black tail coat and trousers, a floppy bow tied at the neck of a white shirt. 'It's a costume perfectly in tune with the times,' she said, with obvious delight, 'androgynous and mildly shocking.'

The real shock was mine. I'd never been much given to gazing into mirrors and had lost track of what the years had done to my appearance. When the prints came from the photographer, I was surprised and dismayed. Here, staring back at me, was an eccentric old auntie, a defiant little woman with an abundance of short white hair and large dark eyes and arched, questioning brows, who seemed to be saying, 'I will not look away. Why should you?'

I was better prepared, I thought, for the reviews of the second edition than the first, determined not to let them push me into a funk. But when, over the next few weeks, they started to appear in newspapers and journals, I asked Alida to read them first and sort them out. The good reviews – and they were numerous – she read aloud to us one evening after Mama had been put to bed. Alida's wonderful contralto lent them almost sibylline gravity. 'Here's what Edith Sitwell says in the *Daily Herald*: "In each poem we find the record of some great and terrible emotional experience, some ardent spirituality, controlled and made understandable by intellect and by an infallible certainty for the right expression."'

Sitting across from me at the kitchen table, Anne clapped her hands and said, 'Well done, Charlotte.' Her blue-violet eyes shone in the light from the oil-lamp. Dear, dear Anne.

Alida picked up another clipping. 'The reviewer in the *Sheffield Telegraph* says your poetry is "full of restrained tenderness and pathos and forceful phrasing which rings absolutely sincere, stirring one knows not what divine sense of tears, voicing one knows not what insistent obstinate questionings of sense and outward things."'

'Is that good?' Anne asked, her brow wrinkling.

'I think it's meant to be, yes,' Alida said. 'It goes on to say, "There is poetry here . . ."'

'Well, I should hope so,' I put in, buoyed by the implied compliment. 'What I wish is that these reviewers would simply say right out it's good stuff and everybody should dash out and buy it.'

That brought a laugh from the two of them, and I proposed we all have a glass of sherry to celebrate.

Later, I found a perfect use for the negative reviews: I twisted them into spills to light my cigarettes.

Best make an end of it; bury it soon.
If there is blood on the hearth who'll know it?
Or blood on the stairs,
When murder is over and done why show it?
In Saturday Market nobody cares.

from 'Saturday Market'

Anne ran out to telephone Alida at the Poetry Bookstore while I dealt with Mama. Neither my sister nor I was unfamiliar with death, but we simply couldn't manage this.

After years of consultations at the Zoo in Regent's Park, I'd persuaded Mr Aldin, the assistant keeper of the parrot house, to accompany me to Gordon Square, to attend Wek. The poor bird had grown so weak he couldn't hold on to his perch and had taken to crouching in his big wire cage, silent, his wrinkled lids only half-open. Faded and tatty, his blue wings drooped along the floor of the cage. Most of his tail feathers were bent or missing, and his feet and toes splayed out like the fingers in a child's drawing. I blamed his decline on the dampness of the dungeon, our basement rooms. It had aggravated Mama's arthritis, too. I hoped Mr Aldin, in his brass-buttoned uniform and billed cap, would have a cure for Wek's condition.

The assistant keeper examined him for several minutes while the parrot watched me from under hooded eyes. 'Sorry, miss,' Mr Aldin said, snapping the cage door shut, 'but he'd best be put down.'

Anne sank into a chair by the kitchen table, her hand over her mouth.

As Mr Aldin explained the procedure to me in a flat, professional manner, my mind refused absolutely to take it in.

Something about chloroform. And a sponge. I watched Mama staring out of the window at the whitewashed area wall, listening impassively. I was afraid that when Mr Aldin left, she'd let go her grip on herself and become hysterical. And she did.

Anne returned from telephoning. She carried a brown glass bottle. She'd stopped at the chemist's on Southampton Row and got the chloroform and instructions for using it. Together, we persuaded a sobbing, exhausted Mama into her bed, and after a large, stiff brandy, she drifted off to sleep.

When Alida arrived, I told her about Mr Aldin's diagnosis. 'Poor Willy. He must be nearly a hundred by now, isn't he?' she asked sympathetically.

'We knew you'd understand,' Anne said, 'why we can't do this ourselves.'

Alida agreed but didn't appear especially eager to do it either. The three of us went along the hall to the windowless bedroom, lighted by a single candle, where all was in readiness: Wek in his cage, the bottle of chloroform, a sponge and some blankets to wrap round the bird cage to shut out the air. As Anne repeated the chemist's instructions, I clapped my hands over my ears. Then she and I left Alida alone in the room.

Soon, she came out into the kitchen and joined us at the table. A trio of reluctant murderers, we sat, waiting the prescribed length of time, our clenched hands thrust before us on the white tablecloth as if to deny our complicity, and too stricken even to put the kettle on for tea.

After long minutes of listening to the gritty shuffle of passers-by on the pavement outside and the low chortle of an occasional motor car, Alida pushed back her chair and left Anne and me to wait some more. I heard a cry of pain from our bedroom. But it may have come from inside my own anxious heart.

Alida reappeared, solemn-faced, with the cardboard box Anne had found to use as an impromptu coffin, and the three of us walked in silent procession through the basement, up the concrete steps and out into the shady garden. The whine and moan of motor traffic sounded from the other side of the house. A twittery flight of sparrows lifted up from the garden wall at our approach.

Even though I couldn't do it myself, I was determined not to turn away when Alida pushed aside the tiny blue stars of the lobelia and trowelled open a small grave. The box was placed in the ground and disappeared under the earth of the flower-bed. Alida stood up, brushing her hands together, and shifted round towards my sister and me.

'Is there a heaven for parrots, do you think?' Anne asked, her voice quietly child-like.

'As certainly as there's one for human souls,' Alida answered.

'And how certain is that?' I heard myself say.

1924

. . . He has never shared with me my haunted house beneath the
trees
Of Eden and Calvary, with its ghosts that have not any eyes for
tears,
And the happier guests who would not see, or if they did,
remember these,
Though they lived there a thousand years.

from 'Madeleine in Church'

I'd wandered into my own short story. I was in a place such
as I'd only imagined years ago in 'Passed': feeble sunshine,
shaggy wind, soot-darkened plaster, rusty iron railings, black
paint peeling from the street door, and behind the cracked,
grimy window glass tattered net curtains. I backed away and
hurried home to Gordon Square.

But it wouldn't be home for much longer. We'd been notified
by the Bedford Estate that the lease on our house was about
to expire. A dreadful man with a thick Northern accent had
come round from a firm of surveyors. Upsetting Mama and
poking his electric torch into every corner on all five floors, he
compiled a fearsome list of thirty-three years' damages and
dilapidation. 'Charlotte, get the police!' Mama commanded.
When I told her the man had a letter of authorization from the
Bedford Office, she cried, 'Get your cousin Walter at once!'
She wouldn't accept that Walter Mew had long since ceased
practising law. 'Retired? Why he's scarcely more than a boy.
The idea, wasting a fine education like that!'

I consulted another solicitor, Mr Hugh Layton. In December
1921, he wrote a letter to the Estate Trustees, explaining that
we couldn't afford to make the repairs and requesting them to

allow us to vacate the premises without penalty. This was granted, and it fell to me to find a decent, affordable home for us somewhere else, by the following March.

Under winter skies the colour of tarnished silver, I tramped the streets of Bloomsbury and beyond, searching out what was available within our means. Nothing Mama could have tolerated. Filthy Dickensian slums. Rowdy, fetid neighbourhoods straight out of Hogarth. I'd about decided we'd have to sell up completely and move to a cheap hotel when I found suitable rooms to let at the top of a terraced house in Delancey Street, between Camden Town and Regent's Park.

The furniture that was ours in the lodgers' rooms upstairs at the Gordon Street house was sold to hire two removal men and their pantechnicon. Mama fretted and raved while Anne and I packed up the household. A melancholy job at best. Alone in the basement bedroom I shared with Anne, I emptied out my travel trunk and prepared to repack it. At the bottom, wrapped in my red paisley Liberty shawl, were Hardy's letters, dating from 1892, thirty years ago. I sat on the edge of my bed and read each of them over, re-experiencing all the old excitement and chagrin and sorrow.

When I heard Mama in the kitchen, speaking loudly to Anne, demanding her tea, I wiped my cheeks with the back of my hand, piled the letters on the shawl, tied them up and carried them out to the kitchen. Anne had stoked up the fire in the stove and put the kettle on. I opened the heavy black-iron fire door and thrust my bundle into the flames and shut the door and, making my mind as bare as the palm of my hand, moved to help Anne set the table.

At 86 Delancey Street, three flights up, we had a small parlour and bedroom in front, with a view of the treetops of Regent's Park. This bedroom was Mama's, nearly filled by the high four-poster bed she'd brought with her when she married Father sixty years ago. Anne and I shared the other bedroom at the back, next to a tiny kitchen and bathroom. The rent claimed two thirds of what remained of our income after seeing to Freda's care, but the new flat was clean and the address a respectable one. As ever, it was necessary to keep up appearances.

Poor Mama, slumped in her threadbare brocade chair, in a strange place with so little round her she could recognize, only the brass candlesticks on the mantelpiece and a few photographs of us as girls. The first week she kept saying, 'Take me home. I want to go home,' over and over again, her tired eyes leaking tears.

Unlike our house in Gordon Street, where the twentieth century hadn't been allowed to intrude, here the rooms had been wired, and Mama was terrified of the electricity. She lighted a candle rather than touch the switch to turn on a light. And she refused to allow us near any switch during a thunderstorm. She waved her arthritic, claw-like hands. 'Stay back! It attracts lightning!' So did a telephone, she declared. We weren't on the telephone, of course, one of the modern luxuries we'd never allowed ourselves. We continued to rely on the mails and the rare telegram sent from the post office in Camden High Street.

Although she didn't go out often, when she did, Mama had to be helped up and down the stairs in case she got dizzy and fell. Soon, she refused to go down them at all and remained in the flat, vexed and bewildered and increasingly confused. 'I named you both for queens,' she told us one evening as we three sat together in the cramped little parlour. Anne had unravelled an old jumper and was knitting the wool into a scarf. I was darning the heel of one of my red stockings, neither of us looking very regal. Mama chattered on, her bent fingers restlessly picking at the buttons on the front of her black bodice: 'When your brother Henry returns to assume his rightful throne, you, Charlotte, will be the Queen of Brunswick, and you will be the Queen of Mecklenburgh, Anne.' My sister and

I gaped at each other. Even though the idea was fantastical and outrageous, neither of us felt much like laughing.

After the move, I was plagued by insomnia. Through the spring, I lay awake after everybody else had fallen asleep and revisited the ghostly rooms of our old house, like a museum of memories. Meeting the dead and near-dead we'd left behind became too painful. I forced myself to think of something, anything, else – Mama's medicine, tomorrow's dinner, the laundry, always a difficult chore in the kitchen sink – until exhaustion dragged me down into dreams of more housework. Months passed, and still easy sleep eluded me. On warm summer nights with our bedroom window open, I stared at the starless ceiling and listened to the lions roar in their cages a few streets away.

At first, my frustration at not being able to write, my sole escape and comfort, had been immense. Then, I'd fallen into numb misery, living a sort of half life, apathetic, all energy drained outwards. When at long last I did sit down with pen and paper, I had great difficulty concentrating. And yet I persisted. Two poems were published in 1922, and in early 1923, three more. One of them, 'Fin de Fête', in the February issue of *Sphere*, was, in a way, a farewell to my younger self and her feelings about Thomas Hardy. He was now past eighty, and I reckoned I wouldn't be seeing or hearing from him again:

> Sweetheart, for such a day
>   One mustn't grudge the score;
> Here, then, it's all to pay,
>   It's Good-night at the door.
>
> Good-night and good dreams to you, –
>   Do you remember the picture-book thieves
> Who left two children sleeping in a wood the long night
>   through,
>   And how the birds came down and covered them with
>   leaves?

His Arms are Full of Broken Things

So you and I should have slept, – But now,
  Oh, what a lonely head!
With just the shadow of a waving bough
  In the moonlight over your bed.

Someone has shut the shining eyes, straightened and folded
    The wandering hands quietly covering the unquiet breast:
So, smoothed and silenced you lie, like a child, not again to be
    questioned or scolded;
But, for you, not one of us believes that this is rest.

from 'Beside the Bed'

Mama lay propped up by pillows, her white hair in lank braids over her shoulders. Her eyes were open but unseeing, in a marble stare. Pathetic and gesturing, she said, 'Nanny!' as if she were calling for her to come. Or maybe it was a cry of recognition, catching sight of her old nurse on the other side of the abyss.

Always small, Mama had shrunk until there was less of her than when she was a girl. Her needs, though, her demands, diminished not at all. She continued to take for granted the punctual fulfilment of her expectations. Years ago, she'd discovered the way to get what she wanted was by being vigorously helpless, and as long as she acted dithery, she couldn't be held responsible for anything she said or did. In the end, she was no longer acting.

Mama had been getting up out of her worn brocade chair in the parlour, shouting at some long-ago maid for not laying the fire properly, when she fell. The doctor diagnosed a possible fracture of the thighbone and confined her to bed. I fed her, bathed her, cared for her, while Anne went out to her studio each day to work. Sapless and lined like a dead leaf, Mama closed her eyes for the last time and succumbed to pneumonia on 12 May 1923, at eighty-six years of age.

She hadn't been an ideal mother, not even a very good

mother, perhaps. But she was our mother, and I was devastated and half-dead myself from months of nursing her and dreading the coming of the end. When she was gone, I felt like a weed dug up and thrown over the garden wall.

We weary, when all is said, all thought, all done.
We strain our eyes beyond this dusk to see
What, from the threshold of eternity
We shall step into.

from 'Not for That City'

The income from Mama's annuity ended with her death. What little Anne and I continued to receive was scarcely enough to meet our commitment to the hospital on the Isle of Wight. Like ageing gypsies, we packed up our few belongings and moved on, this time to Anne's studio in a three-storeyed red-brick building next door to the Scala Theatre near Fitzroy Square. An Italian restaurant occupied the ground floor, and the stairwell reeked of oregano and fried onions.

Anne had a fairly large room on the top floor, windowless but with a skylight of frosted glass, set in the high ceiling. Her easel stood unused in the far corner, old canvases stacked along the wall. Scattered around were paints and brushes and glue pots and pieces of antique furniture awaiting restoration – chairs, side-tables, fire-screens decorated with nymphs and satyrs and pudgy cupids, wreathed in wavy ribbons and festooned with fruit and flowers.

The walls were a dull tombstone grey, and the room smelt of damp and mineral spirits and coal oil from the small stove we used for heating and cooking. Its black flue pipe vented through a pane in the skylight, and when it rained, water leaked in round it and trickled into a bucket. We hadn't much furniture – a sideboard with a mirror at the back, a deal table and a few odd chairs – which we arranged as a sort of parlour in one corner. Our bed – Mama's wedding four-poster – was screened off by a cotton curtain across the other.

Mama would never have approved of our situation. However, my insomnia, thank God, had been left behind in Delancey Street. *The Farmer's Bride* continued to sell, the reviews of the American edition made new friends for my poetry there, and Alida Monro had begun to urge me to complete another chapbook to be published by the Poetry Bookshop. Most days, while Anne worked at her painting, I wrote at the 'parlour' table. After our evening meal, she joined me, painting china cups and saucers with violets for sale in a shop in Museum Street. And I entertained her, reading aloud by candlelight – Emily Brontë, Christina Rossetti, Virginia Woolf's new novel, *Jacob's Room*, borrowed from the lending library.

In spite of the dingy inelegance of the place, once we settled in, the two of us were surprisingly happy. We'd not spent so much time alone in each other's company since we were children in the old nursery of the house in Mecklenburgh Square. When I read from Emily Brontë, I thought how much we resembled our namesake sisters isolated in the parsonage at Haworth. One night, reading her poems, I finished with

> Oh, stars, and dreams, and gentle night;
>   Oh, night and stars return!
> And hide me from the hostile light,
>   That does not warm, but burn;
>
> That drains the blood of suffering men;
>   Drinks tears, instead of dew;
> Let me sleep through his blinding reign,
>   And only wake with you!

At that, Anne looked up from her painting and smiled with such sweetness and grace it was as if she had her own starry light beaming from within. Suddenly, I saw her with a new clarity. The years of fretting about myself and struggling with my writing, the months of nursing Mama, in all that time I'd lost sight of my sister when she'd been right there in front of me nearly every day. She was fifty-one, no longer the bright young woman whose image I'd carried in my mind like a souvenir photograph. Her eyes were still the same blue-violet, but creases showed between her brows and radiated from the corners of those startling eyes. She'd never bobbed her hair and wore it in greying waves and twisted into a soft knot at the nape of her neck. And just as suddenly, I realized how she'd come to resemble our mother. Oh, Anne, my poor angel, I cried inwardly. I loved this woman beyond anything I felt for myself, and I prayed I'd go first rather than lose this dearest and truest of friends.

Making no apologies for our surroundings, we asked old acquaintances in for tea. Alida came most often. She thought our new home quite gay and bohemian. Although she never said as much, she understood our circumstances and regularly brought something to make her visit a party – fairy cakes, ginger biscuits, half a dozen éclairs. One afternoon, she brought Sydney Cockerell.

We'd corresponded from time to time, but he and I had never again spoken of our clash over Emily Brontë's death. Sydney Cockerell was always right. *Ergo*, those who held to the contrary in any instance were always wrong. Full stop. On the other hand, his letters were full of flattery and good humour. For myself, I much preferred him at a distance, meeting him by way of his precise handwriting and courtly language. But here he was, bearing red roses and a broad smile. But his eyes darted round the studio, taking in the dingy clutter. With a slight bow from the waist, he offered me the bunch of flowers.

'How nice,' I said, with forced gaiety, tossing my head. 'Thank you, Sydney.' I took them and went out to the cold-water tap on the landing to fill a milk pitcher with water, thrust the roses in it, and came back to set them in the middle of the table. Anne poured the tea. Conversation was light and amiable, and yet I detected a note of concern – or was it pity? – in Cockerell's voice. By the time he and Alida left, I sensed disapproval in his manner and I responded with barely contained anger. Damn it, who was he to judge how my sister and I lived? I would ask Alida not to bring him ever again to the studio. We could certainly do without his disdain.

I was profoundly wrong. Nothing new in that. It was with the deepest shame I read his next letter. He wrote that he'd spoken to Hardy and, at his urging, had composed a petition to be sent to the Prime Minister, Stanley Baldwin. Cockerell enclosed a copy:

We, the undersigned, send you this to recommend Miss Charlotte Mew for a Pension on the Civil List.

In our opinion, Miss Mew is the most distinguished of the living women writers. Her work stands alone in power, quality and suggestion. There has been and is nothing like it.

I was trembling so I had to hand the piece of paper to Anne to read to me:

As she is a poet, writing poetry of a rare kind, she may not be widely known for many years. We feel that it would be a wise and gracious act, worthy of a great people, to give to this rare spirit the means of doing her work until the world can appraise and reward it.

Anne lowered the page, grinning. 'The petition is signed by Thomas Hardy, John Masefield and Walter de la Mare!' she said, with a mixture of awe and excitement.

I sank into a chair, stunned by the high praise heaped on me, like a shower of gold. I was more touched than I could say that anybody would have gone to Downing Street on my account. I'd been rude and suspicious at Cockerell's visit to the studio, and all the time he was calculating how to help Anne and me. This was but the latest kindness in a long and amazing list, and I immediately wrote to him, expressing my deepest gratitude. I was convinced the Prime Minister wouldn't take the petition seriously, but I wrote notes of appreciation as well to the three signatories. I bit my underlip as I signed the one to Hardy, holding back the impulse to express more than was seemly.

In December 1923 His Majesty's government granted me a Civil List pension of £75 per year, the difference between subsistence and starvation for Anne and me. Henceforth, when callers came to the studio, there'd be cake for tea.

In sheltered beds, the heart of every rose
   Serenely sleeps to-night. As shut as those
Your guarded heart; as safe as they from the beat, beat
Of hooves that tread dropped roses in the street.

    Turn never again
    On those eyes blind with a wild rain
  Your eyes; they were stars to me. –
    There are things stars may not see.

from 'Absence'

Over the years since my visit to Max Gate, I'd exchanged occasional letters with Florence Hardy – a way of keeping up with the news of Hardy himself – and we'd had her and her sister to tea at the studio when they came up to London. As long as I thought of her as Florence and not Mrs Hardy, I found her pleasant enough, although excessively talkative. And pathetic. In September 1924, Florence was operated on again by the throat specialist, Macleod Yeastley, and I went to call on her at the Fitzroy House Nursing Home, not far from the studio.

When I came into her darkened room, I found myself unable to look anywhere but into that tragic, wasted face that floated in the glare of starched white, lighted by the small shaded electric lamp on the wall above her head. The operation had left her more drawn and hollow-eyed than I'd known her before. The nursing sister had warned me Florence was temporarily unable to speak, and I felt constrained to keep silent myself, gesturing greetings and smiling dumbly as I came up to the side of the high white bed. She seemed pleased to see me and slowly pencilled 'Thank you for coming' on a pad of paper she kept near her.

Then, I noticed a young woman standing on the other side of the bed. She wore a fashionably waistless frock of eau-de-Nil crêpe and was oddly familiar yet unplaceable, slight, fragile, with a face like a martyr or a Florentine Madonna. Or a French nun.

In spite of myself, I was staring, momentarily smitten. She met my stare and, lowering her liquid, heavy-lidded eyes, glanced away. Our mutual shyness was almost palpable. Neither of us said anything. Almost a vision, a mirage disappearing, she left.

Silence for several moments after the door closed behind her. 'Who was that?' I whispered.

Florence picked up her pencil and wrote: 'Her father great friend of TH – Virginia Woolf.'

The next day, I had a letter in the post from Hardy:

My dearest, dearest Charlotte,

My person and my poetry are one. I tried to imitate your queer, original voice. Forgive me if I offend. Forgive me everything.

Tom

How could I not forgive him? I was so grateful for all he'd done for me. And to think he'd admired my work enough to try to imitate it! I turned to the second page:

Nobody Comes

Tree-leaves labour up and down,
    And through them the fainting light
    Succumbs to the crawl of night.
Outside in the road the telegraph wire
    To the town from the darkening land
Intones to travellers like a spectral lyre
    Swept by a spectral hand.

A car comes up, with lamps full-glare,
    That flash upon a tree:

> It has nothing to do with me,
> And whangs along in a world of its own,
> Leaving a blacker air;
> And mute by the gate I stand again alone,
> And nobody pulls up there.

Such a lovely, affecting poem. I felt the tug of precarious pleasure and tenderness, the pang of joy and misery. I pictured Max Gate and the lonely old man. I was touched and flattered. All the same, I thought I recognized the gesture for what it truly was – a sad call for sympathy while Florence was the one who was unwell and in hospital. And yet I was greatly tempted by the unspoken invitation to take the train down to Dorchester in her absence. It might be my last chance to spend time with him, to see him alone and tell him how very much he meant to me. Restless with my own restlessness, I argued with myself all afternoon and evening. Late that night, the decision was made for me: Anne woke with a moan, feverish, seriously ill, and I was needed in London to care for her.

1926

The walls are standing to-day, and the gates: I have been through
    the gates,
        I have groped, I have crept
Back, back. There is dust in the streets, and blood . . .

                                    from 'I Have Been Through the Gates'

When I told Alida I'd been asked down to Max Gate again,
she took me in hand, led me to the shops, and fitted me out *à
la mode*: an ecru linen chemise, mid-calf length, trimmed in
dun and grey-green, and tan silk stockings and shoes with
pointed toes and straps across the instep. 'Gosh, Charlotte, you
look *très chic*,' Alida said. She tried to persuade me I looked
ten years younger and attractive. I decided to let her.

   In a time when I should have been happiest – my work being
praised by writers and critics on both sides of the Atlantic,
Alida reading my poems on the BBC, a new poetry collection
planned, social invitations coming to me from so many literary
names, all declined – Anne had been very ill. She'd recovered
and fallen ill again over the last year and more. The doctor
said at first it was influenza, then fatigue, then an internal
infection. I rarely left her bedside, suffered fatigue myself and
wrote nothing. By early 1926, thank God, Anne was much
better. She'd had to give up her antiques restoration, but she
was well enough to paint again and had submitted three pictures
to the Royal Academy Easter Show.

   Hardy had been very ill, too. Presently somewhat better,
he'd expressed a wish to see me again, Florence wrote. Might
I be willing to travel down to Dorchester and stop over-
night?

*

The trees round Max Gate had got thicker since my first visit: leafy copper beech and white poplar, elm and sycamore among the ageing pines. The brick wall round the property was blotched with silver-green lichen, hawthorn blossomed between the chalky drive and the house, and the concrete urn at the side overflowed with white geraniums.

I pinched colour into my cheeks before opening the door of the taxi. I stepped out, blinking, into the summer's yellow glare and smoothed down the skirt of the new linen chemise. I felt the key to the trunk of Hardy's letters against the damp skin between my breasts. Ever my talisman. The thin red ribbon had been replaced many times over the years, and still I wore the key, even though the letters had long ago gone to ashes.

Florence opened the door before I reached the enclosed porch, and we greeted each other awkwardly. She directed the taxi driver, a squinting Dorset man in a flat cap, to leave my case in the front hall. I paid him, and he touched the peak of his cap and left. From somewhere down the hall leading to the kitchen came a muffled barking. Florence gestured in that direction. 'Cook's giving Wessex his dinner, or he'd have been here to greet you, too.'

I was just as glad he wasn't, remembering him as a huge, furry menace. I followed her into the parlour. 'How are you feeling, Florence? Was the operation a success?'

Her eyes, round and watery, were sunk deep in their sockets. She seemed weak, unstrung. Her lips pursed and twitched each time before she spoke. 'It's my husband's health that's at the centre of the household.' She sounded resentful.

Dowdy cushions, tassels, fringes still decorated the parlour, the Staffordshire spaniels and whippets sat placidly on the mantelpiece as they had before, and Emma's disapproving portrait hung yet on the far wall. Florence caught me glancing round the room. 'Some things never change,' she said. 'However, you will find a number of changes since you were here last. We've electricity and a bathroom now, with hot water. And we're on the telephone, too. Of course, Thomas won't speak on it. He has a peasant's suspicion of such things.'

I nodded and returned a weak smile, trying not to appear anxious. I wanted to see Hardy.

She offered me tea, and I declined. 'Maybe later,' she suggested. 'How have you been, Charlotte?' She gestured towards a chair by the empty fireplace. 'I was so pleased to hear Anne was recovered.'

I remained standing. Damn it, I wanted to see him. But I was reluctant to say so. Could Florence see that? Was she purposely making me wait, forcing me to ask?

A long, silent minute of shared displeasure. The grandfather clock in the front hall struck twice, with bronze gravity.

'Thomas will want you to come up,' Florence said, as if defeated, surrendering to the inevitable.

Upstairs, she opened the door to his bedroom, allowed me to enter alone, and shut it behind me. The curtains were drawn against the afternoon sun. The room, smelling of liniment, was shadowy and edged round darkly by a heavy wardrobe and chest of drawers and high-backed bed.

And here, propped up by a snowbank of pillows, was a worn old man in a nightshirt, his veined eyelids closed. On his far side, he stroked a sleeping white cat, his hand pale as its fur. His head was ringed in white down, his moustache drooped sadly, his skin was drawn over his beaky nose.

In the stillness, there was almost more of severance and tragedy than I could bear. The world had got smaller and smaller until it was the size of this room, of this bed, lighted by his presence, brilliant and momentary.

The sound of escaping breath. 'Charlotte,' he said.

'How did you know?'

He opened his eyes, eyes grown large and faded to a grey-mauve, the colour of dried lavender. 'How does this cat of mine know when I come into an unlighted room? We know the ones we love.' He left off caressing the cat and extended his hand to me. 'Come here.'

I moved to the side of his bed. His fingers were warm bones.

'They won't let me talk. They tell me to save my strength. For what? The truth is no one wants to listen. You'll listen, won't you, my dear?'

'Of course.'

'They apparently think I'm dying, that I ought to make my peace with God if I want to enjoy some sort of life ever after. I'm not ready to concede any of that. I've another book of verse to finish. I intend to live this life for a good many more years.'

'I'm glad to hear it.' And wished fervently for it to be so.

'I was cast aside at birth as dead, did I tell you? The midwife only noticed later when she came to dispose of me that I was alive. So you see, I've already experienced one resurrection. I can't expect another, in spite of what the Vicar would have me believe.'

I started to say something, but he gripped my hand and said, 'No, no. Let me finish. I want to set things to rights between us. About last time . . .'

I shook my head. 'No, Thomas, it's I who have to apologize. I've the most to regret.' He cocked his head, perplexed. 'So much has changed between people, between men and women, since we first met. What is it, thirty-four years ago? Thanks to Dr Freud, everybody is talking about sex and writing about sex and having sex, it seems, with everybody else.' Hardy chuckled deep in his throat. I smiled and was strong, all shyness, all reticence gone. I was ready to lay down my burden of unutterable thoughts. 'For myself, I never quite managed the sweet acceptance of my body that would allow true intimacy,' I went on, serious again. 'You might have taught me. In spite of my ferociousness.'

'Perhaps.' He sighed it out.

'If I'd known myself – my mind and my nature – then as I

do now, I might have overcome my fears and let you be my lover. If I could have surrendered my self and trust to you, if we could have taken certain precautions, or if I could have been assured a child would have been untainted, if . . . if . . . if . . .'

He focused beyond me. 'I thought once I'd like to have a child.'

I understood, remembered my own yearnings as a young woman. 'It doesn't matter. Our books are our progeny.'

'Yes, I'm only ever truly happy when I'm writing.'

'I can say the same.' I lifted his hand and kissed the backs of his fingers. 'And when I'm with you.'

He laughed a soft, airy laugh. The old light of mischief winked in his eyes. My heart's fire leapt in tongues. A small spasm burnt through me, strange yet distantly familiar.

'You're a fool,' he said and dropped my hand and held both arms out to me. 'And you're my darling.'

I'd stood too long in that narrow space between passion and repression. Like a weary, trusting child, I crawled up on to the bed and laid my head against his chest and listened to the strong beat within. His words resonated against my ear, tingling, arousing and deeply magisterial. My King of Wessex.

Coming away, I carried the memory of his body, his skin white, powdery, translucent, like a moth's wing. His soul was moth-like, too, its wings quivering, poised for flight.

1927

Oh! hidden eyes that plead in sleep
Against the lonely dark, if I could touch the fear
And leave it kissed away on quiet lids –
If I could hush these hands that are half-awake,
Groping for me in sleep, I could go free.
I wish that God would take them out of mine
And fold them like the wings of frightened birds
Shot cruelly down, but fluttering into quietness so soon.
Broken, forgotten things; there is no grief for them in the green
   Spring
When the new birds fly back to the old trees.
But it shall not be so with you. I will look back. I wish I knew
   that God would stand
Smiling and looking down on you when morning comes,
To hold you, when you wake, closer than I,
So gently though: and not with famished lips or hungry arms:
He does not hurt the frailest, dearest things
As we do in the dark.

from 'The Forest Road'

Dr Cowan was wrong. Internal infection, he'd called it. Doctors! They know nothing and can do nothing. Charlatans! Murderers! They couldn't keep my dear, sweet Anne from suffering an agonizing cancer.

I was nearly mad with pity and distress, with fear and rage. And yet I had to hide my stronger emotions and play the ever-cheerful nurse to match her performance as the ever-cheerful patient. I fed her. I bathed her. I read aloud from amusing new novels, from books of poetry Alida brought from the shop, and from the newspaper, while Anne lay thin and putty-coloured on our parents' wedding bed, the bed in which each of us had been born, Anne only fifty-five years ago.

Looking more a girl than a woman, she lay nestled in the white bedclothes. Her eyes were shut, her lids softly lavender. Her white nightgown ruffled round her thin neck and across her shoulders, an intimation of wings, a possibility of flight. A single linen sheet weighed her down. Her full, brown hair lay curved round her, threaded with grey.

Often, we talked about our friends and their families.

'We've become desiccated old spinsters, haven't we?' she said, with faint breathiness.

'Are you sorry you never married?'

'No, are you?'

'No,' I answered with absolute certainty. I picked up the book of Christina Rossetti's poetry I'd been reading to her earlier and turned to 'Goblin Market', an old favourite from childhood, and quoted:

> For there is no friend like a sister
> In calm or stormy weather;
> To cheer one on the tedious way,
> To fetch one if one goes astray,
> To lift one if one totters down,
> To strengthen whilst one stands.

I raised my eyes and saw that hers were brimming, but her lips curved in a gentle smile.

One June evening, dim through the sooty skylight, I arranged on a tray the teapot and the last two of Anne's cups and saucers painted with tiny violets. I carried our tea to her bedside.

I pulled up the dining-table chair and poured out the steaming cups. Hers sat within inches of her fingers, but she didn't open her eyes or make any move to reach for it. *See, dear, your hair – I must unloose this hair that sleeps and dreams / About your face* . . . A fragment, a line or two from one of my poems came to me as I watched her. God, forgive me: I should have been more attentive to her over the years, but my writing claimed so much of my time and my energy. For myself, I wondered if Art isn't a rather inhuman thing after all.

Of late, Anne liked to talk about the childhood we'd shared.

I said, 'I've been thinking about the doll's house we played with in the nursery when we were girls.' I smoked a cigarette and sipped my tea. I went on talking to her even though I'd got no response. 'Father made it for us. It was delivered in the rain. Do you remember?'

I stubbed out the cigarette in my saucer – how Mama would have hated that – and began a new line of recollection. 'Do you remember the time Father took us all on holiday to Bath? He meant Mama to take the waters for her nerves, to go into the hot pool, but she refused to undress anywhere but in the privacy of her bedroom. So we took the return train up to London the next morning. Or were you too young to remember that?'

Anne's lids fluttered but didn't open. 'I remember.' Her words, although faint, were precisely formed. 'You told Father you'd take your clothes off, even if Mama wouldn't.' A hint of a smile. 'He was quite red-faced and upset.' She paused, out of breath. 'Would you have undressed, gone naked in public?'

'At that age, yes, I'm sure I would have done. I hadn't yet learnt to feel shame for my body.' And once learnt, I'd not been able to unlearn it. An intense modesty had lain hidden under the occasional boldness of my public façade.

I stroked a finger across her cool forehead . . . *beyond the faintest star, / Past earth's last bar / Where angels are, / Thou hast to travel.*

I fussed with, smoothed the bedding. 'Are you warm enough?' No reply. 'Anne, dear?'

Her lips moved moon-slow: 'I shan't want a fire soon.'

Through the evening hours and into the night as the skylight grew leaden overhead, I smoked and watched my sister sleep . . . *ghostly and pitiful and white, / A blot upon the night, / The moon's dropped child.*

'Now, at last, you'll be free,' Anne whispered that terrible midnight as I sat beside her bed, pressing her hand against my wet cheek as she faded into the dark.

'No, no,' I said aloud but to myself because she couldn't hear me. 'Not free. Just alone.'

Sweetheart, is this the last of all our posies
    And little festivals, my flowers are they
But white and wistful ghosts of gayer roses
    Shut with you in this grim garden? Not to-day
Ah! no! come out with me before the grey gate closes
    It is your fête and here is your bouquet!

'Jour des Mortes'

Great bunches of flowers heaped and drifted. The petals had curled and dried, dropped to the fresh-turned earth, and blown away.

TO

THE BELOVED MEMORY

OF

CAROLINE FRANCES ANNE MEW,

WHO DEPARTED THIS LIFE

ON JUNE 18TH, 1927.

'CAST DOWN THE SEED OF WEEPING AND ATTEND.'

HERE ALSO LIES HER SISTER

CHARLOTTE MARY MEW,

WHO DEPARTED THIS LIFE

In the months after the funeral, the plain stone slab in Fortune Green Cemetery kept Anne from rising, from escaping the grave. And it waited, grimly, its inscription incomplete, for me to join her there. Henry was under the muddy clods in Nunhead Cemetery. Father, Mama, Nanny. The faces of the dead, pale as feet. An image, like a daguerreotype, of a pathetic little girl in her older brother's shoes came flashing back to me: Freda buried alive in the hospital on the Isle of Wight. I'd buried

Anne alive, too late I was convinced of it. I could scarcely breathe the candle-heated air and clutched Nanny's hand and stared at the baby face, afraid to wake him and start the crying again. What troubled me was the lid of the white box and what would happen when it was closed. And I'd let them close it on Anne. *Oh, my God, what have I done, what have I done?*

> Then lie you there
> Dear and wild heart behind this quivering snow
> With two red stains on it: and I will strike and tear
> Mine out, and scatter it to yours. Oh! throbbing dust,
> You that were life, our little wind-blown hearts!
>
> from 'The Forest Road'

My head felt sore and empty. I lay on my back, across our bed in the night studio, Anne a faint white face hovering over mine, as if she made her own light. Through the months of summer and autumn, she hadn't left me, and I knew now she wasn't dead. I'd buried her alive. I'd killed her. No wonder she wouldn't let me sleep.

November and my fifty-eighth birthday. I was haunted by the memory of Anne's long-ago birthday gift: the china lion and lamb on my mantelpiece in Gordon Street. Where was it? I dug through all the drawers of the sideboard, tossing everything on to the floor. I looked through every shelf and box in the studio. I went out, searching for it.

As I wandered aimlessly through the streets of London, I realized there were lions everywhere, lions rampant, lions seated, lions standing with forepaw raised, lions couchant in Trafalgar Square, winged Assyrian lions in the British Museum, lions roaring in Regent's Park. I waited for Henry between the paws of a lion, and he didn't come. When I saw him again, he had a sword in his hand. No, that wasn't right. He had a knife. He was going to kill me for murdering Anne.

Bits of my poetry buzzed in my sleepless, aching head:

> *What is this singing on the road*
> *That makes all other music like the music in a dream . . .*

There is a Spirit sits by us in sleep
Nearer than those who walk with us in the bright day . . .

There is a shadow there: I see my soul,
I hear my soul, singing among the trees.

1928

The shadeless, sleepless city of white days,
White nights, or nights and days that are as one –
We weary, when all is said, all thought, all done.
We strain our eyes beyond this dusk to see
What, from the threshold of eternity
We shall step into. No, I think we shun
The splendour of that everlasting glare,
The clamour of that never-ending song.
And if for anything we greatly long,
It is for some remote and quiet stair
Which winds in silence and a space of sleep
Too sound for waking and for dreams too deep.

from 'Not for That City'

I'd forgotten how to sleep. After the raw grief of Anne's death, I suffered painful insomnia and dark, ruinous moods. Alone, I forced myself to keep the daily routine, to build up the fire, tidy up, make a simple meal. My spirit ached and dragged. At night, the fire smouldered and winked out. With mingled hope and pain, I lay awake in the dark, where her lighted face no longer came. As I stared into the blackness, I longed to reach out and touch my sister again. Each morning, I rose in half-light, stiff and exhausted, hoping for some momentary relief, tormented by the certainty that, like Henry and Freda, I was going mad.

Then, on 11 January 1928, came the end of hope, like the last stars in the heavens being put out, one and the other. I felt faint as I passed the news-vendor's stand and saw the headlines: THOMAS HARDY DEAD. I nearly collapsed in front of the greengrocer's. I leant against the door jamb of the shop until my vision returned. I staggered like a drunk the short distance back to the studio.

The fire had gone out. Death and death and death. I sank down on to the bed. The weather in Dorset was bitterly cold with deep snow drifts, the papers said. I thought of poor Jude, dying alone. Was that how it was for Hardy, Thomas, my dear, dear Tom? And would it be that way for me? I was all at once overcome with a fear so acute as I'd only known before in dreams of endless falling. My pulse drummed. I was short of breath and bathed in icy sweat. *I can ... feel the darkness slowly shutting down / To lock from day's long glare my soul and me.*

On 13 January his heart was taken from his body, to be buried in Stinford Churchyard, his remains cremated. The funeral service was set for Monday afternoon, the sixteenth, at Westminster Abbey, where his ashes were to be buried in Poets' Corner. When I arrived, I found attendance was by invitation only. I stood shivering in the crowd outside the Abbey, watching the solemn procession of pall-bearers: Prime Minister Stanley Baldwin, the writers Barrie, Galsworthy, Gosse, Housman, Kipling and Bernard Shaw. And Sydney Cockerell, of course. He stared directly ahead and didn't see me there.

Hours later, when the service was over and all the distinguished mourners departed, I slipped into the Abbey by the side door and crossed the echoing centre aisle to Poets' Corner. There, in the middle was a great heap of flowers. Folding chairs were still arranged round the pallid pomp of white lilacs and the bleeding wounds of red roses. I knelt, cold creeping up through me from the smooth-worn stone. I folded my hands in prayer, like the votive figures on the tombs of dead royalty. My King of Wessex. He promised not to hurt me – ever. 'And this is the promise that He hath promised us, even eternal life.' Nanny quoting John's first epistle. She was dead. Dead were those who believed and those who didn't believe.

I found it hard to pray to a God who created mankind and

then washed His hands of them. Try as I might, I could never see things from His point of view. He promised. Our Father promised. He promised eternal life in Heaven. What He asked in exchange was one's entire life here on Earth, and I could not let go of mine, not quite bad and not quite good. God was the subjugator, pressing His will on suffering humanity that He made that way: 'Oh! quiet Christ who never knew / The poisonous fangs that bite us through / And make us do the things we do, / See how we suffer and fight and die, / How helpless and how low we lie, / God holds You, and You hang so high . . .'

I shifted on my aching knees and glanced round where I knelt. No Christ here, no crucifix, no plaster saints, just marble tablets, urns, memorial inscriptions, sculpted likenesses of great men. On the other side of the high-arched nave, an old man in a white coat was flicking at the busts with a feather-duster. As I watched, the cleaner revealed himself to be an angel, the duster his wings, and I prayed under my breath: 'Oh, keeper of this soaring stone warehouse, this storehouse of bones and souls, bless and care for your newest, Thomas Hardy. He was all-in-all to me – father, lover, friend. And now he's gone on without me.' *He laughed when he was covered with grey wings, / – Asking the darkest angel for bright things / And the angel gave – / so with a smile he overstepped the grave.*

I got shakily to my feet and walked to the mound of flowers and snatched up a red rose and hurried away.

The world is cold without
And dark and hedged about
With mystery and enmity and doubt,
But we must go
Though yet we do not know
Who called, or what marks we shall leave upon the snow.

from 'The Call'

Back at the studio, I was confused. My bare hands were chilled and empty. Where was the rose? I must have dropped it in the street. What was happening to me?

One fitful night, I drifted into a drowse and dreamt about Henry and Freda, and again it's he who holds the sword, and he slays our little sister. And Anne. And I'm next. It's in dreams the things that kill us live.

I woke, frightened, to a drizzling morning, skies weeping against the murky skylight. I gathered a few belongings into my handbag, put on Father's dress suit, and took a cab to Dr Cowan's nursing home in Beaumont Street, where I'd been promised safety and sleep. Beaumont Street appeared to be a cul-de-sac, blocked by an ochre brick house with bays on the ground level and ginger-red cornices. But I knew the street turned sharply to the left and connected with Marylebone High Street. Near the corner, there'd been a hot-potato man's cart when I walked here with Hardy last Sunday afternoon. Or was it years ago?

The door to the nursing home closed behind me, silencing the city sounds, motor traffic and defiant bird song. I had a moment of dread and confusion. Just then, Miss Lutch, the matron, introduced herself with starchy solemnity. Her face was doughy-bland, her hair like frayed rope. She took my arm and led me up the linoleum stairs to an arid room. It was as clean and sterile as white paint could make it. The walls, the narrow iron bedstead, the chest of drawers – except for its clouded mirror – were painted white. The rocking chair was painted white. A white cotton spread was drawn up over the bed. For a few hours on sunny days, the room might borrow reflected light from the wall of grey brick opposite the single window. But this day was overcast, making the room dour and shadowy.

Through the melancholy, white-painted days, I sat in the rocking chair. My hands were my dead mother's pale claws. My dead father's ring was on the little finger. I was wearing my dead father's suit. Everything was touched by death. The reflection in the mirror was the sooty bricks outside the window. And I waited for peace to descend like something with wings. An angel with a feather-duster.

Through the nights, I lay on a bed of shadows and tried to lull myself to sleep with a litany of all the foolish rashnesses and regrets of my life. I was the worst sort of sinner. I let them bury Anne alive. I continued to lie awake, God the Father frowning down at me. 'Submit, submit,' He said.

Sometimes, the room filled with white fog, emanating from the painted walls, and I was lost within it. At other times, it cleared, and I felt myself to be myself again.

Alida Monro came to call, seating herself on a white-painted straight-backed chair. She was still a handsome woman, wearing a green crêpe frock, a heavy coat with moleskin collar – the room was like an icebox – and a brown felt cloche pulled modishly low over her dark brows.

We talked about Anne. 'You must be missing her dreadfully,' Alida said, with a sympathetic shaking of her head.

'There is some consolation,' I told her. 'Now, she can never be old or alone.'

Alida diverted the conversation to mutual friends, their misfortunes, the comforts of religious belief. 'At one time,' I said, with a bit of a laugh, 'I rather fancied myself as a nun. Years ago, Anne and I went abroad on holiday, to Brittany. We visited a convent, where the nuns' cells had whitewashed walls and bare floors. All was cool, clean, simple, beautifully pure – a high, pure serenity.'

I'd got that simple whiteness here, but no serenity. For myself, I resisted the requisite surrender. I said to Alida, 'I might have joined the Roman Church, if it hadn't been for the requirement to confess one's sins, aloud.'

She leant towards me. 'Oh, Charlotte, are your sins really so terrible?'

'My life has been an unending tug-of-war between obedience and rebellion. The struggle continues, I assure you.' *Yet will you when you wing your way / To whiter worlds, more whitely shine . . . ?*

'Don't you find any comfort in the prospect of divine forgiveness and eternal salvation?'

I couldn't answer. God was there, somewhere above me. *Then safe, safe are we? In the shelter of His everlasting wings – / I do not envy Him his victories, His arms are full of broken things.*

After some moments, I said, 'I think my soul is red.' Alida moved to protest, but I cut her off with a raised hand. I rocked forward in my chair. 'I've something to show you. It arrived in the post.' From the top of the chest of drawers, I took a folded piece of paper and offered it to her.

She examined it – a call slip from the Reading Room of the British Museum. But when she unfolded it, it showed on the back a poem written out in a spiky, masculine scrawl:

Sweetheart, for such a day
    One mustn't grudge the score;
Here, then, it's all to pay,
    It's Good-night at the door.

Good-night and good dreams to you, –
    Do you remember the picture-book thieves
Who left two children sleeping in the wood the long night
    through,
        And how the birds came down and covered them with
    leaves?

So you and I should have slept, – But now,
    Oh, what a lovely head!
With just the shadow of a waving bough
    In the moonlight over your bed.

Alida looked up. 'Why, this is your poem, "Fin de Fête",
isn't it?'

I sat again in the rocker. 'Yes, copied out by Thomas Hardy
from *Sphere* magazine and kept on his desk at Max Gate.'

'You knew he had this?' She held up the paper.

'No, Sydney Cockerell sent it to me. He's his literary execu-
tor. It seems Hardy told a number of people he admired it.'

'But he never told you directly?'

How much should I reveal to Alida? 'Mrs Hardy told me he
liked to have my poems read to him, when I was first invited
down to Dorchester.'

'What was it like?' Her tone was light and eager. 'You've
never said.'

I paused, remembering, sorting, censoring. 'At Max Gate,
life was orderly and quiet. White geraniums bloomed in the
conservatory, and every day was like Sunday afternoon.'

The white-painted room was growing shadowed at the end
of a late-winter day, and yet I made no move to switch on the
overhead light, a single unshaded bulb hanging from the middle
of the ceiling. Neither Alida nor I spoke for some time. In the

dusk, I was shrouded in reverie. The Hardy I cherished was the robust man in the British Museum, his hair a deep brown, barely touched by the frost of years. His moustache and full beard, his furious brush of eyebrows, his way of seeing through my skin to my soul.

Finally, Alida made to return the poem.

'No, I want you to keep it.' I was unworthy of his admiration, unworthy to keep the poem. The fog was beginning to seep from the walls again.

Alida folded the poem into her handbag and prepared to leave. We parted at the door open into the hallway. I squeezed her gloved hands in mine and stretched up and kissed her cheek. She stepped back, her eyes drowning in tears, surprised, I think, by my affectionate gesture of farewell.

I was sorry now not to have loved more boldly – Hardy, Anne, Alida, everyone – no matter what the consequences. But love – even my love for Anne – had been tied to an overwhelming awareness of sin. It no longer mattered. *I'm a wretched sinner, a sinner who didn't dare sin nearly enough.*

Alida's footsteps down the hall narrowed to a point and disappeared. I dropped into the rocker. I sat into the suffocating gloom of night. Moonlight, reflected off the brick wall outside the window, painted a long, pale rectangle across the lino, stopping at the toes of my black shoes.

It's always night here, and I'm in the house where I was born, the doll's house, my heart's abandoned home. I touch the glass in the window of the nursery, the very room where I'm standing. I shiver. There's a kind of magic to it. I'm large and small. I'm outside. I'm inside. The house has stairways and fireplaces, draperies and carpets. I walk round, going from room to room, pantry to parlour. I search the bedrooms, the nursery, hunting for someone, anyone. Through the open back of the house, I look up at the crucified Christ, like the crucifix in the little Breton church. I ache to fly up to Him, to touch the twisted figure that hangs between heaven and earth, linking the human and the divine. But I'm trapped in the plaything of my childhood.

The next morning, I took my handbag and went out to the shops. At the edge of my vision, a grey smoke. The plane trees of London were burning, and the rain had put out the fire, the rooks cawing in the bare branches, the red roses charred to black. Hardy's voice whispered in my ear: 'Death is an absolution.'

'I will be forgiven?' I asked, with soundless joy.

'We are beyond that – the dead. We are divinely indifferent to sin.'

At the chemist's, I bought a bottle of Lysol. I returned to my white-painted room and drank the bitter disinfectant. *I mean to go through the door without fear* . . . Light streamed into my head, and I was blind, twisted in pain, a biting foam rising to my lips.

'Don't keep me. Let me go,' I told Dr Cowan. *Smile, Death* . . . My fists closed tightly on nothing.

Smile, Death, see I smile as I come to you
Straight from the road and the moor that I leave behind,
Nothing on earth to me was like this wind-blown space,
Nothing was like the road, but at the end there was a vision or a
   face
               And the eyes were not always kind.

   Smile, Death, as you fasten the blades to my feet for me,
On, on let us skate past the sleeping willows dusted with snow;
Fast, fast down the frozen stream, with the moor and the road
   and the vision behind,
      (Show me your face, why the eyes are kind!)
And we will not speak of life or believe in it or remember it as we
   go.